MISS SILVER turned to the chief murder suspect and said: 'You would like to talk to me?'

Quite suddenly Georgina began to feel that she would. She forgot all about Miss Silver looking like a governess in a family group of the Edwardian period. She had been a governess once — Georgina knew that — and now she was a private enquiry agent and Frank Abbott regarded her with reverence. In her own mind Georgina made a correction. There wasn't a Frank Abbott any longer. There was only Detective-Inspector Abbott with the cool cynical gaze which had given her story the lie.

The look which Miss Silver had turned upon her was neither cool nor cynical. It was kind, but it was penetrating. She felt as if it went right through her and out at the other side. Strangely enough it was not a disagreeable feeling. It might have been had there been anything that she wanted to hide, but since she hadn't there was a certain relief in feeling that she wouldn't have to explain too much — Miss Silver would understand.

The Fingerprint

Patricia Wentworth

CORONET BOOKS
Hodder and Stoughton

Set, printed and bound in Great Britain for
Hodder and Stoughton Paperbacks, a
division of Hodder and Stoughton Ltd.,
Mill Road, Dunton Green, Sevenoaks,
Kent (Editorial Office: 47 Bedford Square,
London, WC1 3DP) by
Cox & Wyman Ltd, Reading

ISBN 0 340 18775 1

CHAPTER ONE

FRANK ABBOTT was pleasantly occupied in forgetting that he was a Detective Inspector. Certainly no one meeting him for the first time would have suspected him of having any connection with Scotland Yard or the inexorable processes of the law, though he might just possibly have been a barrister. He had, in fact, been intended for the Bar, but his father's sudden death had necessitated some occupation more likely to solve the immediate problem of food to eat and a roof over his head. With more relations than anyone in England — his paternal great-grandfather had married three times and done his duty by the nation to the extent of having some two dozen children — he had never lacked a social background. In the country he could stay in almost any county without having to incur an hotel bill, and in town he received a good many more invitations than he was able to accept. When he was younger his immediate superior Chief Inspector Lamb, always on the alert for symptoms of wind in the head, had composed a special homily on the subject of Social Dissipation and its Inevitable and Deteriorating Results, which he delivered so often that Frank could have picked it up at any given point and finished it for himself. Although not now so much in use as formerly, it was still liable to be dug out, re-furbished, and delivered with undiminished vigour.

Tonight, however, was a carefree occasion. His cousin Cicely Abbott and her husband Grant Hathaway were up in town and giving a party to celebrate the extremely lucrative sale, for export, of a young pedigree bull. The party was small, intimate, and amusing. It is also memorable for the fact that Anthony Hallam was present, and that he and Frank spent a good part of the evening picking up threads and bringing themselves up to date after a five years' interval during which they had neither met nor written to one another. Out of sight had perhaps been out of mind, but no sooner were they once more in sight and touch than the old liking was strong between them. Old friendships do not always endure as characters develop and circumstances change, but in this case each was secretly a little surprised to find how quickly the five years' gap was bridged. When Anthony urged him to come down to Field End, Frank could very easily have refused, but found that he had no desire to do so.

'It's old Jonathan Field's place. He's some sort of a cousin of my mother's. There's no wife, but he's got two nieces. They are giving a dance, and I've been asked to bring another man. They'll put us up. I suppose you get an occasional Saturday night and Sunday off?'

Frank nodded. If it hadn't been for Jonathan Field's name, he might have said, 'No,' just like that. As it was, he said quickly,

'*The* Jonathan Fields – the fingerprint man?'

Regardless of grammar, Anthony Hallam said,

'That's him. Extraordinary hobby. He has the fingerprints of everyone who has ever stayed there — his version of a visitors' book. I asked him whether some of them didn't object, and he wagged a finger at me and said he would nourish the deepest suspicions of anyone who did.'

Frank said,

'That didn't exactly answer the question, did it?'

'Oh, he didn't want to answer it, but I asked Georgina —'

'And who is Georgina?'

Anthony laughed. The laugh had a warm, pleased sound.

'Wait and see! She's the niece who lives with him, Georgina Grey. I won't attempt to describe her.'

'Didn't you say there were two nieces?'

'Oh, the other one is a sort of cousin, not really a niece at all. Her name is Mirrie Field. She's a recent introduction. Little bit of a thing, with eyelashes.'

It was at this point that Cicely came up and made a face at them.

'If you two think you are going to talk to each other instead of dancing —'

They both groaned. Frank said,

'He was describing the latest girl friend's eyelashes. I can't wait to see them!'

Cicely was still just a little brown thing, but she too had eyelashes, and when she was happy she had her points. She was certainly happy tonight. She caught Frank's hand.

'You can dance with me! And Anthony will be lucky if he gets Vivia Marsden. She's going to be a top star in ballet.'

Cicely herself was like a feather in the wind. Frank looked down at her with the affection which his cool elegance belied. The mirror-smooth fair hair, the eyes of a cold and icy blue, the features which he had inherited from his grandmother the formidable Lady Evelyn Abbott, combined to produce a somewhat daunting impression. But he had never daunted his cousin Cicely. Looking up as he looked down, she showed him the tip of a scarlet tongue and said,

'Isn't Grant clever to have got such a lot for Deepside Diggory? I hope they'll be nice to him. He really is an angel lamb.'

'He'll be on velvet. You are clever, Grant is clever, and let us hope that Diggory will be clever too. And now we won't talk about bulls any more. I have reached saturation point.'

Cicely allowed a very small frown to appear. Then she said,

'I never really can make out whether you hate the country, or whether you won't talk about it because you would really like to live there most frightfully and farm like Grant does, only you can't.'

Frank said,

'Heaven forbid!' Then he laughed. 'I'm coming down to a do at Field End with Anthony next weekend. Any chance of your being there?'

'Oh, yes, we'll be there. It's a birthday party for Georgina. At least it started that way, but now they've got Mirrie Field there it looks as if it was turning into a coming-out party for her. She's a Field relation that nobody had ever heard about before.'

'Before what?'

'Oh, the last couple of months or so. Old Jonathan ran into her somewhere, found out she was some kind of seventeenth cousin, and brought her back on a visit. She hasn't any people and she hasn't any money, but she's got a very clinging disposition, and if you ask me, I should say they'll have her for keeps.'

Frank was not interested in Mirrie Field — not then. He said, 'Did I ask you?' in his most detached manner, and she pinched his arm and told him he would probably fall in love with Georgina Grey.

'Only I warn you it won't be the least bit of good, because if she doesn't take Anthony, it will almost certainly be Johnny Fabian.'

'Oh — what is he doing in your parts?'

'Making love to Georgina, I expect. Or Mirrie. Or both of them, but probably Georgina because of the money. He hasn't got a bean, and she is supposed to be Jonathan's heiress. Personally I should say that Mirrie was a runner-up, but Johnny can't afford to take risks. Anyhow, money or no money, Georgina will be an ass if she marries him. I don't suppose she will — she ought to know him too well for that. His stepmother, Mrs. Fabian, lives at Field End, you know.'

Frank's memory began to wake up.

'Oh yes, I remember. She's some sort of relation, isn't she — used to run the house?'

'Darling, she couldn't run a rabbit-hutch! She's an umpteenth cousin of old Jonathan's, and when he took on Georgina it was considered the right thing to have someone like that in the house. I think he clung to her as a protection against nurses and governesses who wanted to boss him or marry him. Miss Vinnie says there were several determined attempts, so you may say Mrs. Fabian began by being Jonathan's chaperone. Miss Vinnie says he was dreadfully nervous about breaths of scandal. And of course Mrs. Fabian has clung like a leech. No, that's too bad of me — she's perfectly harmless, only quite terribly inefficient. I couldn't stand it myself, but I expect they are used to her. It's all right as long as Georgina doesn't let herself get so used to Johnny that she wakes up one morning and finds she has married him.'

'Any reason why she shouldn't?'

A bright colour came up under Cicely's brown skin.

'As if you didn't know! He makes love to every girl he meets, and if Georgina married him she would have to look after him for the rest of her life — and she's not that sort, you know.'

'What sort is she?'

Cicely's expression changed. Her really lovely sherry-coloured eyes looked up at him.

'She is — ' She hesitated for a word, and then said, 'vulnerable. Most people wouldn't tell you that. They would say that she had looks and — and everything she wanted. But they don't know. She doesn't know either. She thinks everyone is like herself. She — she — oh, well she wouldn't know a snake if she saw one.'

'You're being harsh, aren't you? Is Johnny Fabian the snake?'

Cicely's chin lifted.

'Oh, I don't know — he might be.'

She bit her lip, and her colour went out like a blown flame. He had an impression that if she hadn't been dancing she might have stamped her foot. As it was, she jerked against his arm and came out with a burst of words.

'The trouble is she'll have a great deal too much money.'

Cicely herself had had too much money.* Lady Evelyn Abbot's considerable fortune had gone past her father and Frank to the fifteen-year-old grand-daughter who was the only relation with whom she had not contrived to quarrel, and the first year of Cicely's marriage had nearly come to grief upon the prejudices and suspicions which her grand-mother's twisted mind had implanted. The memory of those miserable months was in her voice as she spoke.

Frank gave her a light answer.

'Most people could put up with that complaint.' And then, as she looked up at him again startled, 'Don't make too much of it, Cis. Johnny wouldn't anyway.'

She said quite sharply like a little scratching cat,

'Anthony might.'

'Anthony? My good girl!'

Her voice turned obstinate.

'I don't think he would like a very rich wife. Some people don't.'

* Eternity Ring.

'Some people might think more about the wife than about the money. Personally, of course, I am waiting for a super heiress.'

'And when you've found her?'

'I shall forsake a sordid life of crime and return to the Sussex Downs and keep bees like Sherlock Holmes.'

'I should have thought you might have found your heiress by now if you had really looked for her.'

He laughed.

'Perhaps I haven't really looked!'

'Frank, why haven't you? Is it because of that Susan What's-her-name? Someone once told Mummy she was the only woman you had ever really been in love with.'

'And you always believe everything that anyone tells Monica?'

Cicely persisted.

'Was there really a Susan?'

'Quite a number of them. It's a popular name.'

'Oh, well, if you won't tell me —'

'So that you may tell Monica, and Monica may tell all her dearest friends? Thank you, my child!'

She made a little cross face.

'Oh, well, you'll have to marry some day. But I don't think Georgina would be any good. She's as fair as you are. You ought to marry a dark girl, or at any rate a brown one.'

'Like you?'

Cicely showed the tip of her tongue again.

'*Exactly* like me. What a pity I'm not twins!'

CHAPTER TWO

FRANK ABBOTT drove down to Field End with Anthony Hallam on the following Saturday evening. They ran into fog and arrived so much later than they meant to that they were shown directly to their rooms and were obliged to hurry over their dressing. They had left the fog behind them, but all that he could see of the house as they drove up to it was the square Georgian look and enough light filtering through the curtains to show that not one of the rooms inside was dark. Memory supplied the rest — two ornamental gates both standing wide, a courtyard designed for the old coaching days, and the whole front of the house hung with Virginia creeper. He had spent school holidays not much more than a mile away at Deeping, when old Lady Evelyn was still reigning in Abbotsleigh and had not as yet had any irrevocable quarrel with him. He knew all this part of the country like the back of his hand. Deeping village still alluded to him as Mr. Frank, and he could remember Field End in an early September frost, standing foursquare with its face to the road, hung with a crimson, vermilion and scarlet tapestry. There would be no leaves now, only a winter tracery of slender brown stems. He could not recall that he had ever been inside the house before, though he had known Jonathan Field by sight, tall and thin, with a habit of walking bare-headed in the wildest weather with his rather long grey hair blowing out behind him.

Coming down dressed with Anthony, they encountered Jonathan in the hall. Frank didn't know what he had expected, but there was a distinct jab of surprise as he realised how little the old boy had changed. The tall, thin figure was just as upright, the grey hair no greyer, the whole look and aspect so entirely that supplied by memory, that he could almost have expected to hear his grandmother announced and to see her make an imposing entrance in the black velvet and diamonds of a state occasion.

The picture was momentarily so vivid that the entrance of Mrs. Fabian struck a jarring note. She came from the direction of the dining-room, and he remembered that she had always been in a hurry. She was in a hurry now — quite breathless with it in fact, her hair, which was no longer brown but had never made up its mind to turn grey, floating rather wildly from a twist of purple chiffon, and the diamond brooch at her shoulder coming undone. It actually dropped off as she shook hands with Anthony. And then, when he had picked it up and whilst she was fastening it, Frank was being explained and she was asserting that of course she remembered him perfectly.

'You used to stay with Lady Evelyn at Abbottsleigh in your school holidays. I don't think I ever really met you, but I used to think how tall and thin you were — and so very much like your grandmother.'

This was not, of course, the most tactful approach. Although perfectly well aware of his resemblance to that formidable lady, it did not please her grandson to be reminded of the fact. Her portrait still dominated the drawing-room at Abbottsleigh with its long pale face, its bony nose, pale eyes, and the sleek fair hair above them.

He said, 'So everyone tells me,' and she went on in a rambling inconsequent manner,

'But Georgina was only a little girl then — you won't remember her, but you will remember my stepson, Johnny Fabian — he was always here a good deal, but perhaps that was later on, because of course there was a family quarrel, wasn't there, and you stopped coming down. Family quarrels are always so distressing — of course any quarrels are. Your cousin Cicely and her husband — everyone was so glad when that was made up, and I believe they are coming here tonight. My dear mother brought us up never to let the sun go down on our wrath. "Kiss and be friends ere night descends" was what she used to say. And there was a verse my German governess made me learn — dear me, I hope I can remember it ... Ah, yes, I can! She held up her hand where a number of inexpensive and very dirty rings clustered like swarming bees, and quoted:

> *Und hüte deine Zunge wohl,*
> *Bald ist ein boses Wort gestagt,*
> *Die Stunde kommt, die Stunde kommt,*
> *Wenn du an Gräbern stehst und klagst.*

'But if you don't understand German, perhaps I had better translate. Fraülein Weingarten used to make me say it every day:

> Guard your tongue well,
> An angry word is soon spoken,

> The hour will come, the hour will come,
> When you will stand and mourn by graves,

'Not really a very cheerful verse to teach a child, but she always said I had a heedless tongue. Oh dear, it all seems so long ago.' She strayed on, saying vaguely, 'I really think I heard a car. Did anyone else hear it?'

From a little distance it was possible to observe that she was wearing what would have been a perfectly good black lace dress if she had not had the bright idea of relieving it with some bits of faded fur, a couple of purple bows, and a large bunch of rather tumbled violets. There her attempts at adornment ceased. She displayed indeterminate features quite innocent of any effort in that direction. It was even doubtful whether they so much as knew the touch of a powder-puff.

Jonathan Field looked at his watch and said,

'Georgina ought to be down. Where is she? She and Mirrie — they ought both to be here.'

A very small voice said, 'Oh, Uncle Jonathan —' and there beside them was a little creature in a white dress. She had dark curls, and the dress was all soft fluffy frills. She hung on Jonathan's arm and looked up at him with pansy-brown eyes.

'Don't — oh please don't be vexed! She won't be long — she really won't. I expect it was my fault — she was helping me. And it's going to be such a lovely party. You mustn't be vexed.' She was tugging at his arm like a child, but so softly as to give the effect of a caress.

Jonathan Field smiled indulgently. Anthony said, 'Hullo, Mirrie!' and Frank Abbott found himself being introduced. The brown eyes transferred their upward look. They were of exactly the same shade as the clustering curls, but the lashes were darker, though whether this was due to nature or to art it was impossible to discern. The words of the introduction had been 'My niece Mirrie Field'. Old Jonathan's smile had been practically a doting one. Distant cousin's daughter my foot — if she didn't finish up co-heiress with the real niece, he was a Dutchman! The eyes alone with their look of trusting appeal could have done the trick hands down, but the eyes plus the curls, that little round soft face, and the mouth with its suggestion of a childish pout made a certainty of it. He wondered what the mouth was pouting for. Sweets, kisses, or anything else that came its way?

Anthony Hallam said,

'Is that the new rig-out? It's very successful. I suppose Georgina was helping you to dress.'

She sparkled at him for a moment, and then the lashes drooped. A very small foot drew circles on the polished floor.

'Well — no — I had things to do and I didn't get them finished, so I had to ask Georgina. She's so good, but I'm afraid she was vexed. I mean, she's so good about everything herself and I haven't had a lot of practice, but I didn't — oh, I really didn't mean to make her late.' Her voice trembled a little and the eyes were raised again.

But Anthony Hallam had turned and was looking past her and across the hall. He said, 'Oh, well, she's coming now,' and just as the lobby door opened to admit the first of the guests Georgina Grey came into sight at the head of the stairs and began to descend them.

A late entrance is nearly always an effective one. Frank wondered a little cynically whether she had planned it. But if she had, there was a flaw in the timing. Guests were streaming into the hall, old Jonathan was greeting them, and the new-found niece was being brought forward with a hand on her shoulder to be presented in the most affectionate manner. Only Frank himself and Anthony Hallam had the leisure to watch Georgina come down the stairs.

She was worth watching too, and it was evident that Anthony thought so. Frank saw a tall girl in a silver dress — a tall fair girl with a lovely figure and pale gold hair. She had a white skin, a red mouth, and eyes of a strange dark grey. Eyebrows and lashes were no more than a couple of shades darker than her hair, but the eyes had a black ring about the iris, and the iris was the colour of deep water under a cloudy sky. It could look grey or it could look green, but always and in any light it was arresting. Frank, who was something of an expert, considered that the eyes were the making of her. If they had been blue the whole effect would have been too pale. If they had been brown — but of course they wouldn't be, not with that hair, and he was prepared to bet that the hair was natural. She had the right skin for it and she wore as little make-up as a girl considered decent. She came down without any appearance of hurry, went past them with a smile for Anthony, and was in the thick of the greetings.

There had been a string of names not always easy to allocate — Lord and Lady Pondesbury, Mr. and Mrs. Shotterleigh, Miss Mary Shotterleigh, Miss Deborah Shotterleigh, Mr. Vincent, Mr. and Mrs Warrender. Frank identified Lord Pondesbury, and remembered the Shotterleigh twins as prim little girls exactly alike, who looked as if they couldn't say boo to a goose. One of them was in pink and the other in blue, and they still looked prim.

Johnny Fabian, latest of the house-party, came running down after Georgina. He was as always in the best of spirits, ignored the brief frown accorded him by Jonathan, and began to talk and laugh with everyone. The Shotterleigh girls brightened perceptibly. Mirrie Field's colour rose. She didn't speak to him, she just stood there and made a picture — brown curls, white frills, a small string of pearls about a soft white throat, dark lashes dropped over soft brown eyes.

When Georgina had spoken to everyone else she came across to Anthony and Frank. She rested a hand on Anthony's arm, gave him a second smile, and acknowledged Frank's introduction with friendliness and charm. He had been thinking that Johnny Fabian really hadn't changed in the least — he probably never would. The dark hair which insisted on curling no matter how short it was cut would probably recede with the passing years, but the dancing blue eyes would keep their merry sparkle and the engaging smile still brings him more smiles in return than fell to most men's lot. It had got him out of scrapes at home, at school, in the army, and it would continue to do so. He turned it on pretty girls and on plain ones, upon the elderly, the clever, the dull, and the disappointed. Frank had never known him well — just a chance encounter here and there — but he was clapped on the shoulder and greeted like an old friend.

'Hullo there! Ages since we met. How's crime?'

Frank said, 'Much as usual.'

Johnny turned to Georgina.

'Our famous detective, in case you don't know. A shining light of what American books talk of as the Homicide Squad. A Lieutenant in the Homicide Squad, that's what he would be over there. Sounds much more imposing than a Detective Inspector or whatever he is at Scotland Yard.'

Frank laughed.

'And what are you doing with yourself?' he asked. 'Didn't I hear about your going into shipping or something?'

Johnny shook his head.

'Not shipping. Something frightfully dreary that I never really got the hang of — I think they call themselves General Importers. There was a second cousin twice removed of my grandfather's who was a sleeping partner, he got me in, and after about six months a partner who wasn't asleep chucked me out. It was practically bound to happen, because if I ever came across a business that was a smell under the nose, that was it.'

'So what are you doing now?'

'Well, a misguided aunt left me her little all a few months ago, and I am looking round for something to put it into. It's difficult of course, because what I want is an amusing job where there isn't any boss and where I don't have to do any work. And meanwhile I do a spot of car-coping — pick 'em up cheap and sell 'em as dear as I can, with a lick of paint and what have you to make 'em go down easy.'

Jonathan Field called across the hall to them.

'Well, we're all here now, I think. Georgina, has everybody come?'

Her hand dropped from Anthony's arm and she went over to him.

'Yes, darling, I think so. And there's Stokes to say that we can go in. Will you take Lady Pondesbury?'

Jonathan Field gave his arm to a muscular lady who looked rather as if she had come out in a brick-coloured mask and short red gloves. Between these two extremely sun-burned portions and the black satin in which the rest of her was encased there were large milk-white arms and a considerable area of milk-white back and chest. She wore what she had no hesitation in describing as a copy of the ancestral diamond and ruby necklace which had been sold to pay the estate duties on her father-in-law's decease some fifteen years earlier. Her husband Lord Pondesbury, a horsy little man with a swivel eye, approached Georgina. Jonathan Field observed the forms of his youth. In his house people still went in to dinner two by two in a seemly and orderly manner. Frank found himself with Mary Shotterleigh, and saw Anthony go in with Mirrie Field.

CHAPTER THREE

LOOKING back on it afterwards, Frank found himself remembering a number of disjointed bits and pieces. The complete picture had been there like one of those large jigsaw puzzles laid out upon a table. It had been there for him to look at, and if it is true that the memory never really loses anything, it was still there to be remembered. But when he came to look back on it, it was as if someone had picked up a handful of pieces here and there and tossed them into his lap. Some of them fell in groups, and others singly. Some of them fell right, and some of them fell wrong. Some made nonsense. He had to unscramble them and try and get them together again. One of the more successful efforts brought back the scene in Jonathan's study. They had finished dinner and there was time to fill in before the dance guests arrived. Now just how many of them were there? Himself and Anthony. It was Anthony who had asked whether Jonathan would show them his collection, and Lord Pondesbury had said, 'Not for me, old boy. I don't know one end of a fingerprint from the other and I don't want to. I'll go and have a word with Marcia Warrender about that two-year-old of hers.'

Mr. and Mrs. Shotterleigh hadn't been interested either, but the girls came into the study, and so did Mirrie Field and

Mr. Vincent, but not Lady Pondesbury, or Georgina, who remained in the drawing-room to play hostess. He thought about the rest of them crossing the big square hall and coming into the study with its book-lined walls and the handsome maroon curtains drawn across the windows. It would be rather a dark room by day, but under modern lighting pleasant enough, with comfortable chairs and a carpet in tones of red and green. Mirrie Field's white frills and the pink and blue of the Shotterleigh girls stood out against the dark furnishings.

When they were all there and the door shut, Jonathan got out his heavy albums and found room for them on the writing-table. Nobody thought about sitting down. Johnny Fabian stayed by the door, amused for the moment but prepared to escape if he was bored, and Mary Shotterleigh stayed with him. She had grown up rather pretty. She looked sideways at Johnny and he said something which brought her colour up in a bright attractive blush. The other girl, Deborah, came up to the corner of the writing-table and stood there looking shy. Mirrie Field was with Anthony Hallam, pressed up as close to him as she could get and holding on to his sleeve rather as if she was afraid that something might jump out of one of the albums and bite her. Frank himself was over by the fire with a man called Vincent, a newcomer to the neighbourhood after some years in South America. According to Anthony there was plenty of money, but no wife or family. As they stood together, Mr. Vincent observed that he couldn't imagine why anyone should want to collect fingerprints, to which Frank replied that it wouldn't appeal to him personally, but he understood that Mr. Field's collection was unique. Mr. Vincent fixed him with a dullish eye and enquired,

'How do you mean unique? I should have thought the police collection would be that.'

'Oh, the police only get the failures. They don't touch the potential criminal or the chap who has never been found out. And that, of course, is where Mr. Field has the pull. He has been collecting for the last forty years or so, and he is so well known that it is quite a compliment to be asked for a contribution. In fact anyone who refused would be sticking out his neck and asking to be suspected of dabbling in crime.'

Mr. Vincent said it all seemed rather dull to him, but then what he was really interested in himself was stamp-collecting and he went on to describe how he had found and subsequently had stolen from him a two cent British Guiana 1851 of which only ten copies had been previously known to exist. It was a tragic tale told in the dullest possible manner. A tepid man with not even a spark of the collector's fire in his belly.

'He went down over the rapids and the stamp with him, and no one would go in to look for the body because the river was so dangerous, so now there are only ten copies again.' He shook his head with faint regret and added the word, 'Pity'.

All this while Jonathan Field was laying out two large volumes on the flat top of his writing-table and hovering over them with an index or a catalogue or whatever he chose to call it.

'Now what shall I show you? Hitler's thumb and forefinger? Most people want to see those. I've got quite a nice little group of the Nazis — Goering, Goebbels, Bormann, and poor old Rommel.'

The book opened easily at the place. Everyone crowded to see, and there they were, exactly like the prints which any of the people in the room might have made. These men had grasped at the world and it had slipped from them. They were gone. There was nothing left but ruined lands and ruined people and some black prints in Jonathan Field's collection.

The prints were all very neatly mounted and set up, a legend under each, with a name and sometimes a date. What an extraordinary hobby for anyone to have. And Jonathan was as keen as mustard, there was no doubt about that. He stood behind his writing-table and snapped off little anecdotes of how he had come by the exhibits. Some of them were amusing, and some of them were tragic, but it was a very good performance. Nobody seemed to look at the prints very much, but they all listened to the stories.

When it had been going on for about half an hour Georgina came in and said that people were beginning to arrive for the dance. Jonathan didn't looked pleased. He said in a pettish voice,

'All right, all right, I'll come.'

He took up the left-hand album and then put it down again.

'The most interesting prints are in here, but I never show them to anyone.'

Looking back, Frank could admire the showmanship. He was going to finish the performance with a bang.

'I don't know the man's name, and I probably never shall, but I've got his fingerprints, and I think — I say I think — I should know his voice.'

Georgina stood in the doorway in her silver dress. She looked across at him and said '*Darling!*' on a note of protest. But Mirrie clasped her hands and breathed in an anguished tone,

'Oh, Uncle Jonathan, *please*! You can't stop there — you must go on!'

There was no doubt which was the popular niece for the moment. Jonathan frowned at Georgina, cast a softened look at Mirrie, and said,

'Oh, well, some other time. It's too long a story for now — quite dramatic though!'

He half opened the volume and shut it again. It didn't shut down smoothly. There was an envelope in the way. Frank had just a glimpse of it over Mirrie's head. And then Jonathan was going on.

'Oh, yes, quite dramatic. We were buried under a heap of rubble in the blitz, not knowing each other from Adam, or caring either for the matter of that, and neither of us thought we'd ever see daylight again. Curious how that sort of thing takes people. I never felt more alive in my life — noticed everything more than I'd ever done before or since — everything speeded up, intensified. There was a pain, but it didn't seem to belong to me. The other fellow was where I could just reach him. He wasn't hurt, just trapped and mad with fright — what they call claustrophobia. I passed him my cigarette-case and matches — that's how I got a fingerprint — and with the third cigarette he began to tell me about a murder he had done. In fact two murders, because he said he had had to kill a possible witness in order to make himself safe after the first one. He had got it all worked out in his mind that the second one didn't really count. He said it was practically self-defence, because she would have gone to the police if he hadn't stopped her, and the only way he could be sure of stopping her was by finishing her off. He was perfectly clear about it, and it didn't seem to bother him at all. But the first one bothered him a bit. You see, he'd done that one to get hold of some money. He said he ought to have had it anyhow and the man he murdered had got it by undue influence, and he seemed to think that would make it all right about the murder. At least he hoped it would, but when a couple of bombs came down pretty near us he didn't feel any too sure about it. He may have been making it up, but I didn't think so then and I don't think so now, so when he passed the case back to me I wrapped my handkerchief round it and slipped it into my breast pocket just in case.'

Anthony said, 'What happened after that?'

Jonathan looked across at him with something that wasn't quite a smile.

'As far as I was concerned that was the end. There was another bomb, and I didn't know anything more until I woke up in hospital with a broken leg. As a matter of fact that last bomb was a blessing in disguise, because it shifted the stuff that was over us and the Red Cross people were able to get me out.'

'And your murderer?' That was Anthony too.

'Never saw hair, hide or hoof of him. He must have crawled out and got away, because there were no corpses lying about. So he's probably walking around somewhere and still trying to make up his mind whether he's a double murderer or not.'

Georgina made a little gesture that said, 'Oh, well —' and turned round and went away, leaving the door open behind her. Now was there any importance in that, or wasn't there? There might have been. Because anyone in the hall could have come up close enough to have heard what Jonathan had said and what Jonathan was saying now. Georgina had stood in an open doorway. She had gone away and left it open behind her. Anyone could have heard what Jonathan said.

CHAPTER FOUR

THE dance went very well. Frank met quite a lot of people he knew. He danced with Cicely Hathaway. She wore a flame-coloured dress and she was enjoying herself. She told him it was said that Mr. Vincent was looking for a wife and she didn't envy her.

'If Mrs. Shotterleigh had her way, it would be Mary or Deb, but either of them would rather have Johnny. Anyhow the Vincent man must be at least twenty years older than they are, and he's the dullest man I ever met in my life. Has he told you how he lost his British Guiana stamp?'

'He has!'

She laughed.

'He tells everyone. Did you go to sleep, or just come over numb with boredom? And you know, it ought to be an exciting story!'

'Yes, he's like that. But we needn't talk about him.'

When he had danced with his Aunt Monica, a charming inconsequent person to whom he was devoted, he approached Miss Mirrie Field, who fluttered her eyelashes at him and said, 'Oh — ' in rather an alarmed sort of way. If that was her game, he was in the mood to play it.

'I don't actually go about arresting people at dances, you know.'

She let him have a good view of her eyes. They were an unusual shade of brown and very pretty.

'But you do arrest them sometimes?' The words were just breathed.

'As occasion offers.'

'That must be horrid — for you.'

He allowed himself to laugh.

'I believe it hurts them rather more than it does me.' He put his arm round her and they slipped into the dance.

Someone had built on a ballroom at the back of the house.

Jonathan's grandmother was an heiress, and she had six daughters. The ballroom had no doubt assisted her in her determination to supply them with eligible husbands. It stood at right angles to the block of the house, and thanks to a wealth of creeper and a charming formal garden which brought it into harmony with the terrace under the drawing-room windows, it was no longer the eyesore which it had been when it was new.

The floor was very good, the music delightful, and their steps went well together. She was a little soft, light thing and she could dance. He had a passing wonder as to how she might compare with Georgina Grey. She passed them at the moment, coping with Lord Pondesbury who had a tendency to treat every dance as if it were some kind of a jig of his own invention. In the circumstances Frank gave Georgina marks for the kindness of her smile.

Mirrie looked up at him and said,

'How *well* you dance!'

'Thank you, Miss Field.'

She gave him a dimpling smile.

'Oh, you mustn't call me Miss Field — I'm just Mirrie. And this is my very first dance.'

'No one would know it. You are very good.'

She said, 'I love it,' in a reverential voice. 'I wanted to go into ballet, but you have to start so young, and there wasn't enough money for me to have lessons. Did you ever want anything dreadfully, dreadfully badly and have to give it up because there wasn't enough money and there simply wasn't anywhere you could *possibly* get it from? I don't suppose you ever did, so you can't possibly know what it feels like.'

Frank knew very well, but he wasn't going to say so. He had been intended for the Bar, and he had had to give it up when his father died. He said,

'It was a pity about that. What are you going to do instead?'

Her colour rose becomingly. The dark lashes came down and hid her eyes. She said in a murmuring voice,

'Uncle Jonathan is being so kind.' And then, 'Oh, don't you *love* dancing?'

They danced.

Later, when they were sitting out, she stopped suddenly in the middle of some artless prattle about this and that to lift a fold of the white frilly skirt which billowed out over the low chair and say,

'Do you know, this is the very, very first dress of my own I've ever had.'

He was stirred to amusement and something else.

'And who did the others belong to?'

She said, 'They were cast-offs.'

'You mean you had older sisters?'

'Oh, no. They belonged to people I'd never heard about — people who send parcels to poor relations. You don't know how horrid it is to get them.'

'It might have been much more horrid if you hadn't.'

'It couldn't have been.' She had a mournful and accusing look. 'You don't *know* how horrid it was. Some of the things were so ugly, and they didn't really fit. I expect some of them belonged to Georgina. She says no, but I expect they did. She is older than I am, you know, and a whole lot taller, so her things would always have been much too large. They used to put tucks in them all over and say I would grow into them in a year or two, but I never did. I expect they kept me from growing. Don't you think if you hated a thing very much it might keep you from growing into it? There was a perfectly horrid dress with yellow stripes exactly like a wasp, and I had to wear it whether it fitted me or not.' She gave a heartfelt sigh and added, 'I did *hate* my relations.'

Frank leaned back lazily. It was not the first time that he had been the recipient of girlish confidences. After a long apprenticeship with female cousins they no longer embarrassed him.

'I don't know that I should make a practice of hating them. I have hundreds, and they all mean well.'

He was thinking that if she didn't know which side her bread was buttered she had better make haste and find out. And then with a touch of cynicism he became aware that she knew very well. There was a soft agitation in her voice as she said,

'Oh, you didn't think I meant Uncle Jonathan — you

couldn't! I wouldn't mind anything from him. He is different.'

'Is he?'

'Of course he is! He doesn't give me old things, he gives me lovely new ones. He gave me a cheque to buy anything I wanted — real, real money to go into a shop with and buy anything I wanted! And a string of pearls for my birthday! Look at them — I've got them on! Aren't they lovely? And he said this was to be my party as well as Georgina's!'

It certainly looked if Uncle Jonathan was spreading himself. Frank said idly,

'And what about Georgina — is she kind too?'

Mirrie fingered her pearls and looked down at the white frills. She said in a childish voice,

'She is very kind.'

It wasn't until a good deal later that he arrived at dancing with Georgina Grey. She made a charming hostess and there was a good deal of competition, but in the end he got his dance and enjoyed it. Voice, manner and step were easy, graceful and charming. He remembered Cicely Abbott's old nurse saying of somebody that everything she did became her. He thought it might have been said of Georgina Grey.

He was prompted to turn the conversation in Mirrie's direction.

'Anthony tells me she has lately come to live with you.'

Georgina said, 'To stay with us.' And then, 'I think she will stay on.'

'She was telling me that she would have liked to go in for ballet.'

'Yes, but it has been left too late.'

'She dances very well.'

'Oh, yes. But ballet is quite a different thing. You have to start when you are about seven, or even earlier, and it means hours of practice every day for years.'

'I suppose it does.'

He was struck by the serious considering note in her voice. And then they were talking of something else. Mirrie Field as a topic didn't crop up again.

One thing he did see which he was to remember afterwards.

Everyone was breaking off and streaming in to supper. He had Cicely Hathaway as a partner, and just as they nicely settled she said that she had lost her handkerchief. She knew just where it would be, and he went back for it — 'The study, Frank. Grant and I were in there and I was doing my face. It's one Gran gave me, with real lace.' He found it easily enough, and then as he stood with it in his hand he heard a small tapping sound from the direction of the window. He pushed Cicely's handkerchief into his pocket and drew back the nearest curtain. It was the one which screened a glass door on to the terrace. The door was ajar and the sound which he had heard was the sound of it just touching the jamb and swinging out again. But as he drew the curtain back it was opened by something more tangible than the wind. Mirrie Field stood on the step in her white dress, staring up at him with her eyes quite wide with fright.

She said, 'Oh!' and put her hand to her throat.

Well, girls did slip out at a dance, though it was a pretty cold night for that fluffy white dress. But where was the man? You don't go out alone into icy gardens. At least if you do, it is sheer lunacy.

He said, 'I'm sorry I gave you a start. Come along and have hot soup. You must be frozen.'

Mirrie went on looking at him.

'I — I was hot — I just went out.'

They went back into the dining-room together. He didn't think of it again until quite a long time afterwards.

CHAPTER FIVE

IT was an agreeable weekend. Frank and Anthony walked over to Abbottsleigh in the afternoon, and went on to have tea with Grant and Cicely Hathaway, after which Anthony returned to Field End and Frank Abbott went on to town by train from

Lenton. The infamous Cressington case broke next day, and he became too much occupied with it to have time or thought for anything else until, as suddenly and dreadfully as it had begun, it ended and the Yard could breathe again. Chief Inspector Lamb lost a stone in weight, a fact which he resented though he could do very well without it. What annoyed him more was that he had lost his sleep, a thing so unusual as to have the most unhappy effect upon his temper. Frank emerged from the affair with a good deal of kudos and the knowledge that he had probably been as near to death as he ever would be until he actually died.

It is curious to reflect that whereas on the stage an actor is within the limits of his own play and is always aware of what kind of play it is — comedy, tragedy, melodrama, or farce — in real life he has no such knowledge and finds himself sliding from one play to another, with the players continually changing, the cues uncertain, and the plot extremely difficult to follow. After a pleasant preliminary scene at Field End in what appeared to be drawing-room comedy the Cressington case was stark melodrama. Frank had left one theatre and been hurried on to the boards in another. But the Field End play went on without him.

Maggie Bell comes into the story at this point. She had been a cripple ever since a car knocked her down in Deeping village street just before her twelfth birthday. She was now a year or two over thirty, and she had not grown or developed very much since what she always spoke of with some pride as 'my accident'. She could not set her foot to the ground, and she never went out. But that was not to say that she did not know all about everything that went on in Deeping and its surroundings. Her main sources of information were three. She lay all day on a couch drawn up to the window in the front room over Mr. Bisset's Grocery Stores, the name imposed by its owner, an ambitious little man, upon what had started life as a general shop. In addition to the Groceries of the title Mr. Bisset sold overalls, strong lad's and men's, vegetables and fruit in season, jams and preserves concocted by Mrs. Bisset, together with the liquorice bootlaces once popular but now extinct in most parts of England. Mrs. Bisset produced them from a recipe of which she boasted that it had come down in her family for two hundred years and during that time had never been imparted to anyone who was not a blood relation. On the days when she was concocting this delicacy the smell would penetrate not only to the two rooms rented by Mrs. Bell, but would pervade the village street for some fifty yards in either direction, which, as Mrs. Bisset remarked, was as good an advertisement as you could have.

Sooner or later everyone shopped at the Grocery Stores, even what Mrs. Bell called the County, since it may happen to anyone to run out of hairpins, safety pins, knicker elastic, to say nothing of apples, onions, tomatoes, or one of the practically universal breakfast cereals. Whenever it was possible to have her window open Maggie could hear everything that was said on the pavement below, where people would stand and gossip as they came and went. She had the sharpest ears in the county and was proud of the fact. On a fine day she would look out and wave, and nearly everyone would wave back. Mrs. Abbott from Abbottsleigh always did. She would look up and smile ever so nicely. But Miss Cicely, that was Mrs. Grant Hathaway now, she would come running up the stairs with that little Bramble dog of hers and half a dozen magazines and books for Maggie to pass the time with. Clever that Bramble dog was. What they call a dachshund — long body and short legs and ever such a knowing look in his eye. Went with Miss Cicely everywhere, and she'd talk to him just as if he could understand every word.

Maggie's second source of information came from the fact that her mother took in dressmaking. Clever at it too, and needed to be since it was all she and Maggie had to live on except what came from the accident money. Very smart ladies used to bring her things to copy or to be altered. Mrs. Abbott had brought her in old Lady Evelyn Abbott's wedding-dressing to make over for Miss Cicely when she was married. It was the loveliest stuff that Maggie had ever seen in her life — pounds and pounds a yard it must have cost. And wasted on a little brown thing like Miss Cicely — only of course that wasn't a thing she would say except to her mother, and when she said it to her Mrs. Bell right down snapped her nose off.

The third and most important means by which Maggie kept in touch with everything that went on lay, quite literally, to her hand. It was the telephone. She had it on a long flex so that it could stand on the table by her sofa all day and be moved to beside her bed in the evening. It is not to be supposed that there were many people to ring her up, or that Mrs. Bell could afford any but the most necessary outgoing calls. There were of course appointments for fittings, and enquiries as to the progress of work in hand, but the strength of Maggie's position lay in the fact that Deeping was furnished with that valuable aid to knowledge, a party line. When the Eternity Ring case was holding the neighbourhood in a state of horrified suspense Maggie had been able to follow the proceedings from the first mysterious call for Mr. Grant Hathaway by a strange woman with a French accent, through two murders and Mr. Hathaway's impending arrest, down to the final and most startling climax.

She had naturally been a good deal interested in the dance. A good many of the guests had had new dresses for it, but some of the ladies came in for alterations to what they already had, Lady Pondesbury for one. You'd think she'd be sick, sore and weary of that old black satin of hers, but in she'd come time after time, and always the same story, somehow or other it had got to be let out. Any money they had went on horses — and why not if they liked it that way? Mrs. Abbott, she had brought in her black lace, and a nice dress it was and didn't need very much done to it — just a little bringing up to date as you might say. Miss Georgina had had a new dress, a lovely silver one. Maggie would have liked to see her in it. She did hear Miss Mirrie Field talking about it on the telephone. The day before the dance it was. She put through a London call, and it was a man she was talking to, telling him all about the party and how excited she was. She said her uncle had given her a cheque and told her to get a real nice dress, and she had, but it wasn't as grand as Georgina's — 'Hers is silver and ever so becoming, and mine is white with a lot of little frills. Don't you wish you could see me in it?' And he said, 'Perhaps I shall,' and Miss Mirrie said, 'Oh no, you mustn't do anything silly.' And he said, 'I've dropped you a line. And you remember what I told you about my letters?' Miss Mirrie said oh, yes, she did, and the man said, 'Well, you go on remembering it, or you'll be finding yourself out on your ear!' and he rang off. Not at all a refined way to talk, Maggie thought. She was surprised at Miss Mirrie putting up with it. She had kept a sharp look-out to see if there were any more of those calls, but if there were she missed them.

The dance was over and there was just the usual amount of ringing up about it afterwards and saying how much they had enjoyed it, but nothing out of the way interesting. Not that week.

It was on the Monday morning a week later that Georgina Grey received her first anonymous letter. It lay beside her plate on the breakfast table, and since she was the first to come down she was alone in the room when she opened it. When she thought about this afterwards she was grateful. She stood there tall and fair in a grey skirt and a twin set of primrose wool, and for a moment she just didn't accept what was happening. She had torn open a cheap flimsy envelope and dropped it on to the table. She held a cheap flimsy bit of paper in her hand. It had lines on it. In spite of the lines the writing was very bad. She got as far as that, and then her mind seemed to stick. There were words on the paper, but it didn't seem as if she could take them in. Her mind shut itself against them, and quite without conscious thought she turned the sheet over to look for the signature, but the writing went on right down to the foot of the page, and then it just left off. There wasn't any signature.

She turned it over again and began to read from where it seemed to begin at the top of the page. There wasn't an address, and that wasn't a date. There wasn't properly speaking any beginning at all. It just started.

'You think pretty well of yourself, don't you, Miss Georgina Grey? You've been brought up soft, and I suppose you think you'll go on living soft to the end of the chapter. You won't. You've got things coming to you that you're not going to like. Some of those who are underneath now will be on top, and you will be underneath. When you have never had anything to speak of you don't miss it so much, but when you have always had everything and then quite suddenly you don't have anything at all you miss it like hell. Up with the rocket and down with the stick, that's you. I suppose you think people don't see how you treat your cousin — looking down your nose at her and being patronising and giving her your cast-off clothes. You needn't think it doesn't get talked about, or that there aren't quite a lot of people who are getting up to boiling-point about it. And all because you want everything for yourself and because she is prettier than you are and with much more taking ways, and because A. H. and *others* have begun to think so. And that hits you where it hurts, doesn't it? Don't worry, there will be lots more coming! People don't like to see a girl spiting another girl and trying to push her down just because she is younger and prettier, and because you think J. F. is getting too fond of her as well as A. H.'

Georgina read it right through to the end. Then she put it back into the envelope. Her first feeling was one of bewilderment. You heard about anonymous letters, but you didn't get them. They were like a lot of things which you read about in the papers. They happened to other people. They didn't happen to you. It took her a little time to assimilate the fact that this was happening to her. It was as unexpected and as unbelievable as if she had been slapped in the face in the street by a stranger. She had to go on from there to wondering why anyone should do such a thing, and to the further question of who could have done it. Who could possibly have written her a letter like that? It must be someone who knew about her and about Mirrie, but she couldn't think of anyone who would do such a thing. She stood there by the breakfast table with the cheap envelope in her hand and felt as if she had missed a step in the dark.

When she heard voices in the hall she went out quickly by way of the service-door and up the back stairs to her room, where she put the letter into a drawer. After which she came down again to find Mirrie and Anthony in the dining-room. They were standing very close together. No. She wouldn't allow that into her thought — it was Mirrie who was standing very close to Anthony. It was just a way she had of coming right up to anyone — to him, or to Johnny, or to Jonathan Field — to stand like that with her head tilted, stroking a coat-sleeve and looking up. It was an artless, unconscious trick and very engaging, but just at this moment Georgina could have done without it.

Anthony turned to meet her, and Mirrie sparkled and said.

'It's a lovely morning. And Anthony's going to show me a place in the wood where a badger lives, only he says we shan't see him, because he only comes out at night. Why do you suppose he does that? I should hate to go out in the dark alone — wouldn't you?'

'But then you're not a badger,' said Anthony in a teasing voice.

After breakfast Georgina took the anonymous letter to Jonathan Field in the study. He looked up with an air of impatience as she came to stand by the writing-table and put the envelope down in front of him.

'This came by the morning post. I thought I had better show it to you.'

When he spoke, the impatience was in his voice.

'What is it?'

'It's an anonymous letter.'

'An anonymous — what nonsense!'

'I thought you had better see it.'

He picked the envelope up, his brows drawn very close and black above his deep-set eyes. He got the letter out, frowned even more darkly, and read it through. When he had come to the end he turned back and read it a second time. Then glancing up he said sharply,

'Any idea who wrote it?'

'Absolutely none.'

He dropped it on the blotting-pad.

'Cheap paper, bad writing. What's it all about?'

'I don't know.'

He leaned back, swinging his chair round so that he faced her.

'A cheap, nasty letter. But why was it written?'

She said again, 'I don't know.'

His voice was suddenly sharp.

'It means there's been talk! About Mirrie and about you! People have been talking! Why? Something must have been going on to make this talk about you! Why haven't I been told?'

'There wasn't anything to tell.'

He brought his hand down hard upon the letter.

'There's no smoke without some fire! No one writes a letter like this unless there's been talk! Talk and *feeling*! If you weren't getting on with Mirrie you ought to have told me! You might know she wouldn't say anything. She is always thinking about what she can do to please you. I suppose that ought to have opened my eyes. I can't think why it didn't. She hasn't ever felt secure — she hasn't felt sure of herself or of you.'

Georgina went back a step.

'Uncle Jonathan!'

'I thought you would be glad to have her here — as glad as I was. She is so grateful for everything — so anxious to please. I can't understand why you should have taken this prejudice.'

'Why do you say that I have taken a prejudice?'

He had always been quick to anger, but not against her. She was not afraid, but she felt herself vulnerable. The whole thing was so sudden, so much a denial of what their relationship had always been. His hand beat on the table and on the letter that lay there.

'I don't understand this about the clothes — giving her old things to wear. It would be very humiliating — very humiliating indeed. For her — and for me, since it seems it has been noticed. I can't think how you came to do such a thing!'

Georgina's eyes had not left his face. She saw it hard and altered. She steadied her voice and said,

'You haven't waited to ask me whether I did do it.'

'Well, I am asking you now.'

She came a step nearer and rested her hand on the edge of the table.

'Will you let me tell you just what happened? You brought Mirrie here, and she had nothing. You said she had come on a visit. You didn't say for how long. You didn't say that you meant to make yourself responsible for her.'

'I hadn't made any plans.'

'Uncle Jonathan, she really hadn't got anything. I took one or two things of my own over to Mrs. Bell at Deeping. She is very clever about alterations, and she took them in and made them fit. If Mirrie minded she didn't say so. She seemed to be terribly pleased. She said she had never had anything so nice before, and I suppose she hadn't. They were very good things.'

His face was closed against her. He said,

'You shouldn't have done it. It was putting her in a wrong position. You should have come to me.'

'I didn't like to.'

She couldn't say — it wasn't in her to say — that there had been an instinct to protect the stray kitten of a creature that he had brought home with him. There had been a trunk full of what was literally rubbish — old musty clothes, chiefly black — old tattered books — and a frightful mangy eiderdown pushed in on the top to keep the other things steady. There wasn't anything that could have been worn in Field End. There wasn't anything at all. She couldn't tell him that Mirrie hadn't a change of underclothes, or a nightgown to sleep in, or practically anything except a cheap shoddy dress she stood up in and the cheap shoddy coat which covered it.

Jonathan echoed her last words.

'You didn't like to? Why?'

Georgina had an appalled feeling that they were sliding rapidly down a steep place to disaster. She had known him for too many years to mistake what was happening. She had seen him involved in too many breaches, controversies, and quarrels, starting often from some infinitesimal seed and ending in bitter estrangement. And always whilst the process was going on he would be impervious to argument or reason. But this was the first time it had happened with her. She had been seventeen years under his roof, and it was the very first time. She couldn't believe that he had gone too far away for her to reach him. She only knew that she had to try. She said,

'It's difficult — '

'I asked you why you didn't come to me. Well, why didn't you?'

'I didn't know what you wanted — what you meant to do. I really didn't like to let you, to let anyone know, how little she had. I didn't know you meant her to stay. Don't you see I wanted to be nice to her? I thought it would be just a thing between us — between two girls. It's the sort of thing that is happening in families all the time, girls passing them on because they've grown out of them, or because they've got tired of them and think they would like to have a change.'

Jonathan broke in on a hard sarcastic note.

'Yes — now we're getting there! You were tired of the things and you wanted a change. They weren't good enough for you, but they were all right for Mirrie. And she was so innocent and inexperienced she didn't see that she was being humiliated. Do you know what she said to me the other day? I thought it was one of the most pathetic things I had ever heard. I had given her a cheque to fit herself out, and she came in here before dinner to show me her dress. She looked a picture, and she held up a bit of the skirt and said, "Do you know, this is the first bought dress of my own I've ever had." Cast-offs, that was all she'd had all her life — other people's cast-offs. Charity parcels! And then after I brought her here, when you might think she had got away from all that, she runs into it again. You pick out some old clothes you don't want any more, let the village dressmaker botch them up, and get the poor child to believe you are doing her a kindness in foisting them on her!'

They had got a long way from the anonymous letter, and a long way from reason and from the likelihood that he could be got to listen to her and to understand. She couldn't get near him, she couldn't reach him at all. The letter lay where he had dropped it on his blotting-pad. She came round to stand beside him and leaned to pick it up. As she turned away with it in her hand, he said,

'Wait! There is something I have been going to say to you.'

He pushed his own chair back and sat there tapping on the arm. Then he looked over to her and spoke briefly.

'It's about my will.'

She was pale above the pale primrose of her jumper and cardigan. The dark grey eyes looked all the darker for it. When he said, 'It's about my will,' a little colour came up momentarily and then was gone again.

'Uncle Jonathan — '

He lifted a hand from his knees.

'I am speaking. What I want you to do is to listen. I suppose like everyone else you have taken it for granted that whatever I have will come to you?'

'Uncle Jonathan, *please* — '

He rapped out, 'I have told you that I am speaking! All I want you to do is to listen! There is nothing more offensive than the intrusion of emotion into matters of business. This is a matter of business. It concerns my will. I don't wish you to be under any misapprehension as to its terms. I have never embarrassed you or myself by discussing them with you, but since I have recently decided to make certain alterations, I feel that you should be informed. I don't want you to think that my decision has been made in a hurry, or because of any indignation which I may be feeling at the moment. I came to the conclusion some time ago that my present will no longer expressed my wishes. I am therefore proposing to make certain alterations. In the main the legacies to the household staff and to charities will remain as they are, but there will be important changes in some other directions. I intend to make provision for Mirrie.'

Georgina drew in her breath. She said quickly and warmly,

'But of course, Uncle Jonathan.'

There was a faint sarcastic lift of the black brows which made so decorative a contrast with his thick grey hair. He said,

'Very nice of you, I am sure, but I would ask you not to interrupt. I intend to provide for Mirrie by making her secure and independent. This will make a considerable difference in what under my present will is left to you.'

'Uncle Jonathan — '

'Disinterestedness can be overdone, my dear. Are you going to pretend you wouldn't care if I cut you off without a penny?'

She said in a quick indignant voice,

'Of *course* I should care! It would mean that you were terribly angry, or that you didn't care for me any more — of course I should care! But not about Mirrie. I should be very glad about your providing for Mirrie. Oh, darling, please wake up and stop thinking dreadful things about me! I don't see how we can be talking to each other like this. It's like some frightful dream — it really is! What has put such horrible ideas into your head?'

He said,

'They are facts, and facts are inconvenient things. You can't get away from them by calling them dreams. If a thing is plain enough for you to be getting anonymous letters about it, it's time something was done. You've been jealous of that poor child from the first, and I was a fool not to see it.'

Georgina said slowly,

'Who has been putting these things into your mind? Is it Mirrie?'

There was bleak anger in his eyes.

'Mirrie? No, it wasn't Mirrie, poor child. She thinks you have meant to be kind to her. It's been all, "Look how kind Georgina is! She has given me an old dress of hers — such a pretty colour," or, "Isn't she kind! She says I can come out for a walk with her and Anthony, but of course I knew she would rather be alone with him, so I didn't go."

'There was something about that in your letter wasn't there? Something about A. H. getting too fond of her. Now, my dear, I'll give you a bit of advice, and if you've any sense you'll take it. There's nothing any man dislikes more than a jealous, spiteful woman, so if you are interested in Anthony Hallam, I would advise you to be careful how you show your jealousy of Mirrie.'

She did not know what to do or what to say. Her every word and look seemed only to feed that strange unnatural anger. It was no use talking to him whilst he was like this — she had better go. But if she said nothing, the whole thing went by default. She made an effort and spoke.

'I never thought of being jealous.'

'Then you had better do so without delay! It is a bad fault and you should try to correct it. If you married it could wreck your life. I tell you frankly that there is nothing which puts a man off so much.'

It wasn't any good. He had worked himself into a state of exasperation where there was nothing she could so or say. She said,

'It isn't any good my saying anything, is it, but I haven't really thought about Mirrie like that. I don't know what had happened between us. I don't know what you want me to do. I think I had better go.'

Her voice had got slower and slower. Now it just left off. She turned with the letter in her hand went across the room to the door. She had her back to him as she went, and all at once she had the feeling that there was something behind her, something that was an enemy. There was the old, old instinct that it wasn't wise to turn your back upon an enemy. She came to the door and found it unlatched and went out. She thought that she had shut it behind her when she came into the room. But it was unlatched now.

CHAPTER SIX

ANTHONY HALLAM was coming down the stairs. Because he always looked at Georgina when she was there to look at he looked across at her now, and saw at once that something had happened. For one thing there was no colour in her face, just absolutely none, and for another the way she was coming towards him across the hall she might have been blind. Her eyes were fixed, but not on him, and if she wasn't exactly feeling her way, she had one hand a little out in front of her and it gave that effect. It was her left hand and it was empty. Her right hand hung down with a letter in it. He ran down the rest of the stairs and met her as she came to the bottom step.

'Georgina — what is it? Have you had bad news?'

He was one step above her. She looked up at him as if she had only just seen that he was there and said, 'Yes.' He could see right down into her eyes, and they had a lost look.

'What is it?'

The hand which had been stretched out took hold of the baluster. The other one, the one that held the letter, motioned him to let her pass. He stepped aside, and she went on up the stair without turning her head. He went up behind her, but she did not seem to know that he was there. She had own sitting-room on the first floor. It was along a passage to the left, a bright room looking south-east with a view over the terrace to the garden with its sloping lawn and the great cedar which had been there since the house was built. He went in with her, and the first time she noticed him was when she put out a hand to shut the door and it touched his own. She moved at once and said,

'I want to be alone.'

'I'll go if you want me to. But can't you tell me what is the matter? You look — '

She went over to a table and put down the letter she was holding. Then she took a yellow linen handkerchief out of her cardigan pocket and rubbed her hand with it. He had the impression that she was wiping something off. He said quickly,

'Is it that letter?'

There was a movement that said, 'Yes.'

'Who is it from?'

'I don't know. Anthony — '

'Don't send me away. I can't go — I want to help you. Won't you tell me what has happened?'

She moved her head in a gesture which indicated the letter.

'Do you mean I am to read it?'

She had a moment of indecision. She had shut her doors. There was an impulse to bolt them against him, there was an impulse to throw them wide and let him in. There was no conscious thought behind the pressure of these two things. Each had its own urge, its own force. And then quite suddenly she was letting the second impulse have its way. She hadn't known what she was going to do until she was doing it. She heard herself say,

'Yes, read it.'

Whilst he was reading it she watched him. She was tall, but he stood half a head above her. He had a tanned skin and pleasantly irregular features, eyes between blue and grey, eyebrows dark with a sort of quirk in them, a good strong line of jaw, and a firm-set mouth and chin. There floated vaguely on the surface of her mind an old and comforting impression that he didn't look as if he would ever let anyone down.

He was frowning over the letter. When he got down to the bottom of the second page where it left off he said,

'The proper place for anonymous letters is the fire. Let's burn it.'

'No, I don't think so.'

'Much better get rid of it, unless — have you any idea where it comes from?'

'No.'

'You had much better put it on the fire.'

She had begun to remember what she ought to have remembered before, that he came into the letter himself. One of the more unpleasant sentences floated up— 'because you want everything for yourself, and because she is prettier than you are and with much more taking ways, and because A. H. and *others* have begun to think so.' *She* was Mirrie, and A. H. was Anthony Hallam. He couldn't miss it, or the place right at the end where it said, 'because you think J. F. is getting fond of her as well as A. H.' She said,

'I ought not to have let you read it.'

'I'm very glad you did.'

She drew a long troubled breath.

'I oughtn't to have let anyone read it. I didn't think — I never thought that anyone would believe those things were true.'

'Of course they wouldn't!'

'Uncle Jonathan did.'

When she said that, he knew where the lost look came from. It wasn't the anonymous letter that had shaken her. It was Jonathan Field.

'He *didn't*!'

'He did. I thought I ought to show it to him. I never thought he would believe it, but he did. He has got very fond of Mirrie, and he thinks I'm jealous. I don't think I am — I really don't think so. But he believes it. I even began to think he might have written the letter himself. Not really, you know, but he did seem to agree with everything it said.'

'But that's nonsense!'

The anger in his voice warmed her. There had been a deadly inner cold, like touching metal with your bare hand in a deep frost. She had done that once and it had burned her hand. Anthony's anger didn't burn, it warmed the things which Jonathan Field's anger had frozen. Her thoughts began to move again, to order themselves.

'Anthony, will you tell me truly, has there been anything for people to notice about the way I've treated Mirrie? If there has, I haven't known it myself — I really haven't.'

'You've been an angel to her. Jonathan must be off his head. Are you sure you understood him properly?'

She walked away from him to the window. The garden lay under a grey sky that was rifting to let through a glimpse of wintry blue. The lawn went on for along way, running down to trees which fringed a stream. The trees were leafless and the tracery of bare branches stood out against the water-flow. The weather had been mild and the lawn was green. The cedar had no winter change to make. Some of last year's cones stood up on the sweeping branches like a flock of little brown owls. Field End had been her home since she was three years old. She had been sheltered and loved there. It was Mirrie who had been the lost waif with no one to care for her. It came into her mind that the anonymous letter turned this upside down. 'You think pretty well of yourself. ... You've been brought up soft ... You've got things coming to you that you're not going to like. Some of those who are underneath now will be on top, and you will be underneath.' The words came out of the hidden places of her thought like rats coming out of their holes in the dark. It was all too fantastic to be real. She could have put the letter in the fire and — no, she couldn't have forgotten about it. But she would have done her best not to let it make any difference to her, or to Mirrie, or to anyone. It wasn't the letter, it was Jonathan's reaction to it that was turning her world upside down. She had expected him to be angry, but his anger hadn't turned against the anonymous letter-writer, it had turned against herself. All the concern, all the protective warmth were for Mirrie whom he had known for just six weeks. There was none to spare for the girl who had felt herself a daughter to

41

him ever since she could remember feeling anything at all.

Anthony had come to stand beside her. He put an arm about her shoulders, but he did not speak. It was she who broke the silence, turning to face him as she did so.

'I think I shall have to go away.'

He said, 'It will pass.'

He wasn't touching her any more, but they were very close. She shook her head.

'He has changed. He hasn't got the same feeling for me any more. I thought he would be angry about the letter, but I didn't think he would be angry with me. He never has been before — not like that. But I've seen it happen with other people, even when he had known them and been friends with them for a long time. It starts with something, anything, it doesn't seem to matter much what, and then he goes on working himself up up until there's nothing left that's worth keeping. I've known it happen half a dozen times, and there's nothing anyone can do. It doesn't pass, and he doesn't come round. The other person is just wiped off the slate for good and all.'

'Georgina!'

As if she had not heard him, she said,

'And now it's happened to me.'

He took her hand and found it very cold.

'It won't happen that way with you — it can't! You mustn't do anything in a hurry.'

There was a momentary flash in the dark grey eyes.

'I don't think I'll wait until he tells me to go.'

'He won't do that.'

'I think he will if I give him the chance. The bother is that I'm not trained for anything. Training takes time, and one has to live.'

He waited a little before he said soberly,

'You know, you are making too much of this.'

'You didn't hear what he said.'

'People say a lot of things they don't mean when they are angry.'

Her eyes were suddenly bright with tears.

'I thought he would be angry about the letter. I couldn't believe it when he was angry with me.'

He said as easily as he could,

'Oh, he just flew off the handle. He does sometimes — everyone does. You know how it is yourself. You say something because you are angry, and you go on getting angrier because you have said it. It's a sort of buttered slide.'

She shook her head.

'No — no, it wasn't like that. The letter touched it off, but what he said — Anthony, what he said was there in his mind already. I think it had been there for a long time — perhaps since very soon after he brought Mirrie here. You see, he told me he was going to alter his will.'

'He told you that just now?'

'Yes, just now. But he had been thinking about it before that — he must have been. He said he didn't want me to think that his decision had been made in a hurry, or because of any indignation he might be feeling at the moment. Those are his own words. And then he went on to say he was going to make provision for Mirrie. And I said, "Of course," and he told me not to interrupt, and he asked me whether I was going to pretend I wouldn't care if he cut me off without a penny.'

'And what did you say to that?'

The colour came up brightly in her cheeks.

'I blazed. I said of course I should care, because it would mean that *he* didn't care for me any more. I said I was very glad about Mirrie, and I asked him what had put such horrible ideas into his head.'

'What did he say to that?'

The ringing tone went out of her voice.

'It wasn't any good. He called Mirrie "that poor child", and said I had always been jealous of her from the first and he had been a fool not to see it. It wasn't any use talking to him after that. I did try, but it wasn't any good. I think everything has gone, and I don't think there is anything that can bring it back. So I shall have to go. I can't stay here if he doesn't want me any longer. I oughtn't to have said anything about it. I wasn't going to, only you were there and it came out. I don't want to go on talking about it any more. I want you to go.'

He went as far as the door and turned round with a jerk and came back again.

'Georgina — '

She shook her head.

'I asked you to go away.'

'Yes, I'll go. I just want to say — to say — '

'Don't say it.'

'It's no good your trying to stop me. It's just that I love you very much.' He caught himself up and repeated with a change of emphasis, 'I love you *very* much. But I expect you must know that already. I've loved you for a long time, and I shall go on loving you always. Will you remember that, and if there is anything I can do, will you let me do it? That's all, my dear.'

He went out of the room and shut the door behind him.

CHAPTER SEVEN

MIRRIE FIELD had seen Georgina and Anthony come up the stairs and go into her sitting-room. She had, as a matter of fact, seen Anthony go down. Her room was very nearly opposite Georgina's bedroom and sitting-room. She came out of it, looked down the passage towards the landing, and saw Anthony at the top of the stairs. He had come from the other side of the house, and a moment after she had caught sight of him he took the first step down and was out of sight. Since there was no one to see her, she ran to the end of the corridor. She wouldn't have run if there had been any chance of her being seen. She just wanted to catch him up as if by accident before he had time to cross the hall and go into one of the downstair rooms. But when she came to the end of the passage he had only got as far as the bottom step, and Georgina was standing just below him, looking up with her hand on the newel.

Mirrie could see that something had happened. She stepped back quickly because she didn't want Georgina to see her. She didn't want anyone to think she was following Anthony Hallam. She waited until they began to come up the stairs, and then she ran back to her room, where she left the door ajar and stood behind it listening. They came along the passage and neither of them said a word. She heard them go into Georgina's sitting-room and shut the door. Then she came out of her room and went downstairs and across the hall to the study.

Jonathan Field was at his table driving a furious pen. He looked up sharply as she came in, but as soon as he saw her his face changed. She had a timid look, standing there by the door, her hand still on the knob as if she were not quite certain whether to go or stay. He put down his pen and said,

'Come along in, Mirrie.'

She shut the door and came a few steps forward.

'I don't want to interrupt — '

'You won't be interrupting — I wanted to see you. Come along over here and sit down.'

He got up, fetched a chair, and laid a hand on her shoulder before seating himself again. Throughout the interview which had just ended Georgina had remained standing, but Mirrie was to sit, and to sit comfortably. His glance softened as it dwelt on her. She was wearing some of the things she had bought with the cheque he had given her, a green tweed skirt, and a jumper and cardigan that went with it. The colour suited her. He said,

'Well, my dear, I'm just off to town to see Maudsley. He is my solicitor. I want to get on with the business I spoke to you about the other day. There's no time like the present.'

'Oh — Georgina didn't tell me — '

'Georgina didn't know. That is to say, I have told her that I am going to make changes in my will, but she doesn't know that I am going up to see about it today. As a matter of fact I have only just made up my mind about that. Wills are gloomy things, and I'll be glad to get the business over and done with. Besides I want to see you in your proper place. I want everyone to know how I think of you. It's only right that they should. From now on it will be just the same as if you were my daughter. You have the name already, so there won't be any need to change it, and under my will you will have just what I would leave to a daughter.'

Her hands were clasped in her lap, her eyes were lifted to his face.

'Oh, you *are* good to me!'

'My dear child — '

'No one has ever been good to me like you are! It's so wonderful I can't believe it! When you brought me here I thought how wonderful it was. And then I thought how dreadful it was going to be to go back. I used to wake up in the night and cry about it. And then you asked me whether I was happy here, and you said — and you said that if I *was* I could stay — always. Oh, you don't know what I felt like — you don't know!'

Jonathan Field was considerably affected. He got out a stiff old-fashioned linen handkerchief and blew his nose, and with a quick graceful movement Mirrie was out of her chair and down on her knees beside him.

'Oh, darling — darling — *darling*! You can't possibly know how grateful I am!'

He pushed the handkerchief down into his breast pocket and put an arm round her.

'Grateful, are you? Well, there's no need for that between you and me. But you're glad to be my little girl? That's all I want from you, you know — just to see you happy and enjoying yourself, and to know that you're a little bit fond of an old fellow who is quite stupidly fond of you.'

She looked up at him through her lashes.

'Is it stupid to be fond of me? No one has ever really been fond of me before.'

'My darling child!'

She said, 'It's wonderful for me. You don't know how wonderful it is.' And then she was dropping a kiss on his hand and slipping back on to her chair, and when she was there she took a small green handkerchief out of her cardigan pocket and dabbed her eyes with it.

CHAPTER EIGHT

IT was not until the rest of the party met at lunch that Jonathan Field's journey to town became generally known. Mrs. Fabian had apparently encountered him in the hall and delayed him to the point of frenzy whilst she considered whether it would be worth his while to go to the Army and Navy Stores and enquire whether a certain kind of rice was now available. As they settled themselves round the dining-table, now reduced to its smallest proportions, she proceeded to relate the incident.

'They always used to stock it before the war, so I thought it would be a good thing if he went and *asked*. The other sort is not really any good for milk puddings — at least that is what Mrs. Stokes always says, though I don't see why. But the trouble is that I never can remember which is which. There is Indian, and Carolina rice, and one of them is good for milk puddings and the other isn't. There wasn't time for me to go and ask Mrs. Stokes. Really men are terribly impatient when they are starting for anywhere, and I don't see that it could possibly matter as he was going by car, and I thought if he were just to ask them at the Stores they would be able to tell him — about which was which and the milk puddings, you know. But he seemed to be in such a *hurry*. Really he might have had half a dozen trains to catch instead of going all the way in his comfortable car! So I thought it would be best to leave it — especially when he said he had an appointment with Mr. Maudsley! Of course solicitors are very busy people, and I am sure they must make a great deal of money — at least my Uncle James always said they did. He was my father's brother but they didn't get on very well, and he kept on having lawsuits, so when he died there wasn't any money at all. He used to get quite worked up about lawyers. I remember his getting a terribly large bill after a lawsuit he had over a dispute about some property on the borders of Wales which had come to him from his grandmother. I know he quoted a verse about it, and my mother was quite distressed. Now let me see if I can remember it —

' "Find me a parson that will not lie — " ' She broke off and cast a deprecating look around the table. 'Really that was very rude and uncalled for, but the person who wrote it may have had some unfortunate experience. Perhaps I had better begin again —

> "Find me a parson that will not lie,
> And a webster that is leal,
> And a lawyer that will not steal,
> And lay these three a dead corpse by,
> And by the virtue of these three
> The said dead corpse shall quickened be."

But I'm not sure that I've got the lines in the right order, because after all it is quite a long time ago.'

Johnny Fabian burst out laughing and said,

'A bit hard on websters, don't you think? I should have thought weaving was a most respectable trade — poor but honest and all that sort of thing. So Jonathan has gone up to see his solicitor, has he? Who is he going to cut out of his will?'

It was purely a matter of luck that Stokes at that moment should have been out of the room. No one who knew Johnny could have deceived himself into imagining that the mere presence of a butler would be any check upon his tongue. Mrs. Fabian said, 'My dear boy!' in a tone of indulgent reproof. Georgina looked across the table at him. But he only laughed.

'Hush — not a word! What an inhibited lot we are. The more passionately interested you are in a subject, the worse form it is to mention it. Everyone is passionately interested in wills, but we mustn't mention them.'

Anthony said, 'Dry up, Johnny!' and Stokes came back into the room bearing a covered silver dish. With the ease of long practice Johnny accomplished a dexterous verbal slide.

'Anyone who pretends not to be interested in money is either a fool or a knave. If you've got any you've got to keep it breeding, and if you're not interested enough to do that you wake up one day and find it's gone and left you! If you haven't got the stuff you have to work frightfully hard to get it, and if I've got to tell the truth and shame the devil I don't mind saying it's a rotten prospect. When you've got to do a twelve-hour grind every day, what's the good of being rich? You just end up like the millionaires who live on tablets and spend their vacations having a rest-cure in some expensive nursing home. On the other hand there's something dreary about being poor.'

Mrs. Fabian was beginning to help a dish of chicken and mushrooms which had been placed before her. She said,

'Georgina, my dear — this is always so good. Mirrie — Anthony — I am sure you must be hungry, and I don't have to ask about Johnny.'

She had an odd slapdash way of wielding a spoon and fork. Stokes, already outraged by not being allowed to hand the dish, watched gloomily whilst what he afterwards described as drips and drabs clouded the surface of a carefully polished table. When she had come down to help herself, and he had been permitted to hand artichokes and potatoes, he was dismissed.

'Thank you, Stokes — you can just leave the vegetables in front of Mr. Anthony.' Then, when he had gone out of the room, she broke in upon the general conversation with a heartfelt, 'Oh, yes, that is so true — what Johnny was saying about being poor. My father had a very good living, but he hadn't any private means, so when he and my mother died in the same year there wasn't anything left, and I went to live with my father's aunts. It was very good of them, because they hadn't really enough for themselves, but they took me in and brought me up, and when they died I wasn't young and I had never been trained for anything. What they had been living on went to another branch of the family, so it really was quite a frightening prospect. One should not concern oneself with money, but it is very difficult not to do so when people keep sending in their bills and you haven't anything to pay them with.'

Johnny, who was sitting next to her, leaned over, patted her arm, and said,

'Darling, desist. We shall all burst out crying in a minute.'

She met his laughing look with an astonished one.

'Oh, no, my dear, that would be foolish — and there is no need, because everything turned out for the best. Your father was a widower and you were only four years old, so of course he needed someone to come and run the house. But after a little he engaged a housekeeper and asked me to marry him, because he thought it would work out better that way. And so it did, and we were all very happy together until he died. And even then we should have been quite comfortably off if he had not put so much of his money into a South American mine. Dear me, I am keeping you all waiting and letting my chicken get cold! Won't anyone else have some more? It is so good.'

Anthony and Johnny responded by passing up their plates, and then Mrs. Fabian thought she would have a little more herself, and perhaps another artichoke and just one potato.

On a formal occasion Georgina would play hostess, but when it was just a family party it was customary to allow Mrs. Fabian the place of honour. Today Anthony Hallam was in Jonathan's place, Georgina on his right with her back to the windows, Mirrie and Johnny on his left. He leaned toward Georgina and said,

'You have been warned! Don't buy South American mines or listen to the confiding stranger with a gold brick or buried treasure. It's better to go through life thinking what a wonderful chance you've missed than to have to go on telling yourself all the different sorts of fool you've been.'

She looked up, and down again. He had a glimpse of something, he wasn't sure what. Why on earth had he said a thing like that? If he had wounded her, made her angry — She said, 'I don't think it arises as far as I am concerned,' and he knew that she was reminding him and herself that she was no longer likely to have a fortune either to keep or throw away. It had gone down the wind of Jonathan's new fancy, and what he had seen in her eyes was a proud reproach.

On his left Mirrie asked in a small ingenuous voice,

'What is a gold brick?'

Whilst Johnny was enlightening her Stokes came back into the room bearing an apple tart.

CHAPTER NINE

JOHNNY FABIAN, coming into what they called the morning-room, a convenient family gathering-place when the more formal drawing-room was not in use, found Mirrie there. She was sitting at an old-fashioned secretaire and she was engaged in writing a letter. She lifted a furrowed brow when he came in, stretched her inky fingers, and said in heartfelt tones,

'Oh, how I do hate writing? Don't you?'

He came and sat on the arm of the nearest chair.

'It depends who I am writing to.'

Mirrie sighed.

'I hate it always.'

'You wouldn't if you were writing to someone whom you passionately adored.'

'Wouldn't I?'

'Definitely not. Think of your favourite film star and im-agine he had just sent you a signed photograph and a flaming love-letter. Wouldn't the words just come tripping off the pen?'

Her brown eyes widened.

'Would they?'

'Do you mean to tell me they wouldn't?'

'I don't know — I haven't got a favourite film star.'

'Unnatural child!'

She continued to gaze at him.

'You see, I've practically never been to the pictures. The relations I lived with only went to improving films with pro-fessors and people like experts showing you things about coal mining or growing beet for making into sugar, and if any of them had written me love-letters I should have put them in the fire.'

Johnny laughed.

'Snubs to the whole race of film stars! It's no use their writ-ing to you! Well, who is the lucky person who is going to get a letter? Let's collaborate, and then I'll run you over to Lenton and we'll do a flick. Perhaps it will make you change your mind.'

'What is collaborate?' She said the word slowly, dividing it into syllables.

'Darling, didn't they teach you anything at school?'

Mirrie's lashes drooped.

'Oh, I'm not clever. They said I wasn't.'

'Well, it means two people writing the same book. Or letter.'

'I don't see how they can.'

'I'll show you. You'll see we'll get along like a house on fire. Who is this letter to?'

She hesitated.

'Well, it's to Miss Brown.'

'And who is Miss Brown?'

'She was one of the people at school.'

'Do you mean one of the mistresses?'

Mirrie gazed.

'There were two Miss Browns. The letter is to Miss Ethel Brown, because I promised to write to her and tell her how I was getting on.'

'All right, that won't take us long. How far have you got?'

She picked up a sheet of paper and read from it:

'DEAR MISS BROWN,

I said I would write, so I am writing. I hope you are quite well. This is a very nice place. The house has seventeen rooms without counting the cellars. Some of them are big. There are bathrooms made out of some of the bedrooms because people didn't worry about baths when the house was built. It is what they call Georgian. There are beautiful things in it, and silver dishes with covers in the dining-room. Everyone is very kind to me, even Georgina. You said she wouldn't be, but she is *quite*. Uncle Jonathan is very kind. He gave me a cheque for a hundred pounds to get my dress for the dance and other things. It was the dress with white frills. He has given me a lot of things. I think he has a great deal of money. He says I am to be like his daughter and he is putting it into his will. It is very kind of him.'

She lifted her eyes from the page and said, 'That's as far as I've got.'

It took a good deal to surprise Johnny Fabian, but this artless epistle actually startled him. He experienced a strong desire to know more, and most particularly to discover why Miss Ethel Brown should be the recipient of these interesting confidences. When Mirrie, pursuing the theme upon which her letter had ended, said, 'It's dreadfully kind of Uncle Jonathan, isn't it?' he said yes it was, and enquired,

'But why write to Miss Brown?'

'I said I would.'

Johnny's eyebrows rose.

'About Jonathan?'

'About how I got on.'

He laughed.

'Well, I should say you had got off! With Jonathan anyhow!'

She repeated what she had said before, but with an added emphasis.

'It's *very* kind of him.'

'He really said he was going to adopt you?'

'Oh, no, he didn't say that. He said he was going to treat me like his daughter, and that I would have what a daughter would have in his will. He said he had told Georgina, and that he wanted everyone to know just how he thought about me.'

Johnny whistled.

'He said that?'

'Yes, he did — after breakfast in his study. I think he had just been telling Georgina. I saw her come upstairs, and I thought she looked as if something had happened.'

'How did she look?'

Mirrie Field said, 'As if someone had hit her.'

He had a quick frown for that. It did just slip into his mind to think, 'How does she know how a girl looks when someone has hit her?' but he let it go.

'Mirrie, look here, I don't believe you ought to send that letter to Miss Brown.'

'Don't you?'

'No, I don't. I don't think Jonathan would like it.'

'But he said he wanted everyone to know how he felt about me.'

'I daresay he did. I don't suppose he wanted everyone to know that he was altering his will. He could be funny about that sort of thing. He mightn't like to think people were counting on what they were going to get after he was dead.'

'People?' said Mirrie in an ingenuous voice.

Johnny Fabian said, 'You, my child!' and laughed.

'Me?'

'Yes, darling. I think you had better tear up that letter to Miss Brown and drop the bits into a nice hot fire.'

Mirrie said, 'Oh!' and then 'Oh, I couldn't! It took me ever so long to write — and I promised.'

Johnny reflected that Miss Ethel Brown was probably a long way off, but he thought he had better find out where she lived. There didn't seem to be any particular call for tact, so he asked right out,

'Where is this school of yours?'

A good deal to his surprise she changed colour.

'It was the Grammar School. It was at Pigeon Hill.'

'And your Miss Browns taught there?'

'Not exactly. I just knew them. They — they were some sort of relation of Aunt Grace's. They taught in another school.'

He thought she was making it up as she went along. But in the name of all that was ridiculous, why? He was looking at her curiously.

'Is it your school you don't want to talk about, or theirs? And why?'

She said in a hurry,

'I didn't like being there. I don't want to think about it or talk about it ever.'

Yet she wrote to Miss Brown — a totally unnecessary performance!

'Well, if it's like that, I think I should let the whole thing fade. People are always saying they'll write letters that never get written. Why not let it go down the drain?'

Tears welled up in the pansy-brown eyes. She said in a little soft, obstinate voice,

'I can't.'

Johnny shrugged his shoulders and got up. He said, 'Well, it's your funeral,' and had got as far as the door, when she stopped him.

'Johnny —'

He turned.

'What is it?'

'I didn't like your saying that about funerals.'

'I am devastated!'

'You're not — you did it to be horrid! I'll just send this one letter, and then I won't write again.'

He said, 'I wouldn't send it at all,' and went out of the room.

Half an hour later he looked from a window and saw a small green figure emerging upon the road. Miss Mirrie Field taking the air? Or going to post a letter? He ran after her and caught her up.

'Air — exercise — or business?'

She had put on the warm topcoat which matched her tweed skirt and pulled a green beret over her curls.

'I just thought I'd like a walk.'

'Then I'd like one too. And after tea we'll go and do that flick in Lenton.'

She sparkled up at him.

'You *are* kind!'

The general shop which was also a branch post office was only a few hundred yards away. He was wondering whether she had Miss Brown's letter in her pocket, and whether she would let him see her post it, when she said,

'I just want to go into Mrs. Holt's and get some safety pins. I think it's such an amusing shop — don't you? Sweets, and cauliflowers, and bootlaces, and nailbrushes, and safety pins, and strings of onions — it's so funny having all those things together!'

The shop stood at the corner where the Deeping road ran off.

It was an old crouched cottage with a new shop-front stuck on to it. On one side there was a garage with a couple of petrol pumps, and on the other a frightful little drab brick house which replaced the picturesque but insanitary cottage demolished by a bomb-splinter in '44, the bomb itself having fallen in the middle of a field without so much as killing a sheep.

As they crossed over to Mrs. Holt's, Mary and Deborah Shotterleigh came out of the shop with two bull-terriers, an Airedale and a Peke. All the dogs barked joyfully and jumped up. Mary and Deborah could just be heard lifting ineffective voices, but the dogs barked on. When the larger of the bull-terriers sprang up in an attempt to lick Mirrie's chin she gave a little scream and clutched hold of Johnny.

'Down, Jasper! Down, Jane! Pingpong, you'll get trodden on! No, Leo!' shrieked the Shotterleigh girls.

Mirrie continued to clutch and the letter which had slipped from her pocket fell down under the feet of the dogs. By the time that she had run into the shop and Mary and Deborah were explaining that Jasper and Jane were really only puppies and the greatest darlings in the world, Johnny had retrieved it. Well, of course there is only one thing to do with a picked-up letter and that is to post it, always provided it is duly stamped and addressed. This letter was certainly stamped. Johnny walked across to the posting-slit which had been let into the old cottage wall and dropped it in. But before he did so he took a look at the address. It may have been one of those instinctive actions, or he may have thought that he would like to know where Mirrie had been at school. Most decidedly and distinctly she had slid away from the question when he asked it, and when anyone won't answer a perfectly simple question curiosity is sharply pricked.

He looked at the address, emitted a practically inaudible whistle, and posted the letter. He heard it fall into the box on the other side of the wall and turned round to wave goodbye to the Shotterleigh girls. They were hauling the bull-terriers away by means of handkerchiefs passed through their collars. The Airedale had come to heel, and the Peke's expression made it plain that he dissociated himself from what he considered to have been a vulgar brawl.

They were safely on the other side of the road before Mirrie ventured out of the shop. She said, 'What dreadful dogs!' After which she put her hand in her pocket and turned bright pink.

'My letter — oh, Johnny, my letter! It's gone!'

He looked at her with laughing eyes.

'It's all right — I posted it.'

She said, 'Oh!' They went over the road together.

When they were on the other side she produced a question.

'Did you look at it? Did it get muddy?'

'I looked at it. It had a paw mark in one corner — Jane's, I think.'

She didn't look at him. She was still rather pink. It was very becoming. Johnny said,

'Perhaps I ought to have asked you before I posted it. It struck me there was something wrong about the address.'

'Oh — '

'Your letter was to Miss Brown, wasn't it? *Or wasn't it?*'

'Of course it was!'

'Well, it wasn't addressed to her. It was addressed to Mr. E. C. Brown, 10 Marracott Street, Pigeon Hill, S.E. That's a London suburb, isn't it?'

She looked up at him sideways then, a creature wary of a trap. A squirrel perhaps? No, a kitten playing with a leaf — playing and catching it — playing and being caught. Only he wasn't so sure that this was play. She gave him a sudden glancing smile and said,

'Didn't I put Miss Brown's name on it?'

'You did not.'

She heaved a small sigh.

'I *am* stupid. But it doesn't matter — she'll get it all right. She is staying with her brother.'

'Mr. E. C. Brown?'

'Oh, yes.'

'And she is staying with him in the middle of the school term?'

She said in a voice of soft reproach, 'She hasn't been well.'

He laughed in a manner which left her in no doubt as to his scepticism. Then he said,

'All right, have it your own way, darling. Mr., Mrs., or Miss — I don't give a damn.'

Her lashes came down.

'You oughtn't to say damn.'

'And you ought not to write letters to Mr. Brown and tell fibs about them, my poppet. Especially when they are the sort of fibs that wouldn't deceive a half-witted child.'

They were turning in at the gate as he spoke. She stamped a small angry foot and ran from him, reaching the front door first and banging it in his face. She was halfway up the stairs as he crossed the hall, but she stopped and turned when she heard him laughing, her cheeks scarlet and her eyes bright with tears.

'I don't want to speak to you!'

He blew her a kiss.

'Darling, you needn't.' Then, as she stamped again and ran up the rest of the way, he called after her,

'It's all right — I won't tell. Don't forget we're going to a flick.'

He wondered whether she would come, and he wondered about some other things too. Just why had she read him her letter to Miss or Mr. Brown? If for some reason she wanted him to know that Jonathan was prepared to treat her as a daughter, just what would the reason be? Something on the lines of 'I'm not a little waif any longer — I'm Jonathan Field's heiress'? Was she, in fact, extending the baited hook, not only to him but also to the rather supposititious Mr. Brown? And where did all this leave Georgina? Was Jonathan Field going to have two heiresses or only one?

Mirrie came down smiling as the tea bell rang, and they made a party of four to see the film that was showing at the Rex in Lenton.

CHAPTER TEN

WHILST they were out Jonathan Field rang up to say that he would be staying in town for the night. Mrs. Fabian came trailing down the stairs to tell the returning party about it. She was wearing a purple dressing-gown in a flowing style with a long black chiffon scarf which imparted a funerary appearance. Since she had removed the bandeau with which she attempted to control her hair during the daytime, it now straggled wildly and she had to keep putting up a hand to push it back from her forehead and out of her eyes.

'Jonathan will be staying the night in town. I thought I had better come down and tell you. I don't know if he was speaking from Mr. Maudsley's office, but the line was extremely bad and I could hardly hear anything he said.'

Johnny laughed.

'Darling, I hope you really did hear whether he was coming back or not, because if you've mucked it up and he gets home in the middle of the night to find everything locked and bolted he won't be at all pleased.'

Mrs. Fabian's first expression of surprise changed rapidly to one of dismay.

'Oh, my dears, do you think — oh, I can't believe — but the line was extremely bad. I couldn't help wondering whether they turn down the current or whatever it is at night.'

Johnny said,

'Darling, you're out of your depth. And anyhow that isn't the point. Exactly what did Jonathan say?'

She had come to a standstill, and was now draped against the newel after the manner of one of those eighteenth-century ladies so often depicted as leaning on a pillar with an urn upon it. She put a hand to her head with an air of distraction and repeated,

'The line was so bad.'

'Darling, you're not trying. Just begin at the beginning and go right on.'

'Well, he said, "Is that you?", and when I said it *was*, he asked where all the rest of you were, so I said you had gone to the cinema in Lenton, and he made a kind of tutting noise as if he was vexed, and I'm not at all sure he didn't say "Damn!"'

'We'll give him the benefit of the doubt. Go on — you're doing fine.'

By common consent the other three were leaving her to Johnny. If anyone could get a coherent story out of her, he would be the one to do it. Mirrie had a hand on Anthony's arm. Georgina sat in the tall carved chair to the right of the door. She had gone with them because she wouldn't let anyone guess, not even Anthony, at the shock Jonathan Field had given her. It wasn't a case of more money or less. It was as if the ground had suddenly opened in front of her and swallowed up the foundations upon which her life was built. Nobody must know how dazed and bruised she felt. Anthony said he loved her, but she had thought that Jonathan loved her very much, and now he didn't seem to love her at all. She wouldn't have minded what he did for Mirrie — she wouldn't have minded his being fond of her. But did you have to take love away from one person in order to give it to another? She hadn't thought so, but it had happened, and there wasn't anything that she or anyone else could do about it. Nobody must pity her or feel obliged to try and pick up the pieces. She would do that for herself, but she must have time, just a little time, and at the moment she was too tired even to think. She sat up straight, her head against the tall back of the chair, and listened vaguely to Johnny and Cousin Anna. Georgina had called her that when she was three years old. Coming into her mind like this, it was a reminder how deep were the roots that Jonathan Field was tearing up.

The sound of their voices came to her with an effect of distance.

'He said he hadn't finished his business with Mr. Maudsley. And then I'm sure he said he couldn't be home tonight — at least I was sure until you asked me if I was.'

Johnny persevered.

'There must have been something to make you sure, or not sure. What did he *say*? Think! He used words — what were they?'

'Something about coming home tonight or not coming home tonight. I really cannot be certain which it was. There was a poem I learnt in the schoolroom, and I have forgotten most of it, but one of the verses began,

'So many things I cannot tell
Linger in memory's haunted shell.'

And they do, you know. You remember some things, but you don't remember others — like putting a sea-shell to your ear and hearing that rushing sound it makes. So I don't think it's any use going on about it. Jonathan will have his key, and we just won't bolt the door. And Mrs. Stokes has got some very nice sandwiches for you all in the dining-room, so do go along and have them.'

Jonathan did not come home in the night, and by breakfast time Mrs. Fabian was recollecting quite clearly that he had said he would stay at his club. In the course of the morning he rang through and said he would be back in time for dinner.

He brought a frowning presence into the house, Mr. Maudsley, an old friend, had ventured on some plain speaking.

'Not quite fair to put a girl forward as your heiress and then suddenly cut her out. You can provide quite adequately for Mirrie Field without doing that.'

'I haven't said that I mean to cut Georgina out of my will.'

'What you are proposing goes very close to it. And she is the nearer relation, isn't she?'

Jonathan gave a frowning nod.

'My sister Ina's daughter, and I repeat, I am not cutting her out of my will.'

'And Mirrie Field — where does she come in?'

'A cousin's daughter. I was on close terms with both her parents. There was — a most unfortunate quarrel which was never made up. They died during the war by enemy action, and the child was left friendless and penniless. I didn't even know of her existence. I heard of it for the first time a few months ago, and I set out to trace her. I found her — ' he paused, bit his lip, and said harshly, 'in a Home. Fortunately, she hadn't been there very long.'

Mr. Maudsley looked down at his blotting-pad. He found points in the story which disturbed him a good deal. He wondered whether he could venture upon a question. In the end he said,

'Where had she been since the death of her parents?'

He thought Jonathan was going to fly out at him, but he controlled himself. He got a curt,

'Some of her mother's relations took her in. They were in very straitened circumstances. She was not an inmate at the Home where I found her — she had a post there.' After a pause he went on again. 'She had had a most wretched time. I am naturally anxious to do all I can for her now. If it hadn't been for my quarrel with her parents she would never have been exposed to such privations.'

He drove himself down to Field End with an obstinate conviction that there was a conspiracy to prevent him from doing what he chose to do with his own. They were all against him, everyone except Mirrie, but they should see — he would show them!

As he opened the door with his latchkey and came into the hall, Mirrie ran down the stairs to meet him in a little white dress and a blue sash. The dress had a childish round neck and puffed sleeves. She looked young and eager as she caught him by the arm and put up her face to be kissed.

'Oh, you're back! How lovely!'

The frown melted from his brow.

'Pleased to see me?'

She squeezed his arm.

'Oh, *yes*! It's *lovely*! Did you get your horrid will signed and everything finished so that you won't have to go up again?'

He laughed.

'It isn't at all a horrid will for you, my child — you know that.'

She gazed up at him adoringly.

'I know how frightfully, frightfully kind you are! But I do hate talking about wills — don't you? I do hope it's all signed and finished with so that you won't have to think about it any more.'

He put an arm round her and kissed her again. It was rather

a solemn sort of kiss, not at all like the first one. Nobody had ever kissed her on the forehead before. It gave her a curious half-frightened feeling, but it only lasted a moment, and then he was saying,

'Oh, yes, it's all signed, with two of Mr. Maudsley's clerks to witness it, so there is nothing to worry about any more.'

The words were said more to himself than to her. They kept repeating themselves in his mind — 'Nothing to worry about — ' But the worry persisted, and the frown returned to his brow.

Dinner that evening would have dragged if Mirrie had not prattled artlessly about the film they had seen in Lenton.

'It was lovely, Uncle Jonathan, and it was almost the first real film I'd ever seen — the first proper story film, you know. Uncle Albert and Aunt Grace didn't approve of them. They didn't approve of such a lot of things.'

The four other people at the table absorbed this, the first mention of any previous family circle. Johnny immediately enquired,

'Darling, who are Uncle Albert and Aunt Grace?' Whereupon Mirrie raised pleading eyes to Jonathan's face.

'Oh, I'm sorry — they just slipped out.'

It was perhaps fortunate that Stokes was not in the room. Jonathan leaned across the table to pat Mirrie's shoulder and murmur, 'Never mind, my child,' and then straightened up to look sternly at the rest of them. 'They were relations of Mirrie's mother. She wasn't happy with them. I am anxious that she should forget about her life under their roof. She has been asked to think and speak of them as little as possible. There are, I hope, a great many much happier years before her in which there will be no need to dwell upon the past.'

Johnny pitched his voice to Georgina's ear.

'This is where we drink confusion to Uncle Albert and Aunt Grace. Do you think it would run to champagne?'

Mrs. Fabian sent a kind vague smile across the table.

'Dear Jonathan, how well you put it! As a poet whose name I have forgotten says;

'Tomorrow comes with flowers of May,
Gone are the snows of yesterday.'

So what is the use of thinking about them?'

Georgina had not meant to speak. She heard herself saying to Anthony very low,

'Sometimes it's the other way round.'

He said, 'It isn't — it won't be.'

She had a startled expression.

'I didn't mean to say it.'

He let his hand touch hers for a moment.

'It doesn't matter what you say to me — you know that.'

Mirrie went on telling Jonathan about the film.

CHAPTER ELEVEN

THE events of the evening which followed were to be told and re-told, weighed, scrutinized, and called upon to corroborate first one speculative theory and then another. Yet upon the surface, and at the time of their happening, these events were ordinary enough.

Mrs. Fabian's remark as she entered the drawing-room had been made upon every occasion of Jonathan's return to the family circle after some brief absence in town — 'Well, I hope that you were able to complete your business satisfactorily.'

The words might vary in some slight degree, but the intention remained the same. It was axiomatic that a man who went up to town, whether for the day or for a longer period, did so in order to attend to business, a word to which she attached no positive meaning. On this particular evening the formula was unchanged. She said,

'I do hope that you were able to complete your business satisfactorily.'

To which Jonathan replied, 'Yes, thank you.'

And with that the gong sounded and they went in to dinner.

When the meal was over they returned to the drawing-room.

Stokes brought in the coffee-tray and set it down on a small table before Georgina — all this in accordance with a routine which went back to her sixteenth birthday. She poured the coffee. Jonathan had his black and sweet. He stood beside her, took his cup from her hand, and remained there without turning away or sitting down, and without speaking.

Georgina went on pouring out. Mirrie liked a lot of milk and a lot of sugar. Johnny took his black. Anthony liked about a third milk. Mrs. Fabian discoursed on how coffee should be made, shook her head over Mrs. Stokes' excellent brew, and drank three cups of it. When Jonathan had had a second cup he went off to the study with the time-honoured excuse that he had letters to write.

A minute or two later Georgina got up and left the room. Stokes saw her go into the study. When she came back to the drawing-room she took up a book. Anthony came over with the evening paper in his hand and sat down beside her. He said in an undertone,

'Why don't you go to bed? You look all in.'

Georgina turned a page.

'No, I'm all right. We'll all go presently.'

By this time Johnny was teaching Mirrie picquet. He could be heard telling her that she had no card sense, to which she replied that she didn't know what it was, and Mrs. Fabian made the comment that serious card games were very fatiguing.

'But we used to play Old Maid, my three aunts and I, and sometimes a visiting cousin, and I used to enjoy it very much — only it vexed me because I was nearly always Old Maid.'

Johnny looked up from his serious game to blow her a kiss and say,

'Darling, it sounds like a riot! And it only goes to show that cards go by contraries, because the aunts didn't marry and you did.'

Jonathan was still in his study when they went upstairs. He often sat there until well after midnight, reading or dozing in his chair. At ten o'clock it was Stokes' habit to take in a tray with a decanter and a syphon, but as often as not they would be left untouched. The entrance of anyone else was neither expected nor desired.

The rest of the party went up to the wide first-floor landing from which a passage led off on either side. Here they said their good nights. Mrs. Fabian quoted:

> ' "Early to bed and early to rise
> Makes a man healthy and wealthy and wise."

Only of course you can't take it literally, because I've never been wealthy, and I don't suppose I ever shall be now.'

Johnny kissed her cheek and said,

'Perhaps you didn't get up early enough.'

And then they separated, Mirrie, Georgina and Mrs. Fabian going to the left, and Anthony and Johnny to the right. For a time there were the sounds of doors opening and shutting and of water running, but all muted by the solid fashion of the walls and the thickness of carpets and curtains. Where the modern house echoes to the dropping of a boot or the sound of a footstep crossing the bedroom floor, Field End absorbed these things and kept its counsel. Stokes and Mrs. Stokes took their way up the back stairs to their third-floor room without the slightest sound coming through by way of wall or ceiling. No one on either floor would hear the opening of the study door or the footstep of the master of the house as he crossed the hall and came up to his own room fronting the stair. Whether he came or did not come, no one in any room heard anything.

Georgina turned out the light, pulled back her curtains, and set the windows wide. She stood in her nightgown and looked out. At first there was nothing but darkness. Then, as her sight adjusted itself, she could see the sky diffusing a faint light through clouds. A light wind moved, and the clouds moved. The garden was all dim, all hidden. There were no stars, there was no moon, and there was no sound except that light moving of the wind.

Quite suddenly the darkness and the silence touched some spring of feeling. Tears came into her eyes and began to run down. It was the first time in those two days that she had had any tears to shed. Everything in her had been shocked and dry.

Now the tears flowed and went on flowing. When at last they ceased there was an extraordinary sense of relief. She washed her face and dried it with a soft towel. Then she got into bed and fell deeply and dreamlessly asleep.

Mrs. Fabian was having a particularly vivid dream. She always dreamed, but as a rule by the time she had waked up in the morning had had her tea brought to her by Doris, one of the two girls who came up from the village, the details of what she dreamed had quite disappeared, merely leaving her with some vague impression of happenings beyond her recollection. But now, at any rate whilst she was asleep, everything in the dream was perfectly clear. She was in a sunny garden with her husband, dear James, and his little boy Johnny about four years old. What she couldn't remember, and it worried her a good deal both at the time and when she thought about it next day, was whether she was married to James, or whether she only knew that she was going to marry him, because even in the dream she knew that they had been married. If it had not been for this uncertainty, which seemed to cast a shade of impropriety over what would otherwise have been most enjoyable, the dream would have been very pleasant indeed. As it was, her thought began to be a good deal disturbed. The sky clouded and everything got dark. She waked suddenly, and the darkness was in her room. Just for a moment she was really frightened. The change had been so sudden from the sunny garden with James and little Johnny to this total darkness with no one there but herself.

Her fear only lasted long enough for her to draw a few frightened breaths and start up on her elbow. As soon as she did that, she could see that a little light was coming in through the window. If the head of her bed had not been against the same wall she would have seen it at once, but she always waked so early if she faced the light. She switched on her bedside lamp and looked at her watch. It was twelve o'clock. She wondered what had waked her. After a minute or two she put out the light and went to sleep again.

Mirrie didn't dream at all — she hardly ever did. As soon as she got into bed and put her head on the pillow she fell asleep, and stayed asleep for as long as possible. One of the things she had hated most about living with Uncle Albert and Aunt Grace was having to get up at six-o'clock. She had to do the stairs and the sitting-room, and make her bed, and sweep and dust her room before breakfast — and breakfast was at half past seven. And then there were the breakfast things to wash, and the potatoes to peel, and a chapter to read before going to school. It took her half an hour to get to school. When she was at the Home it was even worse, because there was more to do and less time to do it in. How she had hated it all! Uncle Albert, with his solemn beard and the mouldy bookshop where he spent his days. If the books had even been new, but they weren't. He went to sales and bought in old rubbishy things which you wouldn't think anyone could want! And Aunt Grace, pinching and paring and scraping and saying what an expense Mirrie was, and she must get on at school so that she could earn her own living as soon as she possibly could. If it hadn't been for Sid.....

She didn't really want to think about Sid, who was Sid Turner and Aunt Grace's step-brother. Uncle Albert and Aunt Grace didn't approve of him. A step-brother wasn't really a relation at all. Sid had been in trouble. He got a year for being mixed up in robbing a till. That was when he was only eighteen. Mirrie thought it was horrid to go on holding it up against him all this long time afterwards, but Uncle Albert and Aunt Grace were like that. She had begun by being sorry for Sid, and when he asked her to meet him and do a flick she pretended she was going round to baby-sit for Hilda Lambton's sister who had married when she was seventeen and had twins. Her name was Floss, and she wouldn't give you away, because it was the sort of thing she used to do herself.

Mirrie had got to know the Lambtons at school. Hilda and she were the same age, and Floss two years older. It was the old Grammar School they all went to. There were some quite nice girls there. Some of them had pretty clothes, the sort she would have liked to have herself. They didn't wear them at school of course, because there was a uniform, but some of them went to the same church as Uncle Albert and Aunt Grace, so she saw them on Sundays. That was when they wore their nice clothes, but she had to go on wearing that hideous uniform. When she was seventeen and hadn't passed those wretched exams, Aunt Grace got her into the Home. They called her Assistant Matron, but she was really there to do the housework. And she still had to get up at six o'clock. Snuggled down warm in her bed at Field End she could remember just how horrid it was to get up in the dark and the icy cold. Not for anything in the world would she go back — not for anything at all. She remembered the day when Jonathan Field had come to the Home and asked to see her. She had been scrubbing and her hands were red. Matron let her have a clean apron and sent her in. She remembered that she was almost crying because she wanted time to brush her hair until it shone, and to put on her Sunday dress. She had a Sunday dress because she couldn't wear the school uniform any more. You couldn't wear it after you had left the Grammar School. The Sunday dress came out of a charity bundle. It was ugly, but it was better than this common print, only Matron said she was tidy enough and sent her in. She had no idea of how much more becoming the print dress was, or just how strong an appeal those little red hands and the tearful brown eyes would have for Jonathan Field. She knew that she was like her mother, because Uncle Albert and Aunt Grace had told her so. They also told her that her mother was flighty and had thrown away her chances, but she had no idea that Jonathan Field was one of the chances that had been thrown away. She walked into the room and into another life. There were interviews with Uncle Albert and Aunt Grace, and with the authorities at the Home. And then Mr. Jonathan Field became Uncle Jonathan, and she went down with him to Field End. It was like a fairy story. The door back into the old life was shut, and barred, and bolted. She would never go back through it again, no matter what anyone said, no matter what anyone did. Never, never, *never*! She was warm, she was relaxed. Her mind was made up and set. The door was locked and bolted. She would never go back. This set purpose went with her into a dreamless sleep.

CHAPTER TWELVE

GEORGINA woke and knew that something had waked her. It was a sound, but she did not know what sound it was. There was the vibration of it on the air and in her mind. If it had been an ordinary sound, she would not have given it a thought at all. An owl crying, a dog barking, or the wind blowing about the house, any of these might have waked her, but they wouldn't have left her with this feeling that something had happened.

She pushed the bedclothes down and sat up. The sound was not repeated. She got out of bed and went to the window. The sky was not as dark as it had been when she looked out before. There might have been a moon behind the clouds. She could discern the outline of the terrace with the raised stone jars at its edge. In summer they would be ablaze with the scarlet geraniums, but they were empty now. The terrace was empty too. Nothing broke the silence or the grey, even gloom. If anything had moved there it was gone. As she looked out now the study was below her and to the left. In the eighteen-nineties her grandfather had replaced one of the Georgian sash windows with a glass door descending by two steps on to the terrace. He had no sense of the sacredness of a period building and felt himself under no obligation to preserve its character. He wanted to be able to step out into the garden as and when he pleased, and when he wanted to do a thing he did it.

As Georgina leaned from her window she saw this glass door move. The wind had risen. It came round the house in a gust and the door moved, swinging out a handsbreadth and swinging in again. She thought she knew now what it was that had waked her. It was the swinging of this door, moving in the wind and swinging out, and moving again and swinging in. Someone must have opened the door behind the curtain and left it open. It was Stokes' business to see that all the doors and windows on the ground floor were fastened, so it must have been Jonathan himself who had opened it. There would be nothing unusual about that. She had often looked out as she was looking now and seen him pacing the terrace, or standing and looking at the sky before going in, and so upstairs to bed. But she had never known him to leave the door unlocked. Stokes would have been very much put out if he had, since it was his rooted belief that an unlocked door or window would instantly attract a burglar. It would really be very much better if Stokes didn't know that the glass door in the study had actually been left swinging to and fro for half the night.

She drew back from the window and put on her dressing-gown and slippers. She couldn't just leave the door banging like that. If the wind got up any more the glass might break. She opened the door of her room and went along the passage to the head of the stairs. There was no light on this upper landing, but a low-powered bulb burned all night in the hall below. Going down into the lighted hall was like going down into bright water — bright, silent water, very still. She came into the hall, and the wall-clock beside the dining-room door gave out a whirring stroke. It struck the quarters by day and night, but the sound waked no one in the house, because it was such an old accustomed thing.

Georgina moved until she could see the face of the clock. The hands stood at one, which meant that by the right time it would be about twelve minutes to, since do what you would to it the old clock gained.

She crossed the hall to the study door and opened it. The room was dark, quite dark, with a light wind moving in it. She put on the overhead light, and the draught between the two doors carried the dark red curtains out into the room and sucked them in again. She turned to shut the door behind her, and it was when she was turning back to go and fasten the door on to the terrace that she saw Jonathan Field fallen forward across his writing-table. She would have seen him before if she had looked that way, but her eye had been caught by the belly-ing curtains.

She had neither eyes nor thought for them now. He must have fallen asleep at his desk. But the banging door would have waked him. If it had waked her on the upper floor, it must surely have waked him here. It was in her mind that he sometimes dropped off in his chair, but not at his desk — not like this. He must have been looking at his fingerprint collection. One of the volumes was there on the right of the table. How strange that he should have got it out to look at, and then have gone to sleep.

She went across to him with a lagging step until she came to the chair where she had sat last night and they had talked. She had got as far as that before she knew why he had not waked. His right arm hung down. A revolver had dropped from the hand and lay upon the carpet. She gripped the back of the chair and stood there quite unable to move. It was the room that seemed to be moving, tilting under her feet as if the solid earth had given way. But she didn't move, and Jonathan didn't move. It came into her mind then that he wouldn't ever move again.

She did not know how long she stood there, but presently the room was steady again. She let go of the chair and came round the corner of the table. She put her hand on the table to help herself whilst she stooped down and picked the revolver up. She had not any intention or purpose in picking it up. It was perhaps the mere instinct which makes any woman pick up anything that has fallen to the floor. She picked it up and she laid it on the table. Then she put her hand upon Jonathan's hand and found it lax and cold.

Anthony waked to the sound of his opening door. Georgina stood there on the threshold calling him.

'Anthony — Anthony — Anthony!'

He was awake and out of bed at the third repetition.

'Georgina! What is it?'

'Jonathan — something has happened — I think he's dead!'

He came over, put on the light, flung on a dressing-gown, thrust his feet into slippers, and came along the passage with her and down the stairs. They came into the study, and the curtains blew out again to meet them. They had not spoken. Now he said,

'Who opened that glass door?'

'I don't know.'

'What made you come down?'

'I heard it bang.'

It was just quick question and answer. And then he was over

at the writing-table, feeling for a pulse that wasn't there, seeing the bullet hole in the dinner-jacket, and turning round to say,

'He's gone! We shall have to ring up the police.'

Georgina had remained beside the door. She had shut it behind her. She went back a step now and leaned against it. Her pale thick hair hung curling upon her shoulders. Her eyes were wide and dark, and her face was white. There was no colour in it at all. Her blue dressing-gown hung down open over a white night-dress. Her bare feet were in slippers trimmed with fur. She had so fixed, so rigid a look that Anthony felt a stab of apprehension. He said harshly,

'For God's sake wake up! I tell you we must ring up the Lenton police!'

She said, 'A doctor —'

'They'll bring one. But it's no use — he's gone. They won't want anything to be touched. You haven't touched anything?'

Georgina opened her stiff lips and said,

'Only the revolver—

CHAPTER THIRTEEN

DETECTIVE INSPECTOR FRANK ABBOTT on his way to Lenton with Sergeant Hubbard emerged from a prolonged silence to remark that he supposed it was too much to expect the locals to warn you when they were going to have a murder and call in the Yard, but it would be a great deal more convenient if they did.

'The trail is always cold before we get on to it. We are never called in until everyone has had time to go over what he is going to say and make sure he isn't going to say too much. Whereas if we could be served with a nice neat notice something on the line of "A murder has been arranged and will take place at twelve p.m. on the thirteenth prox," we should make a point of being on the spot to note any criminal reactions which might be knocking about.'

Sergeant Hubbard allowed himself to laugh. His immediate aim in life was to model himself upon his companion down to the last sock, handkerchief or what-have-you. Since he was dark and stocky, the result of his efforts was merely to try a temper not inclined to suffer fools gladly. Being a cheerful and carefree young man, he continued upon his imitative way without the least suspicion that he was making a nuisance of himself. It was a fine morning, he was a very good driver, and he was being allowed to drive, so all he did was to laugh and say that it might be a pity but he didn't see how it could be helped.

They drew up in front of Lenton police station at no later than eleven o'clock, and after a brief interview with the Superintendent proceeded to Field End, where Inspector Smith was in charge. Frank Abbott, having worked with him before in what came to be known as the Eternity Ring case, was prepared to find that all preliminary measures had been meticulously carried out. Smith was, in fact, a most zealous and conscientious officer. It is of course possible to have too much zeal. It is also possible to have too much imagination. Inspector Smith's most severe critic would not have accused him of this. He was a good-looking, well set-up man with a fresh complexion and a wooden cast of countenance which was sometimes a useful asset. He took Frank and Sergeant Hubbard into the study and described the scene as he had found it on his arrival in the small hours of the morning.

'The body has been taken to the mortuary, but there will be photographs for you to see. There is no doubt about its being murder, though there had been an attempt to make it look like suicide. The weapon had been put into his hand so as to get his dabs on it — a tricky business and it hasn't come off. No one could possibly have shot himself holding a revolver like that, and his dinner-jacket wasn't singed. Nothing in the room has been touched, except that the curtains have been drawn back, but I can show you just how they were.'

Frank Abbott stood in the middle of the room and looked about him. He noticed a number of things — a heavy volume on the writing-table — a choked, untidy grate. His light eyes went to and fro, his mind registered what they saw. It was a little time before he said,

'What was his position?'

'He had fallen forward across the writing-table. Bullet-hole in the left side of his dinner-jacket. Left hand hanging down. Miss Grey, who found the body, says the weapon was lying on the carpet as if it had dropped from his hand. She says she picked it up and put it were it is now, on the table. There are two lots of fingerprints on it.'

Frank's eyebrows rose.

'I don't remember his being left-handed.'

'You knew him?'

'I stayed in the house for a weekend about a fortnight ago. I came down with Captain Hallam. By the way, is he still here?'

'Yes, he is. As a matter of fact it was he who rang us up. Miss Grey says she woke up just before one o'clock. This glass door was banging, and she thinks it was either that or the shot that waked her. She looked out of her window, saw the glass door moving, and came down. The study was in darkness and the door on to the terrace open. She says she thought at first that Mr. Field was asleep. When she saw the revolver she picked it up and went to fetch Captain Hallam.'

Frank Abbott moved nearer to the table.

'That album was there?'

'Just as you see it. Nothing on the table has been touched.'

'Everything been fingerprinted?'

Smith nodded.

The album lay there open. Frank came round the table and looked at it. It was the one Jonathan Field had had spread out before him when he told his story of a murderer's confession in a bombed building. As a tale it had gone down well. Frank had found himself wondering how many times old Jonathan had told it. Perhaps many times, perhaps only just that once. Somewhere idly at the back of his mind he also wondered just what the odds were against the two men concerned ever coming across one another again. If he could be said to think about it at all, it might have been that they were very long indeed. He frowned slightly, put two hands on the book to close it, and then opened it again.

When Jonathan Field had been telling his tale he had opened it like that, but he hadn't opened it fully. He had said, 'It's too long a story for now — quite dramatic though!' and he had put his hands on the volume, opened it halfway, and clapped it to again. What stuck out in Frank's memory was the manila envelope. The book had opened upon it, and when it shut it had not shut smoothly because the envelope was there. It might have been there as a marker. It was there now. He lifted the envelope, and it was light in his hand. It was light because it was empty. But he was prepared to swear that it hadn't been empty when Jonathan was telling his yarn. There was something in it. He would have liked very much to know what that something was, and whether it had anything to do with Jonathan's story. As he turned it in his hand a faint pencilling showed up across one of the narrow ends. He moved it so that it caught the light, and could just make out what had been written and then, it seemed, rubbed out — 'Notes on the blitz story. J. F.' The notes had been there ten days ago, and they were not here today. Someone must have taken them out. It might have been Jonathan himself. It might have been someone else. The notes were gone, but the envelope remained. If it was there as a marker, then full or empty it still served its purpose, for close the album as you would, it opened always at the same place. And at that place a leaf had been torn out.

Inspector Smith, standing beside him, gazed wooden-faced at the album, and said,

'Someone seems to have torn one of the pages out.'

CHAPTER FOURTEEN

GEORGINA GREY came into the study. She had on a dark skirt and a high-necked jumper of white wool. She was very pale indeed and she had used no make-up. Frank Abbott discerned that it was costing her an effort to come into the room in which less than twelve hours before she had found her uncle dead. Now it was he who was sitting at Jonathan Field's table, and he was there to investigate the circumstances of his death. He rose to meet Georgina, shook hands with her, and spoke his condolences.

'Inspector Smith will have told you that Scotland Yard has been called in. It is all very trying for you, but I am sure you will wish to help us as much as you can.'

She said, 'Yes,' and she sat down.

Since he was at the writing-table, there was just the one chair in which she could sit, and it was the one in which she had sat during that last interview with Jonathan Field. She put her hands in her lap and waited. She had made a short statement and Frank Abbott took her through it. The events of the previous evening — quiet and domestic — everyone early to bed except Jonathan Field.

'He was in the habit of sitting up late?'

'Oh, yes. Sometimes he would be very late indeed.'

'What would you call very late?'

'If he dropped off in his chair it might be after one o'clock.'

'Did anyone go in to say good night to him?'

'No – he didn't care about being disturbed.' She hesitated, and then went on, her breath coming a little more quickly. 'I had been in here earlier — I came in to talk to him. I said good night to him then.'

He let that go and went on with her statement.

'Something waked you — do you think it could have been the shot?'

'I don't know. I suppose it might have been. I thought it was the door.'

'This glass door?'

'Yes. It was open. I looked out of my window and saw it move. That is what I came down for — to shut it.'

He looked at her statement.

'You came into the room, put on the light, and saw your uncle at his table. How soon did it occur to you that he was dead?'

She said, 'I don't know. I saw him, and I knew he wouldn't

go to sleep like that — and I came over here and saw the revolver.'

'You picked it up, didn't you? Why did you do that?'

'I don't know, Mr. Abbott — I really don't. I thought he was dead, and then I didn't think at all. I just picked it up and put it on the table.'

'Was it Mr. Field's revolver?'

'I don't know. I didn't know that he had one.'

'You hadn't ever seen it before?'

'No, I hadn't.'

'I see. Was your uncle left-handed?'

She had a startled look.

'I don't know. I mean, I don't know whether you would have called him left-handed or not. He used his right hand in the ordinary way, but I believe he used to be a left-hand bowler.'

He turned a little in his chair and looked round at the fireplace.

'Mr. Field seems to have been burning papers there. Do you know what they were?'

A little faint colour stained her skin as she said,

'They were — private papers.'

'Anything to do with his fingerprint collection?'

She said in undoubted surprise,

'Oh, no, nothing like that!'

'Miss Grey, when you were in here talking to your uncle, was this album on the table?'

'Oh, no, it wasn't.'

'Sure about that?'

'I'm quite sure. It's such a big thing — I couldn't have missed it.'

'But it was here on the table when you found Mr. Field's body and picked up the revolver?'

'I suppose it was.'

'You are not sure?'

She shut her eyes for a moment.

'Yes, it was there. I didn't think about it at the time, but I saw it.'

'Was it open or shut?'

'It was open.'

'And Mr. Field did not tear out a sheet and burn it whilst you were with him?'

She looked steadily at him and said,

'Why do you ask me that?'

'Because a sheet has been torn out and paper has been burned in that grate.'

He opened the album at the place where it was marked and lifted the envelope to uncover the rough edge of the missing page.

'You see?'

'Yes.'

'When was this done, and why?'

'I don't know anything at all about the torn-out page — it wasn't done while I was here. But my uncle did burn something.'

'I am afraid I must ask you what it was that was burned.'

She hesitated.

'Mr. Abbott — '

'You are not obliged to answer, but if you have nothing to hide you would be well advised to do so.'

He saw her wince and then stiffen.

'No, of course there is nothing to hide. It is just — it was all rather private.'

There was a faintly cynical gleam in his eye as he said, 'When it comes to a case of murder there is no privacy.' He had not thought that she could be paler, but suddenly she was.

'Murder?'

'Did you think it was suicide?'

She said slowly and deliberately,

'When something like this happens you don't think. It's there and it has happened — you don't think about it.' After a pause three words came more slowly still. 'It's — too dreadful.'

He nodded.

'Miss Grey, several of the statements I have here say that when Mr. Field was in his study he was not to be disturbed. You said the same thing yourself when I asked you if you had gone in to say good night to him, yet earlier in the evening you followed him into the study and remained there for about three-quarters of an hour.'

'I wanted to talk to him.'

'It was quite a long talk. Papers were burned, either by him at the time or by you later on.'

She said quickly, 'He burned it himself.'

He raised his eyebrows and repeated her own word.

'*It?*' There was a moment before he went on. 'Half at least of what was burned was on stiff legal paper. There are one or two fragments which were not burned through. Did they by any chance form part of a will?'

There was quite a long pause before she said, 'Yes.'

'You came in here and talked to him, and a will was burned. You want to state that as a fact?'

'Yes.'

He came back in a flash.

'Who burned it?'

'My uncle did.'

'Why?'

'He was going to make another.'

'Then you came in here to talk to him about his will?'

'It wasn't like that.'

He said, 'Don't you think you had better tell me what you did come to talk to him about?'

He saw her brows draw together in something that was not quite a frown. Under them her eyes were dark and intent. After a moment or two she said,

'Yes, I had better tell you. Everyone in the house knows about some of it, so perhaps you had better hear the whole thing. You met Mirrie when you were down here before. I don't know what Anthony told you about her.'

'Just that she was a distant cousin, and that Mr. Field had taken a great fancy to her.'

She bent her head.

'I think he was in love with her mother, but she married someone else. There was a quarrel. He didn't know that they had a child. If he had known, he would have done something for Mirrie when her father and mother were killed. It was in the war. She went to some distant relations, and it was all rather wretched. They didn't want her, and there was very little money. She went to a Grammar School, but she wasn't any good at exams, so when she was seventeen they got her a job as Assistant Matron at an orphanage. It was really just a fine name for being a housemaid. In the end Uncle Jonathan heard she was there and fetched her away. Most of this is what he told me last night. I didn't know it before.'

'Yes — please go on.'

It was easier now that she had begun to talk about it. There was even a sense of relief. She said,

'Uncle Jonathan got very fond of her. She has — those sort of ways, you know. And then — he told me last night she is very like her mother. We could all see that he was getting very fond of her. Then one day I got an anonymous letter. It — it was horrible.'

He nodded.

'They mostly are. What did it say?'

Some distressed colour came into her face.

'It said everyone was talking about my not being nice to Mirrie. It — it was trying to make out that I was jealous of her because she was prettier than I was, and because people liked her better — that sort of thing.' The dark grey eyes were honestly indignant.

'Have you got this letter?'

She shook her head.

'I showed it to Uncle Jonathan, and then I burned it. I ought to have burned it at once.'

'Why do you say that?'

A queer blaze of anger came up in her — now, when everything was past and gone and couldn't be called back again. It warmed her voice as she said,

'Because Uncle Jonathan was angry — not with the person who wrote the letter, but with me!'

'Why?'

'I didn't know. I thought and thought, but I didn't know. He had a very quick temper, and it was just as if the letter had set a match to it. He took sides against me with the person who had written it. He seemed to think I had been jealous of Mirrie and had meant to hurt her feelings when I gave her some of my things. And I didn't, Mr. Abbott — I didn't! If you've got sisters or cousins you know how girls pass things round and it doesn't mean anything but being friendly and liking a change — it just doesn't mean anything at all. I suppose things were stiffer in Uncle Jonathan's time, because he didn't seem ever to have heard of such a thing.'

'In fact you had a serious quarrel with Mr. Field. What day was this?'

She let the statement about the quarrel go and said in a bewildered voice,

'Monday — it seems as if it was a long time ago, but this is only Wednesday.' Her eyes were suddenly wet. 'I'm sorry, Mr. Abbott — it doesn't seem as if it could have happened.'

There was a big patch-pocket on her skirt. She drove a hand into it, pulled out a handkerchief, and pressed it to her eyes. Then she turned back to him and said 'Yes?'

'You had this quarrel with your uncle on Monday. And then he went to town? Did he tell you he was going?'

'No, Mrs. Fabian told us at lunch that he had gone.'

'And he stayed the night?'

'Yes.'

'Why did he go to town?'

'I didn't know he was going.'

'But I think you knew why he had gone. Miss Grey, if you are going to tell me any of this, don't you think you had better tell me all of it. It is bound to come out, you know.'

She said, 'Yes, you're right. I was just trying not to say more than I really knew.'

'Yes, go on.'

'My uncle talked to me about his will. He had got very fond of Mirrie and he was all worked up about her. He said he had been meaning to talk to me about altering his will so as to make provision for her.'

'And you quarrelled about that?'

Her colour came up brightly.

'Oh, no — no! I didn't mind about it at all — not at all. I told him so. I just wanted him not to be angry with me, not to believe that I was jealous — because I wasn't, I really wasn't.'

'So you had a reconciliation?'

The bright colour died.

'No, not then. He went on being angry. He said some very cruel things.'

'What sort of things?'

'He said disinterestedness could be overdone, and he asked me if I was going to pretend I shouldn't care if he was to cut me off without a penny.'

'And what did you say to that?'

'I said that of course I should care, because it would mean that he was terribly angry, or that he didn't care for me any more, but I should be very glad if he provided for Mirrie. I kept on saying things like that, but it wasn't any use. He had gone into one of his cold, angry fits and it wasn't any use, so I came away.'

'And when you heard that he had gone up to town on business you believed that he had gone to see his solicitor?'

'Yes, he said so to Mrs. Fabian.'

Frank thought, 'There could be quite a case against Georgina Grey. Quarrel about the other niece — quarrel about the will. I wonder if he got as far as signing a new one. Those unburned scraps of paper in the grate look very much as if one of the wills had been burned there. The question is, which one? And by whom?' He said,

'You did know, then, that Mr. Field had gone to see his solicitor. What happened on his return? And did he say anything about having completed the business he had gone up for?'

'Yes, Mrs. Fabian asked him whether he had. It's rather a family joke, because she always does it, more or less in those very words.'

'What did he say?'

'He said, "Yes".'

'Did you understand that to mean that he had altered his will?'

Georgina said, 'Yes, I did.'

He had been making a brief note from time to time. He did so now. Then he looked up at her again.

'Now, Miss Grey, would you care to tell me why you followed your uncle to the study last night, and what passed between you?'

The strain had gone from her pose and from her voice. She said quietly and sadly,

'Yes, I would like to. Uncle Jonathan had coffee in the drawing-room, then he came in here. The more I thought about everything, the more I wanted to go to him. You see, I did think that he had altered his will. Mirrie ran down to meet him when he arrived. I think he told her then that he had altered it. She was terribly pleased, and he put his arm round her — I was up on the landing and I saw them. And afterwards at dinner and in the drawing-room he kept looking at her, and she — you could see that he had told her something. She was all gay and lighted up. So I thought, "Well, if that is settled and done with, there isn't any need for him to go on being angry with me. I can go and talk to him now without his thinking that I am trying to influence him or get him to change his mind. I can go and tell him that I'm glad about Mirrie — really glad, and that the only thing I mind about is that he should be angry with me or think that I ever meant to be unkind to her." I thought perhaps he would listen now because he had done what he wanted to. So I came in here and talked to him.'

'What did you say?'

She wasn't looking at him now. She was looking down at the hands in her lap and the handkerchief they were holding. There was a remembering sound in her voice as if she were speaking more to herself than to him.

'I asked him if he had done what he wanted to do about Mirrie. He said that he had and he didn't want to discuss it. I said no, I didn't want to either. I only wanted to say that I was glad, and that I was glad about his being fond of her, because she hadn't got anyone else and I knew it was making them both very happy. He hadn't listened to me before, but he began to listen to me then. We talked about Mirrie, and he told me about having cared for her mother. He told me that he had cared for her a lot, but that she had married his cousin. He said he had begun to feel as if Mirrie was his daughter as well as hers. He had quite stopped being angry with me. We didn't talk about it — it had gone. He was just the same as he had always been to me, except that I felt he was really giving me his confidence in a way that he had never done before. Just at the end he said that it had made him very happy my coming to him like that. Then he said that he had been unjust, and that he had let his unjust anger carry him away. He said, "Maudsley told me I was doing wrong, and I was angry with him, but he was in the right of it. I let myself be carried away by some very strong feelings." He said my coming to him like that had touched him very much. He took an envelope out of the drawer in front of me and said, "I signed an unjust will this morning, and I'm going to tear it up and burn it!" I said, "No, don't," and he laughed and said, "I can do what I like with my own," and he took a paper out of the envelope and tore it up and dropped the pieces into the fire.'

Frank Abbott had not reached his present length of service in the police without having listened to a good many plausible stories. He was of the opinion that this was not a very plausible one. His immediate surface reaction to Georgina's account of that last vital interview with Jonathan Field was one of blank scepticism — 'She shot him, and she burned the will which cut her out in favour of Mirrie Field.' And then he experienced a sharp prick of anger, because there was something deep below the surface that protested. Simplicity is the most difficult thing in the world to ape. Yet women had done it and got away with it time out of mind. He wished with all his heart that he could have had Miss Silver there to tell him whether Georgina was putting on an act. He had once said of Miss Maud Silver that as far as she was concerned the human race was glass-fronted, and furthermore that she saw right past the shop window into the back premises. He reflected with cynicism that Georgina had such a lot in the shop window that it was too much to suppose that there was enough to furnish all the other rooms as well.

He was watching her as these thoughts passed through his mind. A very good shop window indeed. Even to his exacting taste she had nearly everything. At the moment, of course, she was too pale, and there was evidence of strain, but he wasn't at all sure that it did not heighten her appeal. He said,

'Mr. Field told you that he had signed a new will that morning?'

'Yes.'

She sat there quite quietly whilst he looked at her. Her voice was quiet too.

'A will which he characterised as unjust — what did you understand by his saying that?'

'I thought — ' She paused. 'I suppose I thought that he was leaving most of what he had to Mirrie.'

'Did you think he had cut you out altogether?'

This time the pause was longer. She looked down for a moment, and then lifted her eyes to his face again.

'I don't know what I thought. You see, I wasn't really thinking about the money at all, I was thinking about his being angry with me. He had never really been angry with me before — not like that. I wanted to be friends again.'

Frank said,

'You weren't concerned about the money?'

'I wasn't thinking about it.'

CHAPTER FIFTEEN

WHEN Georgina Grey had gone out of the room and Mirrie Field had entered it Frank Abbott was sharply aware of the contrast between them. Where the older girl had been quiet and controlled, this little creature with the tumbled hair and tear-stained face brought with her an atmosphere of emotional disturbance. She had, to use a colloquialism, been crying her eyes out. Like Georgina she had on a white woollen jumper and a grey-tweed skirt. She carried a handkerchief crumpled up in one hand, and as she came up to the chair by the writing-table and sat down there she dabbed her eyes and sniffed childishly. Frank found himself speaking as if to a child.

'I won't keep you longer than I can help. I just want to go through your statement with you and see whether there is anything you can add to it.'

Mirrie gazed at him wide-eyed. Her lips trembled, her soft little chin trembled. She said in a small despairing voice,

'It's all so dreadful — he was so kind — '

He picked up her statement and read it over to her. It could hardly have conveyed less information. They had all had dinner together and gone into the drawing-room afterwards. Uncle Jonathan had come in too. He had had his coffee, and then he had gone away and she hadn't seen him again. She had gone up to bed when the others went, and she had slept without waking up until there was a noise in the house and Georgina had come in and told her that Uncle Jonathan was dead. Mirrie punctuated the reading with one or two caught breaths and something that was not quite a sob. The handkerchief was pressed to her eyes again as he finished. He laid the paper down and said,

'Mr. Field had been away for twenty-four hours?'

'He went away on Monday morning.'

'Did you know that he was going to see his solicitor?'

'He said — he said he was.'

'Did he tell you why?'

The hand with the handkerchief dropped into her lap.

'He said he wanted — to provide for me.' Here there really was a sob. 'He was so *kind*.'

'He told you that he meant to alter his will, and that he was in fact going up to London for that purpose?'

The tears welled up in her eyes.

'Yes, he did.'

'Well now, when he came back on Tuesday evening you ran down and met him in the hall.'

'Oh — how do you know!'

He gave her a cool smile.

'There wasn't much secret about it, was there? A hall is what you might call a fairly public place.'

She had a faintly startled air.

'Did someone see me?'

'Someone saw you.'

'It was just that I was so pleased about his being back. I had dressed early.'

He smiled again.

'Well, there wasn't anything wrong about that. I expect he was pleased to see you.'

'Oh, yes, he *was*!'

Frank said,

'What I really wanted to know was whether he said anything about his business with Mr. Maudsley.'

Mirrie brightened a little.

'Oh, yes, he *did*. I said I hoped he had got all his horrid business done, so that he wouldn't have to go away any more. And he said it wasn't a horrid business for *me*, and that it was all signed, with two of Mr. Maudsley's clerks to witness it, so there wasn't anything to worry about any more.'

'He was talking about his will?'

She looked at him with childlike candour.

'Oh, yes.'

Frank Abbott thought, 'She knew he was cutting Georgina out and putting her in. I wonder if she tried for it, or whether it just happened. I wonder whether he had an afterthought and destroyed the will himself. I wonder whether it has been destroyed at all. Georgina certainly had a motive for destroying it. Mirrie wouldn't have any motive at all. I wonder whether Mirrie knows that it may have been destroyed. I wonder whether Georgina was speaking the truth, because if she wasn't — if she wasn't — '

Mirrie had her handkerchief to her eyes again. She said in a muffled voice,

'He was so *dreadfully* kind to me. It doesn't seem as if it *could* be true.'

He let her go after that, and saw Mrs. Fabian, who wandered through the events of the last two days in a characteristically irrelevant manner. She was extremely informative, but it was difficult to connect her information with the death of Jonathan Field. Frank had, for instance, to listen to a good many chance-come anecdotes of Georgina's infancy, together with excursions into dear Jonathan's personal tastes and habits. He permitted her to flow on, because there was always the chance of finding some wheat amongst the chaff, but when she finally settled down to reminiscences of Johnny's school-days he felt that the moment had come to apply the closure.

Neither Anthony nor Johnny Fabian had anything to add to their bare statements. They had gone upstairs with the others, and they had not come down again. Anthony had slept until he was roused by Georgina, and Johnny until he was roused by Anthony.

It was Stokes who produced one important piece of evidence. He had gone into the study with his tray of drinks at ten o'clock. He put it down on the small octagonal table beside the leather-covered armchair usually occupied by Mr. Field. It was not so occupied at the moment, because Mr. Field was over at the bookcase at the far end of the room. He was stooping down as if he were looking at one of the lower shelves. Asked which shelf, Stokes indicated that from which one of the albums containing the collection of fingerprints had been taken. He was positive that at that time both volumes were in their place.

Frank's next questions produced replies of considerable importance.

'Did you make up the fire whilst you were here?'

'I was going to do so, sir, but Mr. Field stopped me. He said to leave it and he would see to it himself later on.'

'Was that unusual?'

'Yes, sir.'

'Did he give any reason for it?'

'Why, yes, sir. He said he had been burning papers, and not to choke the grate until they had burned away.'

So Jonathan really had been burning something himself. Frank went on.

'Just take a look at the grate now, Stokes. How does it compare with the state it was in when you saw it at ten o'clock last night?'

'There's one more log been put on — that one on the right with the knot in it. It was lying right on top of the wood-basket, and I wouldn't have picked it out to put on myself with the fire having got a bit low and knots being as you might say on the tricky side when it comes to burning. No, the one I should have taken was that little one that's on top now — a nice dry faggot that would have got the flame up quick.'

'I see you're an expert. I'm rather good at fires myself, and I'm with you all the way. Now, leaving the wood on one side, what about the papers that Mr. Field had been burning? Would you say he had added any more afterwards, or as far as the burnt paper goes is the grate in about the same state as it was last night?'

Stokes was a pleasant little man with a ruddy russet skin and very thick grey hair which he wore a little longer than a younger man might have done. He said in his soft agreeable voice,

'It's difficult to say, sir, but I should think everything is pretty much as it was — a little more smouldered away, as it were, but no more than you would expect.'

Frank was reflecting that a will usually covered several sheets of extremely tough and intractable paper. It wouldn't be easy to tear and it wouldn't be easy to burn. If Jonathan had burned it himself whilst the fire was medium hot, the grate might be expected to look very much as it did now. If Georgina had burned it at round about one in the morning, it was probable that she would have had to use more wood. According to Stokes no more wood had been used except the awkward piece with the knot in it, which remained as to about three-quarters of it unburned and could very easily have been added by Jonathan. He went over and lifted it gingerly by the knotted end. Under it there was a bed of cold ash. There was also a sizeable piece of that tough paper. It was about a couple of inches long by an inch wide and only the edges were scorched. The words 'the said Miriam Field' were plainly visible. He couldn't imagine such a phrase occurring in anything except a will, and as Mirrie's name would certainly not have appeared in any but Jonathan's latest, it confirmed Georgina's statement that it was this will which had been burned, whilst, leaving undecided the question of who had burned it. If, as Georgina had said, it was Jonathan himself, the presence of the knotted log could be accounted for. The room would have been losing heat and he had obviously had no immediate intention of going to bed, since up to ten o'clock the album subsequently found upon his desk, was according to Stokes, still on its shelf at the time he came in with the tray of drinks. If Jonathan intended to sit up he might restrain Stokes from touching the fire — he wouldn't want any talk about the burned will, fragments of which were probably still in evidence, and yet once the butler was out of the way he could have pitched a log on the fire himself.

But if Georgina had burned the will at some time just short of one o'clock, what motive could she possibly have had for putting that particular log upon a fire which must have been very near to being burned out by then? Looking at what remained in the grate, he doubted very much if there would have been enough heat there to burn as much of the things as had been burned. He stood there looking down at the grey ash, the scrap of paper, the knotted log. If it was Georgina who had shot Jonathan Field and destroyed the will which would cut her out of a fortune, what must her mental state have been? The man stood to her in the relation of a father. She had shot him because he was cutting her out of his will. With his dead body slumped across the writing-table, she had to get his fingerprints upon the revolver, to find and destroy the will, and be ready with a story which would explain its destruction. All this with the vibration of the shot still trembling on the air, and with the possibility that at any moment the door might open and let an accusing witness in.

Was she one of those people upon whom in moments of emergency an icy control descends, co-ordinating thought and action to an unimaginable degree? Or would it have been an affair of shaking hands and pounding heart, a desperate search, and a blind fury of destruction? Or was she speaking the truth when she said that it was Jonathan who had torn up the will and put it on the fire?

He turned round to see Stokes watching him in a sad, patient manner which reminded him of an old dog waiting to be noticed. He went back to the table and asked him, as he had asked everyone else in the household,

'Did you know that Mr. Field had a revolver?'

He got the same answer as all the others had given him.

'Oh, no, sir, I didn't.'

Frank stood with a hand on the table.

'Did he keep any of these drawers locked?'

'The bottom two on the right-hand side, sir.'

He sat down in the writing-chair and found both drawers fast.

Jonathan's keys, handed over by Inspector Smith, were to hand. The upper of the two drawers contained bundles of letters, and lying on top of them a closed miniature case. There would have been no room for a revolver.

In the bottom drawer there were a couple of notebooks with lists of securities and details of investments, and under the notebooks a long envelope endorsed 'My will. J. F.' and a date two years back.

Then it was certainly the new will that had been burned as Georgina had said. What he found hard to swallow was the reason she gave for Jonathan having burned it, or even the bare fact that it had been burned by him. This older will would have been made when Georgina was twenty-one. He put it back in the drawer and returned to the question of whether Jonathan had kept a revolver there as well as his will. There would have been plenty of room for it. But if Jonathan was going to shoot himself, or if Georgina was going to shoot Jonathan, what was the point of locking the drawer again? Yet someone had locked it.

It simply didn't make sense.

He let Stokes go and turned to the telephone. He had the number of Mr. Maudsley's office on a slip of paper tucked into the blotting-pad. Two previous attempts to get in touch having failed, it behoved him to try again. This time he got through and was answered by a clerk.

'I would like to speak to Mr. Maudsley.'

The voice at the other end said, 'Well — I'm afraid — '

'Is he in his office?'

'Well, no, he isn't. As a matter of fact he won't be here today.'

'Then perhaps I could speak to the head clerk.'

There was a delay during which a number of irritating small sounds buzzed in the receiver — a rustling of papers, footsteps, an inaudible whispering. And then a woman on the line, quiet and efficient.

'Miss Cummins speaking. I am afraid Mr. Maudsley will not be in today. Do you wish to make an appointment?'

Frank said, 'No. This is police business. I am Inspector Abbott from the Yard, and I am down at Field End in connection with the murder of one of Mr. Maudsley's clients, Mr. Jonathan Field.'

Miss Cummins became unofficially shocked.

'Mr. Field? You can't mean it, Inspector! He was here with us only yesterday afternoon. Good gracious me!'

'He was murdered last night. It is important for me to get in touch with Mr. Maudsley as soon as possible.'

'Well now — I hardly know what to say. The fact is, Mr. Maudsley has been ordered to take a short holiday. He has been rather run down, and his doctor — '

'Can you give me his private address?'

'Well, I'm afraid it wouldn't be any use to you. He was taking an early train to Scotland this morning. He had not really made up his mind as to where he would stay, but there are one or two hotels in Edinburgh — '

Frank took down a couple of names.

'Don't ring off! You say Mr. Field was with you yesterday afternoon. You had been preparing a new will for him?'

A faint cool note of disapproval tinged the voice that answered him.

'That is so.'

'Mr. Field signed this will?'

'He did.'

'Is it in your custody, or did he take it away with him?'

The disapproval became very decided.

'He took it away with him.'

'I wonder if you can tell me what happened to the will which this one superseded.'

'I am afraid I have no information on the subject. It would have been in Mr. Field's possession.'

There was nothing more to be got out of Miss Cummins. He picked up Sergeant Hubbard and went out to get some lunch.

CHAPTER SIXTEEN

MAGGIE BELL had had a most interesting morning. It had followed upon what she herself would have described as 'one of my bad nights'. She hadn't slept very much, and when she had there were horrid dreams. By a stroke of irony she fell into a heavy sleep just at a time when the telephone would have been of the greatest interest.

She was sick, sore and weary by the time her mother had helped her to dress and got her on to the sofa in the window. As a rule she would put in an hour or two during the day oversewing seams and putting on buttons, and hooks and eyes. She couldn't keep at it for long, but it was surprising what she got through in the day, and Mrs. Bell found it a great help. But this morning she didn't feel like holding a needle, she really didn't. And that made the day stretch out before her ever so long, because however fond you are of reading you can't read all the time. Now if there was something exciting going on that she could listen in to it would be just what she felt like. But of course things never happened the way you wanted them to. Which, as Mrs. Bell said afterwards, only goes to show that you never can tell.

Maggie lay on her sofa with a shawl round her shoulders, a rug drawn up to her waist, and the nearest casement window open so as not to miss anything that might be going on outside. She hadn't been settled that way for more than five minutes before she heard Mr. Magthorpe call out from the roadway to Mr. Bisset inside the shop. Mr. Magthorpe was one of the best news-gatherers in the district, and being a baker to trade and in the habit of doing his own rounds Mondays, Wednesdays and Saturdays, his opportunities were naturally good. He was a little man with a large voice who sang bass in the choir, so you could be sure of hearing every word he said. And what he was saying was, 'Morning, Harry, I suppose you've heard what's happened up at Field End?'

Mr. Bisset hadn't heard a word. He came right out on his doorstep and said so. And there was Mr. Magthorpe with his face pulled down to half as long again, leaning sideways out of his van to say,

'Murder, that's what it was. And as fine an old gentleman as ever stepped.'

'Not Mr. Field!' Mr. Bisset was quite out of breath with surprise.

Albert Magthorpe nodded solemnly.

'Murdered in his own study. Sitting at his own writing-table.'

'You don't say!'

Mr. Magthorpe did say, and at considerable length. Maggie, listening spellbound, heard all about Miss Georgina waking up in the middle of the night with the sound of the shot or maybe the banging of the glass door on to the terrace, together with a number of other details imparted to Mr. Magthorpe at the back door by Doris Miller who was one of the two daily helps at Field End and a cousin of Mrs. Magthorpe's. So of course it was all true, and what a dreadful thing to happen.

Palpitating with interest and alternatively listening for the telephone to give one of those clicks which meant that someone on the party line was either ringing up somebody else or being rung up, and leaning as near to the window as she could in order not to miss any of the talk in the street, Maggie hardly had a dull moment. Field End being on the Deeping party line, she was able to hear Inspector Smith ringing up Lenton police station, and Lenton police station ringing up Inspector Smith. In this way she learned that Scotland Yard was being called in, and a little later that Detective Inspector Abbott was on his way from town. To Deeping, who remembered him as a school-boy, there was actually no such person. He was, as he always had been, Mr. Frank, and the news that he was coming down to enquire into the Field End murder heightened the interest considerably.

Maggie, listening passionately, heard Miss Cicely who was Mrs. Grant Hathaway calling her mother at Abbottsleigh.

'Darling, is that you? Isn't it too dreadful! I suppose you've heard —'

Mrs. Abbott at the other end of the line said she had, and it was, and the milkman had brought the news. Then Miss Cicely again.

'They say that Scotland Yard is being called in. Do you suppose they'll send Frank down?'

'I don't know — they might.'

'They did before. Darling, weren't you having a Miss Silver down for a weekend some time about now?'

'Yes, we were, but she wasn't sure about the weekend because one of her nieces — the one who is married to a solicitor at Blackheath — might have been wanting her to go down there and . . . Where had I got to?'

'You were just wandering, darling. Is Maudie coming, or isn't she?'

'Cicely, some day you'll call her that to her face!'

'Help! I believe Frank *did* once. Darling, you haven't told me whether she's coming or not, but I rather gather she isn't. What a pity!'

Mrs. Abbott's voice came over the wire without hurry.

'You shouldn't jump to conclusions. I didn't say she wasn't coming — on the contrary. Your father has just taken the car to meet her at Lenton.'

It was pain and grief to Maggie Bell not to break into that conversation and let Mrs. Abbott and Miss Cicely know that it really was Mr. Frank who was coming down from Scotland Yard, only of course it wouldn't have done and she knew better than to do it. In theory everyone in Deeping knew that she listened in on the party line, but she had been doing it for so many years that in practice it was generally forgotten. When you are talking in your own room to a friend in hers, the illusion of privacy is quite overwhelming. Besides, as Mrs. Abbott had been heard to remark, 'If it amuses Maggie to listen to me ordering the fish in Lenton she is welcome.' This applying to most other people, Deeping's telephone conversations continued on pleasantly uninhibited lines, and Maggie Bell went on finding them a great solace.

Maggie went on listening. No less than three calls from Field End to the London solicitor, and two for him by name all the way to Scotland. It seemed to Maggie that the police were in a great hurry to find out about poor Mr. Field's will. That was what all those calls were about. She had heard Mr. Frank speaking to a lady in the London office herself.

Later she heard Miss Cicely ring up Field End. It was Miss Georgina Grey she wanted, but she had to get past one of the police officers before they would let her come to the phone. Quite a song and dance about it there was, and when Miss Georgina did come, hardly a word out of her, only yes or no. Miss Cicely was being ever so warm and loving. She mightn't be much to look at, but she had got a real warm heart.

'Georgina, *darling* — I'm so *dreadfully* sorry!'

'Yes.'

'Darling, are you all right?'

'Oh, yes.'

'I mean, is there anything I can do? You know you've only to say. Would you like me to come over?'

'No.' There was a pause after the word, and then like an afterthought, 'You are very kind. Your cousin is here. He thinks — ' The voice steadied itself and went off into a foreign language.

Maggie felt seriously affronted, but at her end of the line Cicely was appalled, because the words which Georgina had put into German were 'He thinks I did it.' She said in the same language.

'But he can't!'

'He does.'

'He mustn't! I don't care what you say — I'm coming over to see you!'

Georgina was talking on the extension in her sitting-room. She didn't want Cicely, she didn't want anyone. She just wanted to be let alone, to tighten the control in which she was holding thought, and will, and action. She heard herself say, 'No,' and she heard Cicely say,

'Darling, it's no good — I'm coming!'

And with that the line was broken and she was left with the receiver dead in her hand.

Only the last sentence was intelligible to the exasperated Maggie, Cicely Hathaway's determination not to be rebuffed having been expressed quite plainly in English. Maggie would have been at one with Chief Inspector Lamb in his disapproval of lapses into a foreign tongue. What couldn't be said in your own language was either not worth saying, or else it was something you'd be ashamed for people to understand. The Chief Inspector had never met Maggie Bell, and was never likely to do so, but on this point at least they were two minds with but a single thought.

She hung up the receiver and occupied herself with guessing at what it was that was so secret about what Miss Cicely and Miss Georgina were saying. They were ever such good friends, though there must be a matter of four or five years between them and you'd be put to it to find two that were less alike. Miss Georgina had brought in some things to be altered for her cousin not so long ago. Maggie had admired her very much. Lovely figure she had, and all that pale gold hair, and a real beautiful look about the eyes. Miss Cicely was nothing at all beside her, but the cousin, Mirrie Field, she was a real pretty little thing. Nice ways with her too. She had thanked Mum ever so pretty. 'Oh, Mrs. Bell, how beautifully you've done it! Nobody would think it hadn't been made for me, would they?' Ever so nice the things were, but Miss Georgina's things were always nice and no wonder Miss Mirrie was pleased to have them. What she had on wasn't at all the thing for anyone that was staying at Field End. Cheap and nasty, that was what Maggie called it, and no good Mum hushing her up either. If there was one thing you did get to know about in the dressmaking line it was the difference between good stuff and bad. Do what you would to a poor material, poor it was going to look and you couldn't get from it, but a good piece of stuff looked good right through to the end.

CHAPTER SEVENTEEN

FRANK ABBOTT drove away from Field End with Sergeant Hubbard and took him to the Ram for lunch. The hospitality of Field End had been offered and politely but firmly refused. The Ram afforded a good plain meal. When it was over he left Hubbard to take a bus into Lenton and went up to Abbottsleigh to see his relations. A word or two with Monica might be useful.

Ruth, the house-parlourmaid, gave him a beaming smile as she opened the door. Lunch was over, she informed him, and they were in the morning-room. After which she ran ahead and announced him as 'Mr. Frank'. He came into the charming small room which everyone preferred to the large, stiff drawing-room furnished in the late Lady Evelyn Abbott's taste and dominated by her portrait. The morning-room, of a more comfortable size, had been done over by Monica and happily delivered from brocade and gilding. The only family portrait it contained was a charming water-colour sketch of Cicely as a child. Frank always came into it with the feeling that he was coming home. He did so now.

But he had hardly taken a single forward step before he was brought up short by the spectacle of Miss Maud Silver very comfortably ensconced in a low armless chair which might have come out of her own flat in Montague Mansions. He stood where he was, heard Monica laugh and say as she came forward to slip her arm through his and reach up to kiss him,

'Well, Frank, I hoped you would find time to come in. And look who is here!'

He said,

'I am looking. And quite expecting to see her dissolve into thin air! Now how in the world — '

Miss Silver smiled. Her flowered knitting-bag lay on the floor beside her. She wore a dress of dark green wool made after the same fashion as every other dress in which Frank had seen her — longer in the skirt and straighter in the shape than was the fashion, with a little net front, its collar supported by slides of whalebone to fill up the V-shaped opening at the neck. Since she was on a social visit she wore an old-fashioned gold chain and her favourite brooch, a rose carved in bog-oak with an Irish pearl at its heart. She held a coffee-cup in her left hand, and without rising from her chair she gave him the other.

'My dear Frank — how pleasant.'

He seated himself. Ruth came in with another cup. He was given coffee. Colonel Abbott, it appeared, had gone over to see the Vicar on business connected with the church accounts.

Frank said, 'I mustn't stay.'

He looked at Monica, as he always did, with pleasure and affection. Cicely had her brown colouring and her sherry-coloured eyes from her mother, but not the charm, the warmth, the agreeable assembly of features, and certainly not her repose. Frank had once told her that she was the most restful woman he had ever met, and she had laughed and said that what she supposed he really meant was that she was lazy. She poured him out a second cup of coffee, exclaimed that he ought to have come to them for lunch, and arrived at the tragedy at Field End.

'The milkman told the maids. It really does seem too dreadful to be true. And only a fortnight ago we were all there dancing! Have you found out anything about it yet? Was it robbery? Stokes says the glass door on to the terrace was open, and that poor Georgina heard it banging and came down and found him. She was so devoted to him. It must have been a terrible shock.'

He said in a non-committal voice,

'I thought it was the other one Mr. Field was so devoted to.'

Monica put down her cup.

'Oh, well, she is a taking little thing. The rippling sort, you know.'

Miss Silver smiled.

'What an expressive word. It reminds me of Lord Tennyson's charming poem about the brook —

> "I chatter over stony ways,
>   In little sharps and trebles,
> I bubble into eddying bays,
>   I babble on the pebbles." '

Frank laughed.

'That's just what she does! You couldn't have hit her off better. Go on — isn't there some more of it?'

Miss Silver obliged with another verse.

> ' "I slip, I slide, I gleam, I glance
>   Among my skimming swallows;
> I make the netted sunbeam dance
>   Against my sandy shallows." '

Frank picked up the last word and repeated it.

'Shallows — that's just where you do get ripples, isn't it?'

Monica Abbott looked distressed.

'That's too bad. I didn't mean anything of that sort, and you know it. And Miss Silver was only quoting what Lord Tennyson said about a brook. Mirrie is a dear pretty little thing, and very fond of her uncle too. I don't think she had ever had much of anything until she came to Field End, and it seemed as if she couldn't do enough to show how grateful she was.'

He blew her a kiss.

'Calm down, darling. I agree with every word you say. I was just wondering how deep it all went. Alfred's fault for putting on the word "shallows"! Now you can tell me — how do she and Georgina get on?'

Monica said warmly, 'Georgina is the kindest girl in the world.' And with that there were footsteps in the hall and Cicely Hathaway came running into the room. She said, 'Mummy!' in a protesting childish voice, and then she saw Frank and turned on him.

'Oh, you're here! Well, I'm glad — ' But she didn't sound anything except angry.

'Cicely darling, you haven't seen Miss Silver.'

The colour was high under Cicely's brown skin, the sherry-coloured eyes were blazing. She swung round, holding out both her hands.

'No, I haven't, have I? I'm frightfully rude, but I'm much too furious to be polite to anyone. You'll forgive me, won't you?' She bent, kissed Miss Silver rapidly on the cheek, a mere snatch of a kiss, and straightened up to storm at Frank again.

'I don't know how you can stand there and look at me — I really don't.'

He looked back with an infuriating indulgence.

'Actually at the moment you are quite easy on the eye. Being in a temper suits you, but perhaps a little strenuous so soon after lunch. And what is it all about anyway?'

'As if you didn't know!'

Monica said, '*Cicely* —'

Cicely stamped her foot.

'If it were anyone else in the whole world! But Georgina! It's the sheer stupid, ignorant, blind idiocy of it!'

There was a glint of angry amusement in his pale, cool stare as he said in a leisurely voice,

'One day you'll run out of adjectives if you squander them like that.'

'Well, I haven't run out of them now!'

'That, darling, is obvious.'

'And you're *not* to call me darling!'

Monica Abbott said, '*Cicely* —' again. She hadn't seen Cicely lose her temper like this for years, and under his cool manner Frank was getting angry too. She made a faint helpless gesture and went over to the hearth, where she stood half turned away with the water-colour drawing of a five-year-old Cicely looking down at her. She reflected that people who lost their tempers were never much more than five years old. In the picture Cis wore a white frock and a very determined expression. She hadn't been easy to manage even then. From behind her she heard Frank say,

'Perhaps you wouldn't mind telling me what I have done, or what I am supposed to have done to Georgina.'

Cicely blazed back at him.

'You think she shot her uncle!'

'Who says so?'

'She does!'

'My child, you can hardly hold me responsible for that.'

'She wouldn't say it if it wasn't true!'

'You meant that like George Washington she cannot tell a lie?' Perhaps I had better remind you that the story is now considered to be apocryphal.'

She threw an exasperated 'Oh!' at him and then melted into a sudden change of mood.

'Frank, you can't really think it — not about Georgina! Even if you'd only met her once you couldn't! You couldn't *really*! She simply hasn't got it in her — not that sort of thing!'

Monica Abbot looked over her shoulder. Cicely was holding on to Frank's coat and looking up at him. Her cheeks were scarlet and her eyes brimmed over. Miss Silver had picked up her knitting — something white and fluffy. Frank said quietly,

'What sort of thing, Cis?'

The answer came in a voice that had dropped to a whisper.

'Envy — hatred — malice — and all uncharitableness — '

The words of the Litany stilled the anger that had been between them. Old, beautiful words — *'From envy, hatred, malice and all uncharitableness — Good Lord deliver us.'* How many of the people who make a glib response have really turned away from the evil in their thoughts before it breaks into word or open deed?

Frank said,

'You're a good friend, Cis.' He stepped back from her and went over to Monica.

'Well, I must get back to my job. My love to Uncle Reg. I expect I'll be seeing him, but at the moment I'm up to my eyes. I'm running out to Lenton now, but I'll be back again.'

'It's no use offering you a bed?'

'I think perhaps not — I may have to go up to town.'

Cicely came between him and the door.

'Frank — '

He said, 'No use, Cis, I can't discuss it with you,' and was gone.

Cicely ran to Miss Silver and dropped on her knees beside her.

'You will – you will go and help Georgina, won't you?'

Miss Silver looked at her kindly.

'You are very much concerned for your friend, my dear.'

'Yes, I am. You see —' she choked on the word — 'if you're going to go by *evidence*, there is quite a lot that would make anyone with a horrid mind like a policeman —' She choked again.

Miss Silver put her knitting down in her lap. It was a white shawl for the baby expected by Valentine Leigh in a month's time. The pattern was a new and delicate one, the wool very soft and fine. A silk handkerchief protected it from contact with the stuff of her dress. As it got larger it would require a pillow-case, but for the moment a handkerchief served. She said,

'Won't you sit down, my dear, and tell me a little more about all this? Evidence which appears very compromising at the outset of a case is sometimes susceptible of quite a natural explanation. Perhaps you would like to tell me what makes you think that Frank suspects your friend.'

Cicely sat back on her heels.

'Well, I suppose anyone would — or at least anyone might if they didn't know Georgina. You see, she was brought up to be Mr. Field's heiress — everyone simply took it for granted. And then all of a sudden about six weeks ago he went up to town and came back with Mirrie Field. Her father was a cousin of his, a fairly distant one, and I've got a sort of idea he had been in love with her mother — I seem to remember Gran saying something about it ages ago. Anyhow there was Mirrie like a kitten with a saucer of cream, and Mr. Field getting fonder of her every day. And Georgina was an angel to her — she really was. Mirrie hadn't anything, and Georgina had some things of her own altered for her — *charming* things. And it wasn't Georgina who told me about giving them to her, it was Maggie Bell. I expect you remember her. She's a cripple, and her mother does dress-making, which is how Maggie knew about the clothes, because Mrs. Bell had them to alter for Mirrie. Though I expect Maggie would have known anyhow, because she listens in on the party line and she always does know everything.'

Monica Abbott stooped down and put a log on the fire. She said,

'Everyone knows she does it, and nobody thinks about it until something happens, and when we all say we must be careful because of Maggie, but actually no one can be bothered and we go on just the same.' She gave Miss Silver her charming smile and added, 'It's such a pleasure to her, and after all what does it matter?'

'It would matter if you had just been committing a murder,' said Cicely.

'Cis!'

Cicely gave a vehement nod.

'Well, it would, wouldn't it? That's why I think Maggie could be useful, you know. I shall go in and see her. I've got a lovely smarmy book about a poor persecuted girl with a cruel stepmother and a frightful step-sister straight out of Cinderella, and wedding bells and golden slippers in the last chapter. Quite a shameless copy really, but Maggie will adore it.

'I really rather like Cinderella stories myself,' said Monica Abbott, 'but I like them well done, and of course sometimes they are just sloppy. But anyhow I think they are better for you than the sort of gloomy book which goes on for about six hundred pages and ends up with someone committing suicide or facing a hopeless dawn. Because really, whatever you feel like, in real life you just have to get on with your job.'

Cicely said,

'Darling, you needn't tell us you're not Third Programme — we've known it for years!'

Miss Silver was knitting. She looked up now to say,

'So Mirrie Field is Cinderella, and Mr. Jonathan Field was a fairy godfather. But according to you Miss Georgina Grey does not fit into the story, my dear?'

Cicely's eyes widened.

'No, she doesn't. She has a story of her own, and it's got to have a happy ending. She just doesn't come into this business of quarrels and wills and murders. Even if Frank doesn't know her at all well he ought to know her better than that. And if he doesn't, he's got no business being a policeman and interfering in people's lives and messing them up by accusing them of things which he ought to know they couldn't possibly have done!' The words came tumbling over each other and left her out of breath.

Miss Silver coughed gently.

'What makes you think that Frank has these suspicions of Miss Grey?'

'Georgina says he has. She isn't stupid, you know — if a thing is there she can see it.'

Miss Silver gazed at her with an air of mild interrogation.

'Perhaps I did not make myself plain. If it is true that Frank suspects Miss Grey of a connection with her uncle's death, there must be some reason why he should do so.'

'No one who knows her — '

Miss Silver put up a restraining hand.

'Calm yourself, my dear. I am not pronouncing any opinion as to whether these suspicions are justified or not, but it is a fact that Frank would not entertain them unless there was some supporting evidence. Did Miss Grey tell you what this was?'

'Yes, she did. And of course there is nothing in it, and no one who knew Georgina could think that there was. It's just that Mr. Field was changing his will.'

'In favour of Mirrie Field?'

'Yes. You see Georgina had an anonymous letter — a really hateful one.'

'They are hateful things, my dear.'

Cicely gave a vigorous nod.

'It said everyone knew she was jealous of Mirrie because Mirrie was prettier than she was and people liked her better. And it went on with silly things like saying she had tried to humiliate Mirrie by giving her cast-off clothes. And they weren't. They were lovely things, and Mirrie was terribly pleased with them.'

'You interest me extremely.'

Cicely sparkled up at her.

'Oh, do I? You don't know how much I want to!'

'Pray continue. Did Miss Grey take this letter to her uncle?'

'Yes, she did! And there was the most frightful flare-up. He seemed to think it was all true about Georgina being jealous, and about the clothes and everything, and he told her he was going to change his will. And I don't think he exactly said he was going to leave her out of it, but I think she thought that that was what he was going to do.'

Monica Abbott made a small shocked sound. Miss Silver said gravely,

'I am sure that I need not warn you against repeating such a conjecture, but I think that you would be well advised to warn your friend not to do so.'

'If people hadn't such perfectly foul minds it wouldn't be necessary! You know, Mr. Field was like that, he did quarrel with people. But Georgina says he had never done it with her before, and she was most frightfully upset. This was on Monday morning, and he went straight off to London and made another will, and didn't come back till Tuesday evening in time for dinner.'

'You say he had made another will. Was that known?'

'Yes, it was — he told Mirrie. And after dinner he went into the study, and Georgina went after him and they had a talk. She says he wasn't angry any more. She told him she was glad about his providing for Mirrie, and he told her about having been fond of Mirrie's mother. They had a long talk, and I think it made them both very happy. And in the end he said he had been angry and unjust and he had made an unjust will. And he got it out and tore it up and burnt it.'

'In Miss Grey's presence?'

'Oh, yes. She tried to stop him, but he said he could do what he liked with his own, and he tore it up and put it on the fire.'

'This was on Tuesday evening?'

'Yes.'

'And when did his death occur?'

'Georgina woke up in the night and heard a door bang — or it might have been the shot. She looked out of her window and saw the glass door between the study and the terrace moving in the wind. She went down to shut it, and she found that Mr. Field had been shot.'

All this time Cicely had been sitting back on her heels. Now, with a characteristically impulsive movement, she thrust at the floor with her hands and came up on to her knees beside Miss Silver again.

'Oh!' she said on a quick-caught breath. 'You can see what it looks like — anyone can see what it looks like! She's got to have someone to help her — she's simply got to! Miss Silver, you will won't you? She must have somebody — she must! Dear, darling angel Miss Silver, say you will!'

Ruth, the parlourmaid, opened the morning-room door and announced,

'Miss Georgina Grey —'

CHAPTER EIGHTEEN

GEORGINA came into the room. She had put on a loose dark coat over her jumper and skirt and twisted a scarf about her neck. It was the first that had come to hand, a mixture of soft greys and blues. She was bare-headed and she wore no gloves. As Monica Abbott went to meet her warmth and kindness came with her.

'My dear child — we have been thinking of you so much.'

Cicely scrambled up.

'I've told her,' she said. Her feet were so numb from sitting on them that she had to catch at Georgina's arm to steady herself.

Georgina Grey had eyes only for Miss Silver. She put an arm about Cicely in a purely instinctive way, and she felt Monica Abbott's kindness as you feel the comfort of coming into a warm room, but all her conscious thought was focused upon the little elderly person who came a step or two to meet her with some white baby knitting in one hand and the other put out to take her own. The hand was small, the clasp firm and kind.

Georgina said, 'How do you do, Miss Silver!' The glowing picture painted by Cicely had been in her thought. She was finding it difficult to relate it to this dowdy little person with her neatly netted fringe and small indeterminate features. Cicely's enthusiastic phrases floated in her mind — 'She's too marvellous — she is really, darling . . . She saved my life over that Eternity Ring business, and I expect she saved Grant's too. They were just going to arrest him, you know . . . She sees right through people . . . Frank practically eats out of her hand.' She didn't know quite what she had expected, but Cicely's fireworks were fading out and leaving a dull greyness behind them. She took the chair she was being offered and sat down.

Monica Abbott came up to Cicely and put a hand on her shoulder.

'If Georgina wants to consult Miss Silver, I think this is where we leave them.'

Cicely got to her feet, looked a reluctant protest, and met a perfectly plain glance of dismissal from Miss Silver. She bit her lip, followed Monica out of the room, and could be heard saying 'Really, Mummy!' in the hall.

Miss Silver turned to Georgina Grey.

'You would like to talk to me?'

Quite suddenly Georgina began to feel that she would. She forgot all about Miss Silver looking like the governess in a family group of the Edwardian period. Mrs. Fabian had a store of old albums. Miss Silver might have stepped out of any one of fifty groups. She had really been a governess once — Georgina knew that — and now she was a private enquiry agent and Frank Abbott regarded her with reverence. In her own mind Georgina made a correction. There wasn't a Frank Abbott any longer. There was only Detective Inspector Abbott with the cool, cynical gaze which had given her story the lie.

The look which Miss Silver had turned upon her was neither cool nor cynical. It was kind, but it was penetrating. She felt as if it went right through her and out at the other side. Strangely enough, it was not a disagreeable feeling. It might have been had there been anything that she wanted to hide, but since she hadn't there was a certain relief in feeling that she wouldn't have to explain too much — Miss Silver would understand.

The searching look melted into the smile which had won the hearts of so many of Miss Silver's clients. A pleasant voice repeated,

'You would like to talk to me?'

Georgina talked, and found it easier than she could have supposed. Chief Detective Inspector Lamb, who had grown up in a country village not so many generations removed from a firm belief in witchcraft, has been accused of cherishing some uneasy suspicions with regard to Miss Silver's powers. He would naturally not have admitted to this, and she would certainly have been extremely shocked. What she did possess was an uncommon faculty for producing an atmosphere strongly reminiscent of the schoolroom over which she had once held so benignant a sway.

It was perhaps on this account that Georgina felt it only natural for Miss Silver to be asking her questions, and for her to be answering them as frankly and as accurately as she could. It no longer occurred to her to hold anything back, or to suppose that her answers would be either doubted or misunderstood. Until Jonathan Field, in that painful interview on Monday morning, had shown that he distrusted her it had never occurred to her that anyone could do so. When after Jonathan's death she discerned that Frank Abbott actually suspected her of being concerned in it, the very foundations of her world were rocked.

Now everything was steadying down and coming into focus again. She said,

'You know, I never thought anyone could imagine I had anything to do with it until I was talking to Mr. Abbott in the study and I could see that he did think so.'

Miss Silver shook her head slightly.

'I think you will have to remember to call him Inspector Abbott, since he is here on duty.'

Georgina was remembering with a prick of surprise that he had been a guest at Field End, and that she had thought him amusing and a very good dancer. He had called her Georgina, and she had called him Frank. And Jonathan Field had been alive. It was only ten days ago, and the world had turned upside down since then. She looked at Miss Silver and said,

'It doesn't seem as if it could possibly have happened.' And then, 'There are two things I can't understand at all.'

Miss Silver pulled on the ball of white wool in her knitting-bag.

'Yes? Pray tell me what they are.'

Georgina leaned forward.

'I don't know why the glass door on to the terrace was open.'

'Do you mean that it was wide open?'

Yes, it was blowing to and fro and banging. That is what woke me. I just can't think why Uncle Jonathan should have opened it.'

Miss Silver was knitting rapidly.

'He might have found the room too hot?'

Georgina shook her head.

'No, he liked a room to be warm.'

'Then we have to suppose that he opened the door in order to let someone in, or else that it was not he who opened it.'

'Who could he possibly have been letting in?'

'I do not know, Miss Grey.'

Georgina said, 'I don't know anyone who would come and see him like that. And if he didn't open it himself who could have opened it?'

'There is no one in the house who might have done so?'

'Why should they?'

'I cannot give you the answer to that, but there might be an answer which neither of us can supply. You say that there were two things which you could not account for. The open door was one. Pray, what was the other?'

'He has a collection of the fingerprints of famous people. They are set up in large albums on the bottom shelf of one of the book-cases in the study. They hadn't been moved when I was there talking to him at about nine o'clock, and Stokes says they were there at ten when he went in with a tray of drinks, but at one o'clock when I found him at his table the second volume was lying open on his right, and Inspector Abbott says a page had been torn out.'

'Dear me! Have you any idea what prints the missing page contained?'

Georgina hesitated.

'I think so, but I'm not sure. Uncle Jonathan had a story about being buried when a house collapsed in the blitz. It's a very good story, and I've heard him tell it quite a number of times. I expect you know we had a dance here about ten days ago. There was a dinner-party first. After dinner some of the people went into the study — Inspector Abbott was one of them. They wanted to see his collection, and he worked round to telling this story. I wasn't there to start with, but I came in just as he got going. I told him people were beginning to arrive for the dance, and he was vexed at being interrupted. Mirrie was there and she begged him to go on, so I came away.'

'Mr. Field went on with the story?'

'Oh, yes, Mirrie was full of it. He and another man were buried under the ruins of a bombed house, and they didn't think they had any chance of getting out. The other man lost his nerve completely. He told Uncle Jonathan he had murdered two people, and he told him how he had done it. Mirrie said Uncle Jonathan didn't get as far as telling them that part of it. I had left the door open and he could hear people coming into the hall, so he just said he thought he would know the man's voice if he heard it again, and that he had got his fingerprints by passing him a cigarette-case. Mirrie said he half opened the album to show them the prints, and there was a long envelope there marking the place. I knew that because I had heard him tell the story before. What he kept in the envelope was a note of what the man had told him. You know, it's quite on the cards that Uncle Jonathan made the whole thing up. If he did, I can just see him bolstering it up with a lot of notes in an envelope and using it to mark the place where he had put some fake fingerprints. Only — ' she hesitated — 'why did he, or why did anyone, tear out that page and burn it?'

Miss Silver said, 'Dear me!'

'The page is gone. It has been torn out — Frank Abbott opened the album and showed me the rough edge. And there is something else. The long envelope that I told you about was there, but it was empty. The notes Uncle Jonathan kept in it were gone.'

'Did you tell Inspector Abbott that?'

'No, I didn't. He went straight on to ask about my uncle burning his will. That was when I could feel what he was thinking about me — and of course I couldn't help seeing why he thought it. It doesn't sound reasonable for anyone to make a new will and to destroy it the same day. And that is just it — people who do things when they are angry are not reasonable. Uncle Jonathan made that will because he was in a rage with me, and he wanted to show everyone how fond he was of

Mirrie. Then when I went in and talked to him after dinner last night the anger just melted away like a bad dream and he couldn't have been sweeter. He took the new will out of his drawer and tore it up and put the pieces in the fire. I tried to stop him, but he wouldn't listen, and I didn't want to make him angry again. He said he would make a new will that would be just to both of us, and that I wasn't to think he loved me any less because he loved Mirrie too.' Her eyes were full of sudden tears. 'Oh, Miss Silver, it doesn't seem as if it could have happened.'

Miss Silver said very kindly and gently,

'It will always be the greatest comfort to you that any misunderstanding between you and your uncle should have been so completely removed. As Coleridge so truly says —

> 'For to be wroth with one we love
> Doth work like madness on the brain.' "

Georgina bit her lip. For a moment she could not speak. When she could command her voice again she said,

'Miss Silver, Cicely thought — she said — you might consent to come to Field End and help us. Will you?'

Miss Silver laid down her knitting and folded her hands upon it, after which she said in a voice of deceptive mildness,

'In what capacity?'

Georgina was a little taken aback. Perhaps she had offended — perhaps Miss Silver would not come. She was surprised to discover how very much she wanted her to come. She said, 'Oh — ' and then,

'You do take cases, don't you?'

'You are asking for my professional assistance?'

'Oh, yes!'

Then I must say to you what I feel it my duty to say to every client. I cannot come into a case with the object of proving the innocence or the guilt of any person. I can come into it only with the object of discovering the truth and serving the ends of justice. I can neither compromise with facts nor gloss them over, and I cannot undertake to conceal material evidence from the police.'

Georgina met her look with one as direct. She said in a steady voice,

'That is all I want — to find out what really happened. I haven't got anything to hide.'

CHAPTER NINETEEN

MISS SILVER packed her suit-case and was driven to Field End, where she found that a pleasant room had been prepared for her. It was opposite Georgina's and next to that occupied by Mirrie Field. Whilst she was unpacking Georgina went downstairs to announce her presence.

She found Mrs. Fabian in the drawing-room, ensconced upon the sofa with her feet up. The sincere grief which she felt for Jonathan's death was accentuated by a painful uncertainty as to her own future. Field End had been her home for nineteen years, and beside being relieved of all anxieties on the score of board and lodging she had drawn a substantial salary, and there had always been a welcome for Johnny. Now she had no certainty about anything. What had been left from the collapse of her husband's means would barely suffice to pay the rent of a cottage, and though it is necessary to have a roof over your head, it does not help you very much if all that it can do is to afford you a shelter where you may die quietly of starvation. Of course Johnny wouldn't let her starve if he could help it, and nor would Georgina. But suppose dear Jonathan had left everything to Mirrie Field. He had gone up to town to make a new will, and he had made it. Mirrie herself had been artlessly confiding on the subject. She had wept and dried her eyes, and wept again as she said how kind Uncle Jonathan had been. All very natural, but what was a proper subject of gratitude for Mirrie could be something quite different for the rest of them. Suppose there should be very little for Georgina. She hadn't said so to anyone, but when Jonathan had told her that he was going up to town to see Mr. Maudsley she had asked him whether he had let Georgina know. Not meaning anything by it or wishing to pry into his affairs, but just wondering whether he had told her he was going to town. But Jonathan had looked at her angrily and said in what, even though he was dead, she could only describe as a nasty voice that Georgina had nothing to do with his affairs.

In retrospect Mrs. Fabian found that this alarmed her very much. She had never really expected anything for herself, though she had sometimes felt that it would be nice if he were to remember Johnny. But during all the years that she had lived at Field End it had never occurred to her to doubt the security of Georgina's position. She was his own flesh and blood, his poor sister Ina's daughter and such a dear child. Naturally she would be Jonathan's heiress. But now there was Mirrie Field, and Jonathan had changed his will. Anna Fabian's body might be comfortable, but her mind was in a sad turmoil. There were visions of Georgina and herself in a garret, though just why it would have been a garret she could not have explained. It was really a great deal more likely to be some tumbledown cottage with no water laid on and only outdoor sanitation. The thought that Georgina would have to find a job brought an added touch of gloom, since it left her to face the garret, or alternatively the cottage, alone. She looked up in a distracted way as Georgina came in, and said,

'It is very wrong of me, I know, and we shouldn't be thinking of anything except poor dear Jonathan, but oh, my dear, I don't know what I am going to do — I really don't. Because you see, though I would be willing to take any kind of post, I am afraid —'

Georgina came over and sat down on the end of the sofa.

'Now, Cousin Anna, what is it?'

Mrs. Fabian burst into tears.

'Dear Jonathan — always so kind! And of course I have no claim, no claim at all, but if he has left everything to Mirrie —'

'I am quite sure that you have nothing to worry about.'

Mrs. Fabian pressed a solid linen handkerchief to her eyes.

'He went up to town to make a new will, and Mirrie says — '

'Yes, I know. But I am quite sure that you needn't worry.'

'Did Jonathan tell you so? Oh, my dear, when you went out of the room last night, did you see him? I have been so hoping that you did, because of course I couldn't help noticing that there was something wrong, and it would have been so dreadful if he had gone like this without any chance of making it up.'

Georgina looked past her.

'Yes, it would have been dreadful, but it didn't happen. We talked — everything was all right between us. And everything is going to be all right for you. You won't cry any more now, will you, because we have a visitor and she will be coming down to tea.'

'A visitor!'

Georgina began to explain Miss Silver.

'I think you will like her. I think she will be a great help to us all.'

'But, my dear — an enquiry agent! Of course that is only another way of saying she is a private detective, and even nowadays, when people do the most extraordinary things, it doesn't seem to be a proper occupation for a lady.'

'Darling Cousin Anna, Miss Silver is one of the most completely proper people I have ever met. You must have heard Cousin Vinnie talk about her.'

Mrs. Fabian gave her eyes a final dab and sat up. Miss Alvina Grey, daughter of a previous Vicar of Deeping and now for many years resident in what had been the sexton's cottage, had had quite a lot to say about the events in what had come to be known as the Eternity Ring case. It was into her room that Mary Stokes had rushed, declaring that she had seen a murdered girl in Dead Man's Copse. Mrs. Fabian had certainly heard the tale a number of times. It was only because of her present distress of mind that she had failed to connect Georgina's guest with the little lady from London who had been staying with Monica Abbott, and who had played such a helpful part in unravelling that mystery. She said quite briskly,

'Yes, yes, of course. You were away at school, and the name

had slipped my mind. Some people are so good at names, but they never seem to me to mean anything, and I don't pretend to be able to remember them. After all, as Shakespeare says,

'What's in a name? That which we call a rose
By any other name would smell as sweet.'

'Silver — yes, that was it, I remember perfectly now — Miss Maud Silver, and everyone spoke very well of her. I remember your Cousin Alvina took a great fancy to her, and she gave her the recipe for those particularly good afternoon tea-cakes of hers.'

The ground thus prepared for a meeting between the two ladies, Georgina left a restored Mrs. Fabian and was crossing the hall, when Anthony came out of the morning-room. When he saw her he turned back. She followed him into the room and he shut the door. She said,

'Where are the others?'

Johnny has taken Mirrie out in his old ruin of a car. She's been crying herself sick, and he thought a little fresh air.'

Georgina nodded.

'She really was fond of Uncle Jonathan. I suppose he was the most wonderful thing that had ever happened to her, poor Mirrie. Uncle Albert and Aunt grace sound fairly grim.'

Anthony had walked over to the window. He turned round now and came back to her.

'Never mind about Mirrie just now. I want to talk about us.'

She looked up faintly startled.

'What is it?'

He said abruptly,

'Mirrie says that Jonathan did make a new will when he was in town. He told her so.'

'I thought we weren't going to talk about Mirrie.'

'We're not. It's what she said about Jonathan's will.'

She moved to the hearth and stood looking down into the fire.

'I don't think I want to talk about wills, Anthony.'

'Nor do I. I want to talk about us. I only mentioned the will to get it out of the way. Jonathan told Mirrie that he was treating her as a daughter, and if that means anything at all it means that she will get the bulk of whatever he has to leave. And that means — oh, Georgina, don't you see — it means that I can ask you to marry me.'

There was an applewood log on the fire. It sent out a very sweet smell. About half of it had burned to a grey ash, but it had not fallen away. Little glowing sparks ran to and fro in the ash under the draught from the chimney.

Georgina looked down at the sparks. Her colour had risen a little. She said in a low voice,

'I don't know that I care very much about a conditional offer of marriage, Anthony.'

'What do you mean? I couldn't ask you if you were going to have all that money.'

'That would depend upon whether you thought more of the money than you do of me.'

She looked up at him for a moment. He had time to see that her eyes were bright with anger, and then she was watching the fire again.

'Georgina!'

'What else? If the money didn't matter more to you than I do, you woudn't let it come between us. I can't see that it's any better that way than it would be if you asked me just because I had got the money. In either case you would be letting the money matter more than I do. I won't marry anyone who does that.'

He took her hand and held it to his cheek.

'You don't really think I care about the money?'

'You do if you let it come between us.'

'But if you haven't got it — darling, don't you see that it makes everything quite easy? I mean, he has probably left you something, but from what you told me yesterday it doesn't sound as if it would be very much.'

She turned a quiet look upon him.

'I'm wondering just how much your pride would let you take. It might be as well to think it out. Suppose he had left me five hundred a year — '

He broke into angry laughter.

'What are you trying to say?'

'It's a case of what you would say.'

'Do you know that he has left you that?'

'No, I don't. I just wondered where you would feel you had to draw the line. And you haven't answered me. Could you or couldn't you bear to marry someone with five hundred a year?'

Before she had any idea of what he would do he had taken her by the shoulders.

'If you think I'm going to be haggled with — '

'Anthony!'

'You don't really think I care about the damned money!'

Georgina looked at him.

'We could always give some of it away, you know. Supposing — just supposing it was more than you felt you could bear — No, Anthony, you are not to kiss me! Not until I say you can. If you won't be haggled with I won't either. I don't know what Uncle Jonathan has left me, and I don't want to know. I want to get this settled between us first, and it's not going to be settled on any question of money. If I have anything, it will be ours. If I haven't got anything, what you have got will be ours. If I've got more than you are going to feel happy about, we can get rid of it. We can talk it over and decide how much of it you can bear to keep. Now don't you think we might stop going on about the money?' Her voice faltered on the last words.

He put his arms round her and they kissed. It was some time before she said, 'You mustn't!'

'Why mustn't I?'

'Because — because — oh, I oughtn't to have let you! I was just thinking of getting the money out of the way.'

'What else is there?'

'Something that matters more than that.'

'Jonathan? I know, darling. But I think he would have been pleased.'

'Yes, he would have been pleased. He liked you very much, but — but — '

'There aren't any buts.'

Now that it came to the point, it was too difficult to say. She leaned against his arm and felt the comfort of it. Why couldn't they just stay like this, knowing that they loved each other and neither thinking nor caring about the future? All through the world's history lovers have wished that it would stand still for them, but it still goes on. The enchanted moment flies, no matter how much they cry to it, '*Verweile doch, du bist so schön!*' Georgina said in a strained voice,

'It's no use, Anthony. Frank Abbott thinks I did it.'

CHAPTER TWENTY

MIRRIE had been at Field End for six weeks, but she had had eighteen years of drab poverty before that. It hadn't been want. There was a decent roof over her head, and there was enough to eat. The charity clothes had often been of quite good quality. If they required mending they were mended very neatly indeed, at first by Aunt Grace, and afterwards by Mirrie herself under Aunt Grace's eye. But it was all very penny-plain. There were no extras, there were no treats, there was no fun. The child who craved for colour and enjoyment began to snatch at them wher-ever and however they might be come by. She learned, to start with, in a perfectly innocent and accidental manner, that a child who burst into tears in a bus and sobbed out her dismay at having had her fare stolen was practically never made to get out and walk. There was always some kind person who would press the pennies into a trembling hand. She really had lost her fare the first time, but the incident had shown her how to save the fares provided by Aunt Grace and use them for cinema tickets. Her remark to Johnny that she had hardly ever seen a film fell a good deal short of the truth, but of course she couldn't tell him about the bus fares. There were other ways of coming by a sixpence or a few coppers here and there. There was the broken milk-bottle trick. She had picked one out of a dust-bin, lurked near a likely dairy, and let it fall on the pavement as a well dressed woman came out of the shop. Confronted with a weeping and most attractive child who said she was afraid to go home because she would be beaten, Mrs. Jones readily produced a shilling and told the child to keep the change. Of course the time spent on visits to the cinema had to be accounted for. There was a child called Beryl Burton of whose parents Uncle Albert and Aunt Grace were pleased to approve. Mirrie could always say that she had gone home with Beryl. It said much for her ingenuity that she was only found out once, and even then she managed to lie her way out of it — there had been a sudden change of plan and she had gone with Hilda Lambton instead.

Hilda was one of the people she didn't want to think about now. Not that she had anything against her, but because of her being all mixed up with Sid Turner. She used to tell Aunt Grace that she was going to a museum or a picture gallery with Hilda, and they used to meet Sid and his friend Bert Holloway and go off to the pictures. Aunt Grace didn't mind how much you went to museums, because of their being free, and Uncle Albert said they were educational. There was a most frightful row when they found out about meeting Sid. Uncle Albert did nothing but quote texts out of the Bible for days and days, and Aunt Grace never stopped scolding, and got Mirrie that frightful job at the Home, where the only outings were to church on Sundays and straight on to Uncle Albert and Aunt Grace for dinner and tea, after which Uncle Albert saw her back to the Home. No more pictures, no more Hilda, no more Sid. It just didn't bear thinking of, so she didn't bother to think about it.

Six weeks is not enough to destroy the influence of this kind of background. It remained as a compelling reason for escape. When she came to Field End on a visit it was with the knowledge that here, if she could take it, was her chance. She must not only please Uncle Jonathan, she must please everyone, so that they would like her, and want her to stay. If she could stay a good long time she might get off with someone and never have to go back to the Home. At first her ambitions went no farther than this. And then Jonathan Field had begun to get fond of her. It didn't happen all at once. She began to feel a warmth and an indulgence. She didn't have to try any more. She pleased without effort and just because he found her pleasing. The visit stopped being a visit and Field End began to be her home. By the time Jonathan said that he regarded her as a daughter and told her he was going to change his will she had travelled a long way. It had not been altogether smooth going. There had been rough places and rather frightening places, and there had been difficult turns, but now it was all over. She had cried with the abandonment of a child, but even whilst the tears ran down she was conscious of something to which she could not have given a name. Uncle Jonathan had been so kind, and she was crying because he was dead. Uncle Jonathan had said he was going to make a new will and treat her as his daughter, and he had really made that will. He had gone up to town, and he had come down again and told her that the will was made. She would never have to go back to Aunt Grace and Uncle Albert again. She would never have to get up at six o'clock and vacuum the Orphanage floors. She would never have to wear anybody else's clothes, not even Georgina's. Richards', which was the best shop in Lenton, had lovely clothes. There was a grey coat and skirt in the window which was marked twenty-five guineas. She could buy it tomorrow if she wanted to. Or if not tomorrow, just as soon as it was given out about Uncle Jonathan's will.

Johnny took her out into the country. They went up over the common and through the woods which lay beyond it. The sky was a pale, cold blue with dark clouds moving down from the north. The leafless trees made a lovely tracery against the sky. But Mirrie had no eyes for anything like that. She liked the light of big electric lamps and the Glorious Technicolour of the films. She did like the feeling of the air on her face. Her eyes were hot and sore from having cried so much. It was nice to have the windows down.

They didn't talk at first, but when they came out upon another common he drew off on to the grass verge and stopped the car. There was rough ground that sloped away from them on every side, with here and there a clump of birch. Last year's bracken made a brown carpet. There was blackberry, and gorse, and faded heather. The dark clouds were coming up behind them. Soon they would cover the sky. Johnny turned to her and said,

'Feeling better?'

'Oh, yes. You *are* kind — everyone is very kind.'

He thought she looked like a kitten that has been out in the rain. You wanted to comfort the little soft thing, to warm it, dry it, give it a saucer of milk — cream if you could lay your hands on it. Certainly Mirrie would prefer cream. Astonishing how quickly a creature accustomed to nothing but skim could become cream-conscious. He had watched this happening with Mirrie, and to his own surprise it had not only amused but touched him. He had it in his mind that looking after her and seeing to it that she got her cream might be an agreeable as well as a highly remunerative job. If she was going to be landed with most of Jonathan's money she was certainly going to need someone to look after her — and it. He said,

'Don't cry any more, will you?'

Mirrie's eyes brimmed over.

'I'll try —'

'That's a good girl!'

She said, 'He was so — good to me.' Her voice caught, and broke the sentence in two.

Johnny said, 'He was very fond of you.'

'Yes — he said he was. He said he felt as if I was his daughter. Johnny — you know he said he was altering his will and he told me he had done it — but you don't think, do you, that he hasn't left anything to Georgina?'

Johnny whistled.

'What makes you think of that?'

Her voice went small and tight.

'He was angry with her. I don't quite know why, but I could see that he was. I wouldn't like her to be left right out.'

'Oh, he wouldn't do that. She's his own niece, and she's been with him ever since she was three years old.'

'Yes, I know. Johnny — if I've got a lot of money — what am I going to do?'

'What would you like to do?'

She looked at him in a considering manner.

'I don't know. I should like to go on being at Field End. Could I do that?'

'I expect so, if you wanted to. It would depend on who the house was left to.'

'He said he wanted it to be my home.'

'Then it would depend on whether he had left you enough money to keep it up.'

'He said he wanted everyone to know that he thought about me like a daughter.'

If words meant anything at all, that meant that at the worst she shared with Georgina. It might mean a good deal more.

She was gazing at him.

'Do you think I could have a car?'

Her tone was so solemn that he almost burst out laughing.

'Darling, I don't see why not.'

She continued to gaze.

'I should have to learn to drive.'

'I'll teach you myself.'

'Oh, Johnny, you are good!'

Johnny Fabian's conscience had been brought up to know its place. Like an eighteenth-century child it spoke when it was spoken to, but not otherwise. But when Mirrie's soft little voice told him how good he was it broke all rules and gave him a decided twinge. He said in a hurry,

'People will always be good to you, darling.'

'Will they?'

She put her hands to him and he took them. She was wearing loose warm gloves. They were too large and too loose, because they had been Georgina's. He pulled them off and lifted the little cold hands to his face, kissing first one palm and then the other.

'Oh, Johnny —'

He said, 'How could anyone help being fond of you? I oughtn't to be, but I am.'

'Why oughtn't you?'

'You're going to have a lot of money, darling.'

'Does that matter?'

'It wouldn't if I had a lot too, but I haven't.'

'Haven't you got any?'

He gave a rueful laugh.

'A little from an aunt and what I make by honest toil.'

'You buy cars and sell them again?'

'I buy them as cheap as I can and sell them as dear as I can — that's the idea. If Jonathan has left me anything, I could put the lot into some decent going concern and make quite a good thing of it. I do know about cars.'

'This one isn't very pretty.'

'Darling, it isn't a car — it's a has been. But I do get it to go, which is more than most people would.'

She said with the air of a child dispensing birthday cake,

'If I really have a lot of money I'll give you some.'

Johnny's conscience gave him another twinge. He kissed her fingers and said in a laughing voice,

'It can't be done, darling. At least not just like that.'

'I don't see why.'

'Well, for one thing you'll have a guardian till you're twenty-one, and whoever he is he wouldn't let you. And even if he did, there's a silly prejudice against men who take money from girls. You wouldn't like everyone to cut me, would you? And think how bad it would be for business.'

He felt her hands flutter in his.

'Johnny, you said it couldn't be done *that* way. Is there a way it could be done?'

'Well —'

She pulled her hands away and clapped them together.

'What is it — what is it?'

He had a laughing, teasing look.

'Quite impracticable, darling, I'm afraid.'

'Tell me what it is! Tell me at once!'

He said, 'Well, I suppose you could marry me.'

Her look changed. Something came into it which was too fleeting for him to be sure of what it might be. She drew in a quick breath and said,

'Could I?'

'Well, people do get married. You will some day. I'm not really suggesting that you should marry me.'

Another of those quick breaths, and then,

'Why aren't you?'

'Darling, you're too young.'

The colour flushed into her face.

'Heaps of girls marry when they are eighteen!'

He went on smiling.

'I'm too poor.'

'But if I don't mind about your being poor?'

He laughed.

'If I was one of those high-minded noble characters, I should say, "How can I, darling? People might say I was marrying you for your money"!'

'I don't call that noble, I call it silly.'

'As a matter of fact so do I.'

'Is that why Anthony doesn't ask Georgina?'

'I shouldn't wonder.'

'He's in love with her, isn't he?'

Johnny laughed.

'You had better ask him!'

Mirrie looked up through her eyelashes.

'I've seen him look at her. I would like to have somebody look at me like that. He doesn't even seem to know I'm there.'

'No — I've noticed that myself. Cheer up, there are lots of good fish in the sea.'

'Are there?' Her voice was small and sad.

Johnny said, 'What about me, darling?'

They were late for tea. Mirrie came in with rosy cheeks and shining eyes. She shook hands with Miss Silver, who regarded her indulgently, and slipped into a place beside her. Mrs. Fabian, who was pouring out the tea, announced that it was stewed, and that she considered stewed tea to be most unwholesome.

'My dear father was so very strict about the way that it was made. He always insisted on double the usual amount, two spoonfuls for each person and two for the pot, and it was never allowed to stand for more than just one minute by his watch. Very extravagant we should consider it now, but in his own house when he said a thing it had to be done. I can never remember my mother disputing his wishes in any direction. I can't think what he would have said about the tea ration.'

Johnny laughed.

'That, darling, we shall never know, and perhaps just as well. I'll have another half cup of tannin.'

CHAPTER TWENTY-ONE

DETECTIVE INSPECTOR FRANK ABBOTT was at Field End by nine o'clock next morning. The first person whom he saw after Stokes had admitted him was Miss Maud Silver coming downstairs. Since she was hatless and was carrying her flowered chintz knitting-bag, he could come to no other conclusion than that she was staying in the house. He waited for her, received a leisured greeting, and said,

'Is it permitted to ask how you got here?'

'Certainly, Frank. Miss Grey drove me over in her car.'

'I thought you were paying Monica a visit. She seemed to think you were, yesterday when I was there after lunch. You had only just come, hadn't you?'

She said with composure,

'Miss Grey has retained my professional services.'

He cocked an eyebrow.

'A fast worker. She came, she saw, you conquered — she whisked you back here. All just a little bewildering, don't you think?'

'She is a friend of your cousin Cicely's.'

'Which of course explains everything! Have you had breakfast?'

'Not yet. The bell rang as you arrived.'

He stood aside to let her pass.

'I shall be in the study. Perhaps you will look in there when you have finished. I should like to have a word with you.'

Miss Silver made her way to the dining-room, where she found Mrs. Fabian, Georgina, and Anthony. Mirrie arrived a moment later. She was out of breath, because all her life it had been such a crime to be late and she had dropped off again after that early morning cup of tea which was one of the high lights of life at Field End. No more tearing out of bed the minute the alarm clock went, the room all dark, bare feet on an icy floor. Instead, hot tea and a lovely warm snuggle in bed. She didn't usually go to sleep again, but this morning she had just sunk down into a queer mixed dream in which Johnny and she were being married and someone came up the aisle behind them and said, 'No'. She woke up all frightened, because she hardly ever dreamed and she didn't like it when she did. And then it was late and she got the old rushed feeling, which was silly, because no one would scold her here, no matter how late she was. Uncle Albert and Aunt Grace and Matron were miles and miles away. She need never see them again, she need never go back to them now.

Johnny came in behind her. He put a hand on her shoulder as he passed, and said,

'Sleep well?'

And then they all sat down. Mrs. Fabian was holding forth on the passing of the country house breakfast.

'Three or four things on the hot plate, and eggs just any way you fancied them, and cold ham and cold tongue. Scottish families used to have porridge first, but my dear father always said oats were horses' food. He disliked them greatly and would never have porridge on his table. And of course there were none of those breakfast cereals before the first world war. Or at least I don't think there were. Things are so apt to slide together in one's mind, don't you think?'

The question appeared to be directed to the company in general. Miss Silver, whose thoughts were far too well ordered to allow of any such slipping and sliding, contented herself with the observation that two world wars had certainly brought about many changes. After which she partook of a medium-boiled egg, two slices of toast, and a cup of tea, and presently came into the study, where she found Frank Abbott at the writing-table. He greeted her with a serious,

'Do you know, I'm sorry Cicely has dragged you into this.'

He was immediately made aware that he had offended.

'I am not in the habit of allowing myself to be dragged into a case.' She was seating herself as she spoke, having first moved the chair a little farther away from him.

He shook his head.

'You know what I mean, and I'm going to tell you why.

You like girls. Georgina Grey is an extremely attractive one, but it looks as if there was very little doubt that she shot her uncle.'

'She is aware that you think so.'

He said,

'Look at the evidence. He quarrels with her on Monday morning and tells her he is going to change his will. He tells the other girl too — Mirrie Field. She is enchanted and goes round prattling. Jonathan Field goes off up to town, sees his solicitor, and makes his new will. He comes back here on Tuesday evening and tells Mirrie what he has done. The rest of the family is given to understand that his business had been satisfactorily completed. I imagine they could all put two and two together. Not many hours later Jonathan is shot dead while he is sitting here at his table. Georgina says it was just before one o'clock when she came down and found him. That glass door on to the terrace was open and banging — she says that is what woke her. She also says she picked up the revolver and put it on the table. There are no fingerprints on it but hers. In addition to all this, the grate was full of charred paper, some of it quite easy to identify as part of a legal document. Georgina says it was his new will, and that he burned it himself after a reconciliation scene with her. She did follow him to the study after dinner, and I have no doubt they had a scene, but as to whether it was a reconciliation or another quarrel we have only her word for it. She didn't shoot him then, because he was alive when Stokes came in at ten o'clock. But if, as seems most likely, she did shoot him at some time during the night, she could very easily have burned the will before she called Anthony Hallam. It all hangs together, doesn't it?'

Miss Silver had been listening with an expression of extreme gravity. She said.

'Circumstantial evidence often does. I do not think you should make up your mind that Miss Grey is guilty.'

He had to subdue a touch of impatience.

'Do you find it so difficult to believe? It must have been a severe shock to her to find that she was being disinherited. She has been brought up to believe that she will be Jonathan's heiress. He has no other near relation, and he is fond of her and proud of her. And then everything changes. He comes across Mirrie Field, brings her down on a visit, and falls for her like a ton of bricks. I have no doubt she was jealous.'

Miss Silver coughed gently.

'I could see no signs of it.'

'Oh, well, she would hardly be human if she wasn't — at any rate to some degree.'

Miss Silver said mildly,

'It is not everyone who has a jealous disposition.'

This time he did not entirely keep the impatience out of his voice.

'Someone seems to have thought that Georgina had one, because she got an anonymous letter accusing her of being jealous of Mirrie and not treating her properly! When she took it to Jonathan he took sides with the letter-writer. That is when he told her he was going to change his will. I suspect that the change was going to be a very drastic one. There was, in fact, a good deal that might have made her see red. And right on top of it he went off to town, made this new will he had told her about, and came back with it in his pocket in time for dinner on Tuesday night. Georgina saw him after that, and she says he burned the will himself. It doesn't seem very likely, does it?'

Miss Silver said in a thoughtful voice,

'I do not know, Frank. By any interpretation of the facts Mr. Field would appear to have been a person of sudden changes of mood and impetuous decisions. He had taken one such decision when influenced by an unexpected quarrel. Might he not have arrived at another under the influence of a reconciliation?'

He looked at her sharply.

'Then who shot him?'

She said, 'That is what remains to be found out,' and as she said it the telephone bell rang sharply.

Frank Abbott leaned forward and took up the receiver. A voice said, 'Is that Deeping 10?'

He said, 'Yes.'

The voice said, 'To whom am I speaking?'

'Detective Inspector Abbott.'

The voice said, 'I am Mr. Maudsley, Mr. Jonathan Field's

solicitor. I have just seen the news of his death in the morning papers. I am speaking from Edinburgh.'

The line was very clear and good. Miss Silver was able to hear every word.

Frank said,

'We have been most anxious to get into touch with you.'

'Yes. I was travelling yesterday. I stopped to see a client on the way up and got in late. I am very much shocked at the news. Is there any possibility of its having been an accident?'

'None whatever. He was murdered.'

Mr. Maudsley repeated the word he had used before.

'How very shocking! Why, he was with me on Monday and Tuesday.'

'Yes, we have been anxious to get into touch with you about that. I believe he made a new will?'

'Yes — yes, he did — but — '

'Your chief clerk says he took it away with him.'

'Yes, he did.'

'It had been signed and witnessed?'

'Oh, yes — but — '

'That was your last contact with Mr. Field?'

'Well, no, Inspector, it wasn't.'

'You saw him again after he left your office?'

'No — but he rang me up.'

Frank was aware of Miss Silver looking extremely intelligent.

'He rang you? When?'

Mr. Maudsley, speaking in the call-box of his Edinburgh hotel, was perfectly distinct and audible to them both.

'It was at about half past nine on Tuesday evening.'

'You are sure about the time?'

'To within five minutes or so.'

'Had the call any connection with the will which he had signed that morning?'

'Yes — a very serious connection. He gave me to understand that he had destroyed it.'

The intelligence of Miss Silver's expression became intensified. Frank Abbott said,

'He told you that he had destroyed his latest will?'

'He said he had just been burning it.'

'The will which he had only signed that morning?'

'Mr. Field was in some ways a man of impulse. He had acted on impulse when he made this latest will. I may say that I had protested very strongly against some of its provisions. We were old friends, and he let me have my say. When he rang me up in the evening it was to tell me that he had come round to my way of thinking, and that he had just burned the will in the presence of his niece Georgina Grey. He thanked me for the representations I had made, and said he had become convinced that he was on the brink of committing an injustice. He added that there was no real hurry, but he would come and see me as soon as I got back to discuss the details of a will which would be just to everyone concerned.'

'I take it that the will superseded by the one which Mr. Field burned will now stand.'

'Undoubtedly. Have you come across it?'

'It is in a locked drawer of his writing-table. May I ask when you expect to be back?'

'I am booking a sleeper for tonight. I will come straight down to Field End. I am an executor, and it will be more regular if I take charge of the will.'

CHAPTER TWENTY-TWO

FRANK ABBOTT hung up the receiver.

'That was Mr. Maudsley the solicitor. He says Jonathan Field rang him up at about half past nine on Tuesday evening and told him he had destroyed the will signed only that morning. Mr. Maudsley had made rather strong representations on the grounds of its being unjust. Jonathan had come to feel that this was the case, and he had just finished burning the will.'

Miss Silver inclined her head.

'Yes, I was able to hear most of what was said.'

Frank lifted an eyebrow.

'Very convenient for Miss Georgina Grey. Jonathan Field must have rung up as soon as she left him and went back to the drawing-room, and before Stokes came in with the drinks. Now the question is, did she come down later on and shoot him, or have we got to find another suspect?'

Miss Silver's voice took on a tone of reproof.

'My dear Frank, with the will destroyed, what possible motive could she have had?'

'My dear ma'am, I don't think one has to look very far for a motive. He had always allowed her to be considered as his heiress. I have no doubt that under the will of two years ago she would have come in for practically everything. When she saw him destroy the will which, as far as one gathers, put Mirrie Field in her place Georgina was back in the position of sole heiress. And she held that position for just so long as Jonathan didn't make another will. He had acted on impulse once when he cut her out. He had acted on impulse again when he destroyed his new will. For all she knew, he might cut her out again, if not tomorrow, then the next day, or the next, or at any time when she chanced to vex him or he had an access of affection for Mirrie.'

Miss Silver looked at him very directly.

'Do you really believe her capable of such a line of reasoning?'

'Oh, she is quite intelligent.'

'I think you know very well that I was not referring to her intelligence. What I meant was that so unprincipled a line of thought would never occur to her.'

There was a sardonic gleam in his eye as he said,

'Discharged without a stain upon her character? Then we must have our other suspect. Unfortunately, we are handicapped by the fact that though there is some evidence that he may exist, he is for the moment featureless and nameless. In fact we haven't a clue as to who he may be, or where to look for him.'

Miss Silver fixed him with a bright, expectant look.

'You interest me extremely. Pray go on.'

He leaned forward to lift the heavy album which contained a

part of Jonathan Field's collection of fingerprints and set it down upon the blotting-pad.

'This album was on the table when Jonathan was shot. You may have heard that he had a very extensive collection of fingerprints. Some of them were in this volume. Anthony Hallam brought me down to a dance here last Saturday week. I stayed the night. There were people to dinner before the dance, and Jonathan brought some of us in here and showed off his collection. He told us a tale about being buried under the ruins of a house during the blitz. There was another man there too. He never saw him, but they could just reach each other. Jonathan said this man was nearly off his head with claustrophobia. He talked all the time. He confessed to a couple of murders, described how he had done them — all that sort of thing. Well, it could have happened. Practically anything could have happened in one of those bad raids, and Jonathan could have got the chap's prints by passing him a cigarette-case as he said he did. But I did think it wasn't the first time he had told the tale, and I thought it had probably got touched up a bit. He said they got him out unconscious next day, and he came round in hospital with a broken leg. And he said there wasn't any sign of the other man. He had to hurry over all that part of it, because Georgina came along and said that people were arriving for the dance, but he did just open the album halfway to give us a sight of the prints. There was an envelope there marking the place.'

As he spoke he parted the leaves, and there the envelope lay. Miss Silver put out her hand for it. He was interested to notice that it took her no time at all to become aware of the very nearly indecipherable pencilling at one end. She turned it to get the best of the light and read what he himself had seen there — 'Notes on the blitz story. J.F.' She said,

'It is empty.'

Frank nodded.

'Yes, it's empty. But it wasn't — I could swear to that. Twelve days ago when he brought us in here and spun that tale the envelope was there at the place where he opened the album, and it wasn't empty then. The notes, whatever they may have been, were inside it. He didn't open the album wide, you know.

He only opened it halfway, and when he parted the leaves the envelope fell over on the left-hand side. And it didn't fall in the way that an empty envelope would have fallen. It dropped because there was something inside it. There was something in it then, and there isn't anything in it now. But of course whatever was there could have been taken out at any time between then and Wednesday morning. It is convenient to suppose that the notes were removed at the time of the murder — that is, during the night between Tuesday and Wednesday. But there isn't any proof that this is what happened, any more than there is any proof that the page with the murderer's fingerprints on it was torn out at the same time.'

'A page has been torn out of the album?'

'The page where the envelope lay.'

He lifted the album over to the edge of the table so that she could see it. She scrutinised it with interest. The page had been somewhat roughly torn out and the jagged edge was plain to see.

'It would be somewhat of a coincidence if the removal of this page and of Mr. Field's notes upon the fingerprints preserved there had no connection with his death.'

'Coincidence or not, there were all the days between the Saturday night of the dance and the murder when the notes might have been removed and the page torn out. But the door to the terrace was open, and though the revolver with which Jonathan Field was shot may have belonged to him, he had no licence for it, and no one in the house will admit to knowing anything about it. A German make — and heaven knows how many thousand odds and ends of firearms were smuggled into the country while demobilisation was going on! Jonathan may have wangled one in himself. He was in France in '44 — some kind of a Red Cross job. Anthony Hallam was in Africa. Johnny Fabian was turned eighteen when the war ended — he did just get over to France. Either of them could have brought a revolver back as a souvenir. Neither of them had any reason to shoot Jonathan. In fact one is thrown back upon the exasperating theory that the unknown murderer of the blitz story had somehow become aware that Jonathan was in possession of his fingerprints and an account of his confession, and that he was in the habit of regaling favoured visitors with a tale which featured them.'

Miss Silver said,

'You would call it an exasperating theory?'

'My dear ma'am, we haven't a clue as to who the blitz murderer may have been. We don't even know that there was such a person. Jonathan Field may have dreamt the whole thing after concussion, or he may simply have invented it. From what I used to hear about him, he would have been perfectly capable of it! Then we don't know how many times he had told the tale before, but when I heard him tell it, there were also present Anthony Hallam, Mirrie Field, Johnny Fabian, the Shotterleigh twins who are local young things, a man called Vincent, also local but a newcomer recently back from South America — lots of money and no family. I may say that he was one of the dullest men I have ever met, and that I nearly passed out with boredom whilst he was telling me how he lost a valuable postage stamp in a rapid. That makes seven of us. Oh, and Georgina Grey came in just as he started the story, but that is neither here nor there, because she had obviously heard it all before. Well, there were seven of us without her, and the only possible candidate for the part of the blitz murderer would be Vincent, because apart from the fingerprints Jonathan's only chance of identifying the man was by recognising his voice. He did say he thought he would be able to do that. So you see, that cuts out all the people with whose voices he was familiar, and it really cuts out Vincent too, because there he was, a guest in the house, and Jonathan obviously hadn't recognised his voice. *But* when Georgina came in it was to tell him that people were arriving for the dance. She stood there on the threshold with the door open behind her. Jonathan played obstinate and insisted on finishing his yarn, and in the end she said, 'Oh, well — ' and went off without him. But she didn't shut the door, and if there had been anyone out in the hall who wanted to listen in, I suppose he could have done so. That would extend the number of people who might have heard about the murderer's confession and his fingerprints. There could be a further and quite indefinite extension of the number owing to the fact that it had been a very good story, and that any or all of the seven or eight people who had heard it first-hand from Jonathan on Saturday week could have told and retold it a dozen times before his murder took place. So that, in fact, it could have spread like the ripples in a pool.'

Miss Silver had been listening with attention.

'It is certainly the kind of story that people would repeat. You may even have repeated it yourself.'

He laughed.

'I could take credit for having been discreet, but as a matter of fact I was far too busy. The other seven would have had plenty of time to spread the tale, and coincidences do happen. It could have reached the murderer, and he could have decided that his confession and his fingerprints would be better in the fire — especially if there were even the remotest chance of his bumping into Jonathan and giving him the opportunity of identifying his voice. Let us suppose for a moment that that is what happened. We can call the chap X. He comes down here, probably by car — there is quite a line in stealing cars for this kind of work. He parks it unobtrusively and walks round the house. He may just possibly have had an appointment with Jonathan — perhaps something in the way of fingerprints to offer. Or, seeing the light, he may have just knocked on the glass door and pitched some likely tale. Anyhow he gets in and they talk. At some period the album is got out and the finger-prints are exhibited. At some point X produces a revolver and shoots Jonathan Field, after which he tears out the page with his own fingerprints, takes the notes out of the envelope, and makes off. I don't think he would have stopped to burn anything at the time in case of the shot having been heard. Once he was clear there would be nothing to connect him with the crime, and there would be all the time in the world to burn the page and the notes at a safe distance from Field End.'

Miss Silver's hands were folded in her lap.

'I can imagine no reason why he should have left that re-volver behind him.'

'Oh, well, I don't insist on the revolver being his own. Let us suppose that it belonged to Jonathan. He is having an interview with a man whom he knows to have been a murderer. Wouldn't it have been natural for him to have taken the precaution of having some means of protection handy?'

Miss Silver said,

'I do not know. I should have said it would be most improbable that Mr. Field would either make an appointment for so late an hour or admit a stranger to his house without one.'

Frank looked a little taken aback.

'Well, someone shot him, and it was someone who knew the story of the man who was buried with Jonathan under a bombed building in the blitz, because otherwise he would have had no motive for tearing out the page with the man's fingerprints and removing Jonathan's notes on the incident.'

Miss Silver gave a gentle unobtrusive cough.

'He tore the page from the album and he removed the notes from the envelope. Can you tell me why he left the empty envelope in the album, where it marked the torn-out page?'

CHAPTER TWENTY-THREE

MR. MAUDSLEY arrived at half past ten, having taken the night train from Edinburgh and breakfasted at his own house. He was a man of about sixty with a pleasant voice and an agreeable manner. His features were good, and if he had put on a couple of stone in the last year or two he carried it well. After a short interview with Detective Inspector Abbott during which the main facts of the case were put before him he suggested that the will should be opened and the beneficiaries acquainted with its contents.

They came into the study. With Mrs. Fabian and Georgina Mr. Maudsley was on terms of old acquaintance. Johnny Fabian and Anthony Hallam he had known as boys. Mirrie Field and Miss Silver were strangers to him. Mirrie came in with her hand on Johnny's arm, her eyes wide and enquiring, like a kitten in a place it does not know. Whilst greetings and condolences were passing she stood as close as she could and kept her hold of him. Mr. Maudsley's 'I needn't say how shocked I was to hear the news' having met with its due response, and a few more murmured words having been added, he went over to the writing-table and sat down there. When everyone was settled he spoke.

'I have here Mr. Field's will, of which I am executor. In the circumstances I think the best thing I can do is to acquaint you with its provisions.'

His manner was grave and formal. His glance travelled from one to another. Chairs had been placed in a rough semicircle — Frank Abbott sitting close up to the table on the extreme right; beyond him Miss Maud Silver in a small armless chair; next to her Mirrie Field and Johnny Fabian, their seats pushed close together and her hand still holding his sleeve. She wore the white wool jumper and grey skirt which she had put on yesterday. Anthony Hallam came next, his face set and rather gloomy, and beyond him Georgina, very pale.

Mrs. Fabian had been given Jonathan Field's big chair, but for all the comfort it afforded her she might just as well have had a wooden stool. She sat stiffly upright in a black coat and skirt usually reserved for funerals and held her hands tightly clasped together in her lap. She mustn't, mustn't let herself think that Jonathan had possibly made any provision for her. It was true that she had been asked to come in and hear the will read, but that would just be because she had lived for such a long time at Field End and had brought Georgina up. At the most there might be some small legacy that would cover the expense of a move, say ten or twenty pounds. But no, she mustn't even let herself count on that, and she must be on her guard against displaying the least sign of disappointment. Dear Mamma had brought her up to believe that a lady did not show her feelings in public. She had done her best to bring dear Georgina up in the same way, and look how beautifully she was behaving now — such self-command, such true thoughtfulness for others. But she didn't like to see her looking so pale and strained. She had loved Jonathan very much and she would miss him greatly. Perhaps she and Anthony . . . She felt a little fluttered pleasure at the thought.

Mr. Maudsley was speaking.

'Captain Hallam is also an executor. With his permission I will at this time merely give you a summary of the main bequests. There are, to begin with, legacies to Mr. and Mrs. Stokes — twenty pounds for each year of service, with the same to the gardener John Anderson. There is a legacy of five thousand pounds to Anthony Hallam, and a life-interest of four hundred a year to Mrs. Fabian. Everything else is left in trust to Miss Georgina Grey, the trustees being myself and Captain Anthony Hallam.'

A little colour came up into Georgina's face. She did not look at Anthony. If she had done so she would have seen that he was frightfully pale. It was evident both to Mr. Maudsley and to Frank Abbott that he had received a very considerable shock.

He was not the only one. Mirrie Field turned a bewildered gaze on Mr. Maudsley. Her voice shook childishly as she said,

'But I don't understand. That isn't the will he made when he went up to town on Monday — it can't be.'

'No, it isn't that will, Miss Field. It is the one which he signed two years ago.'

'But he made the other one — he did make it! He told me he had made it!' She stared incredulously, her fingers digging into Johnny's arm.

Mr. Maudsley said with gravity,

'Yes, he made another will, but he destroyed it.'

'Oh, he couldn't!'

'It is a pity that you came to know anything about it. He seems to have told you that you would benefit under that will.'

'Oh, he did — he *did*! He told me he was treating me as if I was his daughter! He said he wanted everyone to know that was how he thought about me!'

Mr. Maudsley had come down to Field End with a very definite prejudice against Miss Mirrie Field. He had not been prepared to find her so young, or for his own feeling that fate had played her a shabby trick. If Jonathan Field had not burned his new will before he was murdered, she would now have been standing in Georgina's shoes. If he had lived to make the will which he had intended to make, she would no doubt have been generously provided for. As it was, she had no standing at all. Two years ago, when this will which he was expounding had been drawn up, he did not so much as know that she existed. He said in a kindlier voice than he had used before.

'Your uncle rang me up on Tuesday night. He had come to feel that this new will of his went too far. He did not think that the provisions were just, and he told me that he had torn it up and burned it. On my return from Scotland he intended making a further will which would provide for you without being unjust to anyone else.'

'I don't get anything?'

'Not under the present will.'

Mirrie let go of Johnny's arm and stood up. She came a few steps nearer the table and said,

'It was Georgina. She went out of the drawing-room and she came in here and made him burn the will. She can't do that to me — oh, she *can't*! Not after what he said about treating me like his daughter! She can't *do* it!' It came out in soft heartbroken snatches, her hands at her breast, her face colourless, her eyes brimming over.

Georgina got up and came to her.

'Mirrie — don't!'

But Mirrie shrank away from her touch.

'You want to send me away! He was going to look after me, and you talked him round!'

'Mirrie — you mustn't say that. It isn't true — it isn't really. I told him I didn't mind about the money. I only wanted him not to be angry with me any more. I didn't know why he was angry and I couldn't bear it. I didn't know he was going to burn his will. He just did it.'

They might have been there alone. It might have been a play, with the others in the audience looking on. Mirrie looked sideways and said,

'Perhaps he didn't burn it. Perhaps it was you.'

Mr. Maudsley came in on that.

'Mr. Field rang me up and informed me that he had burned that will.'

Mirrie flung round on him.

'You are on her side! You'll take her part! Everyone will! You'll try and send me back to Uncle Albert and Aunt Grace, and to that awful Home! But I won't go — I won't go — *I won't go!*' Her voice had risen almost to a scream, and at every repetition of the word go she stamped like an angry child.

Johnny Fabian had got up when she did. He took a step towards her. Turning away from the writing-table, she came face to face with him. No one was sure whether he said anything or not. Afterwards he wasn't sure himself. With the tears running down her face she said,

'Oh, you won't want to marry me now — will you?' and ran out of the room.

CHAPTER TWENTY-FOUR

JOHNNY went after her. His mind was in a state of the utmost confusion. She wasn't going to have the money after all. Jonathan had signed the will that made her his heiress, and he had destroyed it the same day. Mirrie wasn't going to have a penny, and he could no more stop himself going after her than he could have stopped himself blinking at a flash of lightning or ducking to avoid a blow. There was neither thought nor reason behind his action, there was only one of the strongest forces in the world, and it had taken charge. He came up with her at her bedroom door. She had got so far and stopped there as if she had been flung against it by wind or water. Her hands were flat against the panelled wood, her forehead pressed against her hands, and she was crying with big choking sobs which shook her from head to foot.

Johnny put his arm round her. He turned the handle and the door opened inwards. He took her over to a comfortable chintz-covered chair and put her into it. Then he went down on his knees and took both her hands in his.

'What are you doing crying yourself sick, you silly little thing? You're to come off it, do you hear — at once!'

She couldn't cover her face any more. It was quite distorted with misery. The tears ran down, whilst more and more brimmed up to take their place. She pulled her hands out of his and sobbed.

'He said I would be like his daughter — he said I would have the money. He said he had signed the will — and that everyone would know how he thought about me. And then he went and burned it — or perhaps it was Georgina. Oh, Johnny, do you think it was Georgina who burned the will?'

Johnny shook his head.

'No, of course she didn't. She wouldn't, you know — she isn't like that. And don't you go round saying that sort of thing, because if you do you'll put her off doing anything to make up for Jonathan burning it. She won't do anything if you start fighting her of course, but if you don't she might rally round with quite a nice little nest-egg for us to set up house on.'

'But you don't want to marry me now. You told me you were too poor to marry me, but I thought if I had a lot of money I could give you some.'

'And I told you that sort of thing wasn't done.'

'I thought it was very stupid of you. I was going to get you to see how stupid it was, and then everything would have been all right — but now I haven't got any money to give you — '

The words were broken into by sobbing breaths. And how true they were. If he didn't marry money, he was going to have to work for it, and work hard. The thought revolted him. Mirrie and a fortune had been an uncommonly pleasant prospect, but Mirrie without anything at all would really mean hard work. The thought should have been an efficacious deterrent, but he found himself kissing her hands and saying the sort of things which ought to have made his blood run cold, only they seemed to be having the opposite effect.

'Mirrie — say you like me a bit. I want to hear you say it. I've gone in off the deep end about you — I expect you know that. I'll work my fingers to the bone if you'll take me on. I didn't think I'd ever want to do that for any girl, but I do for you. I've got that bit of capital my aunt left me. I was going to put it into a garage business. I'm looking round for one. There might be a flat over it.'

Mirrie's tears had ceased to flow. She gazed at him between dark wet lashes and said,

'Should we have television?'

'Not quite at first — unless Georgina thought it would be a bright idea for a wedding present. Darling, does that mean you will?'

She sniffed.

'I haven't got a handkerchief.'

'Girls never do have one. Here's mine.'

She blew her nose and sat up.

'Johnny, you oughtn't to be in here. Aunt Grace said *most* particularly that a nice girl never lets anyone come into her bedroom.'

'Darling, not even a housemaid?'

Mirrie's eyes were wide with reproof.

'She meant a *man*.'

He broke into rather shaky laughter.

'You are a funny little thing!'

'I'm not! You — you must go away.'

He got up, set the door halfway open, and came back again.

'That ought to satisfy anyone's sense of respectability.'

Her eyes were brimming.

'Johnny, I thought you were going away.'

'Didn't you want me to?'

Her head was shaken and the tears ran down.

'Oh, no, I didn't. It was just Aunt Grace.'

He knelt down beside the chair again.

'Darling, let's give Aunt Grace a rest. Shall we? I'm not really so hot on her or on Uncle Albert. Suppose we forget them. I want to talk about us.'

She shook her head in a slow, mournful manner.

'There's nothing to talk about. I haven't got any money.'

'I know — it's too bad. Do you think you could bear to be rather poor for a bit?'

'I shall have to be. Oh, Johnny, don't — *don't* let them send me back to Uncle Albert and Aunt Grace!'

'Darling, we were going to forget about them. What about marrying me and living over the garage business? Can you cook? Because that's very important, and if you can't you'll have to learn.'

She brightened a little.

'Oh, but I can! Even Aunt Grace said I wasn't bad, and Uncle Albert liked my omelettes better than hers.'

'Tactless of him. I don't suppose it went down very well.'

'N-no — it didn't. He liked my soups too. Johnny, shall we be very poor?'

At that moment Johnny Fabian became aware of an extraordinary willingness to do without practically everything else in order to look after Mirrie and have her making omelettes for him. He would even be prepared to work really hard in order to provide the necessary eggs.

He said so. They kissed. And Mrs. Fabian walked in upon the scene. She had come to console Mirrie upon the loss of a fortune, and found her flushed and radiant. But she took Aunt Grace's view of bedroom interviews. They could go and talk in the morning-room, and Johnny ought to have known better.

'Yes, Johnny, you ought — and Mirrie such a very young girl! And she had better wash her face before she goes downstairs.'

CHAPTER TWENTY-FIVE

THE inquest on Jonathan Field took place next morning, and the funeral in the afternoon. At the inquest only formal evidence was offered and the proceedings were adjourned. The funeral was at Deeping and was attended by a very large number of people.

Miss Silver removed the bunch of flowers from her second-best hat and covered her olive-green dress with the black cloth coat whose years of service were now becoming legendary. Such an excellent material. Pre-war of course, and still so warm, so serviceable. A small scarf of black wool kindly lent to her by Mrs. Fabian enabled her to dispense with the rather yellow fur tippet of an even greater antiquity than the coat. It had been a good fur once, and was still most cosy, most comfortable. Since she considered the country draughty, it invariably accompanied her when she left London, but the colour being a little bright for a funeral she gladly accepted the loan of Mrs. Fabian's scarf.

Georgina and Mirrie walked side-by-side behind the coffin. They stood together at the grave. When Mirrie was obviously overcome, Johnny Fabian came forward and put an arm about her shoulders. But Georgina stood alone, tall and slight in her plain black coat and skirt, her face pale and her eyes fixed darkly on the line of trees against a sky of wintry blue. When it was all over, simply and quietly she spoke to the old friends who came up in twos and threes.

Frank Abbott, on the edge of the crowd, found himself buttonholed by Mr. Vincent.

'Very odd thing, don't you think — very odd indeed. Wealthy, prominent man shot dead in his own house in a country village — not at all the sort of thing that you would expect.'

Frank had never found country villages immune from crime. He said so, quoting Sherlock Holmes as reported by Dr. Watson in support.

Mr. Vincent stared.

'Ah, but that is just in a story. Must have things happening in a story or it goes dull on you. But not the sort of thing you expect in real life — oh, no, definitely not. You don't think it can have anything to do with that yarn he told us after dinner in the study on the night of the dance? You were there, weren't you?

'Oh, yes, I was there.'

'What did you make of it?' pursued Mr. Vincent. 'Personally I thought he was telling the tale, if you know what I mean. I remember fourteen years ago when I was in Venezuela — '

Frank recalled him to present-day Ledshire.

'Well, of course he might have been making it up. It made quite a good story.'

Mr. Vincent agreed.

'I have told it several times myself — dining out and that sort of thing, you know. Lord and Lady Pondesbury were kind enough to invite me, and as neither they nor any of their guests had been present when Mr. Field was showing us his album, I took the liberty of repeating what he had told us on that occasion. I am afraid I did not tell it as well as he did. I could not, for instance, remember whether he mentioned the exact date of the occurrence, or even whether he referred it to any particular year of the war. I told them about the experience it reminded me of in Venezuela in the thirties — but I cannot be sure of the year — '

Frank said abruptly,

'Did you tell Mr. Field's story anywhere else?'

'Twice — or it may have been three times,' said Mr. Vincent complacently. 'I have a friend who runs a boys' club on the outskirts of London in the Pigeon Hill direction. I spent an evening there with him — Tuesday, or was it Wednesday, last week. Not this week, definitely — and I think it must have been the Tuesday, because I seem to connect it with my sister-in-law Emmeline Craddock, and it was on the Tuesday that I had a letter from her in which she proposed to come and stay with me for this weekend — a most inconvenient date, but I am afraid she was offended when I wrote and said so. A charming woman and I am very fond of her, but a little inclined to take offence if things do not go quite the way she wants them to.'

'You told Mr. Field's story at the boys' club?'

'Oh, yes, to several people — and afterwards in a little speech which I felt prompted to make. It went down very well, and I was able to finish it — the story, though unfortunately not the speech — before my friend felt obliged to draw my attention to the fact that the time was getting on, and that I was in danger of missing my train. But you must really let me tell you of the incident in Venezuela . . .'

Mirrie had never been to a funeral before. The part in the church was bad enough. All those flowers and the long coffin upon which they were heaped, and everybody in horrible clothes that reminded her of the worst things out of the charity parcels. Even Lady Pondesbury and Mrs. Shotterleigh looked as if their clothes had come out of a second-hand shop. She and

Georgina had new coats and skirts. She had a dear little hat that was more like a cap only it had a little bit of veiling on it, and it was very becoming. She had never had anything that was all black before, and it suited her, but not like it suited Georgina. The new clothes were sustaining, but when she looked at the coffin and thought of Uncle Jonathan being there she just couldn't help crying.

It was worse in the windy churchyard. She and Georgina had to stand right on the edge of the open grave. She very nearly couldn't do it. Her throat was all choked, and the tears welled up in her eyes so fast that she could hardly see. That was when Johnny Fabian came up and put his arm round her. She didn't stop crying, but she stopped feeling as if she was going to choke, and just at the end she turned and hid her face against him.

People came up and spoke to Georgina, who said all the right things in a sad, quiet voice. Some of them said something kind to Mirrie. Lord Pondesbury patted her shoulder, and several people called her 'poor child'. After a little they began to go away. Georgina was speaking to the Vicar. Mirrie dabbed her eyes for the last time and put her handkerchief in her pocket. Johnny had moved a step away. They would all be going home now. It would be nice to go home. She looked about her at the moving groups of people, and saw Sid Turner coming towards her from the other side of the grave.

It was a really frightful shock. He was wearing a dark suit and a black tie. He had a bowler hat on his head. Everything he had on was new and good. Sid always prided himself on being dressy. Lord Pondesbury's suit looked as if he had had it since before the war. Mr. Shotterleigh's black tie was frayed at the edges. Colonel Abbott wasn't nearly so smartly dressed as Sid. But here in this country churchyard amidst these old grave-stones they looked all right and Sid looked all wrong. For the first time it occurred to Mirrie that clothes could look too new.

Sid came over to her and lifted his hat. Something inside her began to shake. She ought to have been pleased to see him. She wasn't pleased. She wanted to run away and hide before he met Johnny. He said,

'Well, Mirrie?'

He was about the same height as Johnny. She tilted her head to look up at him, met his bold dark eyes, and looked down again as quickly as she could. He had crisply curling black hair. Even in that once brief glance it occurred to her that it curled too much, and that he wore it too long. She moved a step nearer to Johnny, and knew at once that it was a mistake. Sid came a step nearer too.

'Well, Mirrie? You look very nice in your black. What about getting along to your place for some tea?'

Johnny had been speaking to Grant Hathaway. He looked round, to see Mirrie looking flushed and distressed, and a strange young man who appeared to be embarrassing her. He said, 'I think we ought to be going now,' and Mirrie turned to him with relief. Over her head she heard Sid say,

'My sentiments to a T. Sorry — no pun intended. Time we all got out of this, isn't it? But of course you don't know who I am. It's a case of meet the boy friend. Mirrie, my dear, introduce us.'

She said only just above a whisper,

'It's Aunt Grace's step-brother Sid Turner, Johnny,' and with that Georgina came up to them and she had to say it all over again.

Sid came back to Field End with them. She and Georgina went upstairs, and she had to explain a little more about him. It was a very faltering explanation.

'He — he used to be kind. I used to go to the pictures with him sometimes. Aunt Grace didn't know. She never let me go anywhere. She — she and Uncle Albert didn't approve of Sid.'

Georgina didn't approve of him either, but she didn't say so. She asked,

'Did you know he was coming down to the funeral?'

'No — no I didn't. He saw about it in the paper. I don't know why he came.'

In her own quaking mind she knew very well. He had come here because he thought — he thought that Uncle Jonathan had done what he said he would. She had told Sid about the will, and he didn't know that Uncle Jonathan had burned it. There

149

wasn't any will, and there wasn't any money. She was just Mirrie Field without a penny like she had always been, and that was what she would have to tell Sid. It frightened her so much that she couldn't stop shaking.

Georgina said, 'What is it Mirrie? Is it that man? Because if you don't want to come down — '

'No — no, I must. He wouldn't like it if I didn't — '

'Are you afraid of him? You needn't be, you know. We'll have tea, and then Anthony or Johnny will drive him into Lenton to catch a train. Let's go down and get it over. The relations and people will be coming in.'

Downstairs Sid Turner had made it quite plain that tea was not his idea of a drink after a funeral. He was given a whisky and soda, and Johnny kept him company.

Tea was being served in the dining-room. Sid's eye flicked over the silver on the sideboard and the family portraits on the walls. It was a slap-up place, and no sign of the seen-better-days kind of look there was about so many big houses now. He had done some buying at auctions in his time. You could turn a bit there if you were in the know — commission from a dealer who didn't want to be seen bidding himself, or an inside tip that there was something worth spotting at an otherwise dull country sale. If you got round a bit there were always chances, and he knew how to make the most of them.

He began to see pretty soon that it wasn't going to be easy to get a word with Mirrie. She would know how she stood by now, and he wasn't committing himself till he knew too. She was a pretty little thing and rather fetching in her black, though he liked a bit of colour himself. But it was the other girl who was the beauty. Class, that's what she'd got — class. With her height and figure and all that light hair she'd be right in the big money if she went in for modelling. She might be glad to do it too if the cash had really all been left to Mirrie. He wondered just how much it would work out at. It wasn't going to be easy to get near her. A good many people had come back for tea and she was hemmed in.

CHAPTER TWENTY-SIX

SID TURNER found himself rather a fish out of water amongst all these people who were using Christian names and talking about their family affairs, and he didn't like the feeling. In his own surroundings he was very much accustomed to playing the lead. Boys copied his shirts and ties and the way he had his suits cut, and girls waggled their eyelashes and their hips at him. He began to hate all these people, none of whom took any more notice of him than if he had been a bit of furniture.

And then all at once a voice was saying, 'I am afraid that no one is looking after you, Mr. Turner.' He looked round and saw the dowdy little woman who had driven back with them from the cemetery. He thought she seemed very much at home, offering him tea or coffee, or another drink if he would care about it. Since she had taken off her hat, he supposed that she was staying in the house — governess or something like that. Yes, that would be it, Georgina Grey's old governess. He said he could do with a drink, and whilst he was waiting for it it occurred to him that it might be a good plan to get her to talk a bit. Old maids were nosey and generally knew everything that was going on, and they liked the sound of their own voices. It would please her no end to be taken a bit of notice of, and he might quite easily pick up a useful tip or two. A modified version of the smile which made girls waggle was turned upon Miss Silver.

'You the governess or something?'

There is no one better qualified than Miss Maud Silver to set impertinence in its place. It is done in the simplest manner, and like all simple things it is best described by its effects. The offender is aware of a noticeable drop in the temperature. Miss Silver appears to recede to a rather awful distance and he develops sensations of embarrassment which he believed to have been left behind with his early schooldays. Even Chief Inspectors have been known to have this experience. That Mr. Sid

Turner escaped it was due to the fact that Miss Silver desired to converse with him. She had noted his approach to Mirrie at the graveside and her reception of it. She had watched his manner to her, and hers to him, during the drive back to Field End. She therefore replied mildly that it was now some years since she had retired from the scholastic profession.

Sid Turner was pleased with his own acumen. The old governess — that was what she was. He was smart at sizing people up. He said,

'Well, I'm a kind of relation of Mirrie's. Her Aunt Grace's stepbrother, that's me. Thought I'd come down and see her through the funeral, but there doesn't seem any chance of getting anywhere near her, not for the moment. I suppose the old man has done the right thing by her?'

Miss Silver gave a hesitant cough.

'The old man?'

'Mr. — Jonathan — Field, if you like it better that way. He said he was going to treat her like a daughter, didn't he? Told her he'd made a will in her favour. I expect you know all about it. Does she get the house?'

Miss Silver permitted a puzzled look to cross her face.

'I really could not say.'

He laughed.

'Can't say doesn't always mean don't know — does it? I don't mind betting you could tell a thing or two if you wanted to! Come on — be a pal! It's nothing but what Mirrie herself would tell me if I could get near enough to talk to her. What about the house? She gets it, doesn't she?'

Miss Silver's voice fluttered a little. She said,

'I believe not.'

He stared.

'Then who does?'

'I understand Miss Georgina Grey.'

Sid Turner used a regrettable expression. It passed unrebuked except by a mild 'Pray, Mr. Turner —'

'All right, all right. What does she get?'

'I really could not say.'

He took off the rest of his drink at an angry gulp and set the glass down hard. Miss Silver gave a timid cough.

'I am sure that he intended to do all that was kind, but I really do not know about the house. Big houses are so very expensive to keep up nowadays. And the associations — so tragic, and Miss Mirrie is quite a young girl. She would not, perhaps, care to be reminded of Mr. Field's tragic death every time she went into the sstudy, even though it was not she who found him but her cousin Miss Georgina Grey. Stretched on the floor in his own room and shot through the head. Such a shock for a young girl.'

He said, 'But — ' And then, very quickly, 'You've got it all wrong, haven't you? The papers said he was sitting at his desk.'

Miss Silver's manner became uncertain and agitated.

'Oh, I do not know. One does not care to dwell upon such a painful subject. I certainly understood, but I may have been mistaken. What paper did you say you had been reading?'

'I didn't notice. It doesn't matter that I can see. He's dead, and we've just been seeing him buried, so what's the odds? All I want to know about is whether Mirrie is going to get her rights.'

Miss Silver did not respond. She appeared unable to detach herself from the tragedy.

'Such a very sad thing. A man with so many friends, so many interests. His collection — really quite famous. Even at the last he seems to have been occupying himself with one of the albums. Famous fingerprints, you know. A strange hobby to take up. Did your paper mention that the album was found beside him?'

'I believe it did I say — that's a thought! You don't suppose those fingerprints he collected had anything to do with his being murdered, do you?'

Miss Silver gazed as if in horror.

'Oh, Mr. Turner!'

'Well, just look at it. There's the album, and there's the old man shot through the heart. Stands to reason the police would be wondering whether someone who didn't care about having his dabs in an album had bumped him off. You don't happen to know whether anything had been torn out of the album, do you?'

Now that he had set down his drink he did not know just what to do with his hands. At one moment they were in his pockets, the next he was tapping on the edge of the handsome mahogany sideboard against which they were standing. He appeared, in fact, to be beating out some tune which was running in his head.

Miss Silver permitted herself the use of her strongest expression.

'Dear me! Was there something about it in the paper you spoke of?'

'Then a page *was* torn out?'

'I could not say, Mr. Turner. I wondered whether you had seen it in the paper. There was nothing about it in the papers that are taken here. Oh, no, nothing at all. But perhaps the police — I suppose they would have looked to see whether any of the pages had been torn out.'

'If they haven't, they ought to get on with the job right away — at least that's what I should think. But of course it's nothing to do with me. Apt to get a down on anyone who tries to show them how to do their business.'

Miss Silver coughed in a deprecating manner.

'Oh, but they are so truly competent. I have the greatest respect and admiration for the way in which they carry out their duties. I am sure that they will not have over-looked any clue however slight. And they say, do they not, that murderers always do make some mistake and leave a clue behind them. Detective Inspector Abbott is an extremely intelligent officer, and I am sure he would be most zealous in following up any clues which have come into his hands.'

Mr. Turner's attention became more concentrated, his tune-tapping more vigorous.

'Did you say he had a clue?'

Miss Silver allowed a slight perturbation to invade her manner.

'Oh, no. I really would not like it to be supposed that I had said anything of the sort. My position as a guest in the house would impose the utmost reticence. Anything I knew would be considered as a confidence, and I could not possibly disclose it.'

She was aware of a sharp change in him. His face showed nothing, its smooth pallor did not alter. There was, in fact, no outward manifestation, but she had an impulse to step back. Since she was not in the habit of yielding to impulses she remained where she was, looking up at him and waiting for what would come next. It was he who took that backward step.

The people round them were thinning out and beginning to go away. He saw Mirrie moving in the direction of the door, and turning abruptly, he went after her. She had come out into the hall with some old girl who seemed to be a very important person if the fuss they were making about her was anything to go by — Georgina Grey kissing her — Mirrie being kissed — Anthony Hallam and Johnny Fabian going out to see her off. He came up behind Mirrie and took her by the arm.

'Who on earth was that? Royalty?'

She turned a startled look on him.

'It was Mrs. Borrodale. She is Georgina's godmother.'

He laughed.

'All that fuss, and not even a title! I suppose she's got money?'

'No — I think she's quite poor. They are all very fond of her.'

He said, 'I want to talk to you. Where can we go?'

'Sid, I can't — '

He said brutally,

'Do you want me to talk right out here in front of everyone?'

'Sid, you wouldn't!'

'You just watch me! Where can we go?'

She took him into the morning-room, and it was he who shut the door.

'Now — what's cooking?'

'Sid why did you come?'

'To see you of course! I've got to find out how the land lies, haven't I? And I'm not taking any chances on the phone — people in villages are nosey. I could tell you some stories about that! And as for putting things down on paper — not much!' He whistled expressively. 'Not for yours truly!'

'You told me to write to you.'

She had written, and now she wished so much that she hadn't. She had told him things, and what had he done with what she had told him?

She went over to the fire and stood drooping beside it. Why had she come in here with Sid? She oughtn't to have come. He was going to make her tell him things, and when she had told him he was going to be dreadfully, dreadfully angry. She ought to have stayed close to Johnny, and then Sid couldn't have made her come. But Johnny was out on the steps seeing Mrs. Borrodale off.

Sid came over to the hearth. She used to think he looked wonderful when he leaned against the mantelpiece like that with his elbow on it as if the place belonged to him. What he was thinking was that perhaps it did, and she had to tell him that it didn't, nor to her either, and the more she thought about it the less she felt as if she could. She risked a glance at him, and wished she hadn't. He had the black look which had always frightened her.

'Well, come on, out with it! How much has he left you? I suppose they've read the will?'

Mirrie hesitated. He spoke more roughly.

'That was the lawyer in the car in front of us, wasn't it? The old woman — Mrs. Fabian, isn't she — said he was catching a train. Said her son was driving him to Lenton. Meant me to take the hint and go with him, I wouldn't wonder, but I put her off. What I want to know is how we stand. The old man told you he was treating you as his daughter, and he told you he had actually made and signed a new will.'

'Oh, yes, he did. I told you.'

He gave a short laugh.

'I didn't wait for you to tell me! I've a friend in the lawyer's office and she tipped me the wink. And you know damned well you'd no business ringing me up like you did. A place like this'll have extensions all over the shop, I wouldn't wonder. How do you know there wasn't someone listening in on the line?'

'Oh, there wasn't! They were all in the drawing-room just after dinner before the coffee came in, and everyone busy in the kitchen. You said to let you know, and I was ever so excited because of what Uncle Jonathan had just told me. When he came back from London on Tuesday evening.'

'All right, but don't do it again. He said he had made the will, and Maudsley will have told you what's in it. You get the house?'

That horrid shaking was beginning again, but Sid didn't like it if you kept him waiting. She had to answer. She said,

'No — no, I don't.'

'Who gets it?'

'Georgina does.'

'And what do you get?'

'I — I —'

'Come along — out with it!'

'I don't — I don't — get anything. Oh, *Sid*!'

His hand had shot out and caught her arm above the elbow. She stared up at him, her eyes wide and frightened.

'What do you mean, you don't get anything? You wouldn't be lying about it — not to me, would you? You'd better not!'

'I wouldn't! Oh, Sid, you're *hurting*!'

'I'll hurt you worse than that if you lie to me! He signed the new will. How much do you get?'

A flood of terrified words came stumbling out.

'It wasn't my fault. He did make the will — he told me he had. He told me I hadn't got anything to worry about. And then Georgina went and talked to him after dinner and he tore the new will up and — and burned it.'

Sid had turned a really horrid colour — like a tallow candle, only there isn't anything frightening about a tallow candle, and there was about Sid. She went on looking at him, because she couldn't look away. He said in a kind of choked voice,

'He — burned — it?'

Mirrie burst into tears.

'It wasn't my fault —'

There was a moment when Sid Turner thought of so many things to say that they hung back, jostling as it were for first place. It was during that moment that the door opened and Johnny Fabian came in. He saw the perfectly horrible young man who had blown in from London, with a hand on Mirrie's arm. He saw that Mirrie was crying and he couldn't get across the room quickly enough.

Sid let go of Mirrie and stepped back. He didn't like the look in Johnny's eye, and it was no part of his plan to get let in for a rough house. He said,

'She's upset.'

Mirrie sobbed, and dabbed her eyes with a handkerchief which had begun the day very smooth and clean and was now a crumpled wreck. Johnny said briskly,

'It's been an upsetting day. I'm driving Mr. Maudsley to Lenton for his train in ten minutes. Can I give you a lift?'

The thing hung in the balance. Sid Turner wasn't sure. He hadn't known Mirrie as long as he had without finding out how slick a liar she could be. He came down on the side of a check-up on what she had told him.

'She's upset because of being let down flat — that's what. I'm a family connection, I expect she's told you, and I'd like to know what's going to be done about getting her her rights.'

Johnny's eyebrows rose.

'I'm afraid I don't know what you mean. Mirrie, you'd better go up and lie down.'

'Not yet, she won't!' said Sid Turner. 'Not till we've got this clear! Mr. Field said he was going to provide for her. He told her so. And he told her he'd done it. And now she says somebody burned that will and she doesn't get anything.'

'Not somebody — Mr. Field burned it himself.'

'Sez you!' His tone was a nasty one.

Johnny went to the door and threw it open.

'If you want that lift you can have it. And if you want to know what happened about the will you can ask Mr. Maudsley on the way to Lenton. And after that I think it would be a good plan if you were to mind your own business and leave Mirrie alone.'

Sid looked at Mirrie, who went on crying. He looked at the open door and remembered that it was three miles to Lenton. He said,

'If that's the way it is I'll take the lift.'

CHAPTER TWENTY-SEVEN

WHEN the door was shut behind them Mirrie gave her eyes a last vigorous rub and stood on tiptoe to look at herself in the oval glass which hung over the mantelpiece. It had a faded gold frame, and it didn't give back a very good reflection. That was one of the things she didn't understand about Field End, and Abbottsleigh, and the Pondesburys' place, which was called Reynings. There were a lot of shabby old things in all these houses, and instead of throwing them away and getting new ones the people they belonged to seemed to be proud of how old they were. And they didn't call them shabby, they said they were antiques. Johnny had said it to her about this very mirror. She couldn't see herself properly in it at all, but what she did see was enough to make it quite plain that she had better stay where she was until there was a chance of getting away upstairs without meeting anyone. She had really been crying and her eyes were all puffed up. She thought she looked dreadful, and it was no good trying to persuade herself that the glass was to blame, because her eyelids were stiff and sore and even her nose felt swollen. She waited until the sound of voices in the hall had died away and then opened the door a little and looked out.

There was no one in sight but Georgina. She had her hand on the newel-post at the bottom of the stairs and her foot on the first step, and there whilst Mirrie looked at her she stayed. Well, it didn't matter if Georgina saw her with her eyes swelled up. She came out of the morning-room, and as she did so Georgina moved and went on up the stairs. She had reached the door of her sitting-room and was opening it, when she looked round and saw Mirrie behind her. She was tired, and she was sad, and she wanted desperately to be alone. There had been the inquest in the morning, and short and formal as the proceedings were, it had been a strain.

There had been a business talk with Mr. Maudsley. And

then the relations and a few old friends from a distance who had to be given lunch — elderly people for the most part and all meaning to be kind, but expecting to be considered and to have their endless questions answered. Well, it was over now, and the funeral and that rather dreadful gathering of the mourners for tea. It was over and they were gone, and she wanted to be alone and just stop thinking. Anthony hadn't come near her all the day, or all yesterday after Mr. Maudsley had told them about the will. That was one of the things she wanted to stop thinking about. He looked hard and stubborn, and as unhappy as she was herself. She just wanted to stop thinking about it all.

She turned her head and saw Mirrie a yard or two behind her — a little damp, tousled Mirrie like a kitten that has been out in the rain. It wasn't in her to go on and shut the door between them. She said, 'Oh, Mirrie, what is it?' and Mirrie began to cry again, not loudly, but in a piteous, heart-broken way. There seemed to be only one thing to do and she did it. She took the little sobbing creature in and put her into a chair. When she had shut the door she came back and sat down by her.

'Mirrie, what are you crying about?'

Mirrie said, 'It's all so dreadful — '

'I know. But don't go on crying. Uncle Jonathan wouldn't want you to.'

There was a fresh burst of tears.

'He was so good to me!'

'He was very fond of you.'

Mirrie gave a choking sob.

'Are you going to send me back?'

'I want to talk to you about that.'

'Oh, you *are*! Oh, Georgina, don't — don't — *please* don't! Uncle Albert and Aunt Grace — and that dreadful Home — you don't know what it's like — you don't really! And I should never see Johnny again! He likes me now, but he'll forget me if I go away — I know he will! Oh, don't make me go!'

Georgina said, 'I'm not making you do anything. I've been talking to Mr. Maudsley about you.'

'What did he say?' Then, as Georgina hesitated, she went on quickly, 'He doesn't like me. He was *glad* about the will being burned. He won't let you do anything — I know he won't.'

'Listen, Mirrie. Uncle Jonathan was going to provide for you. He burned the will he made on Tuesday because it was made when he was angry with me about something. I don't really know what was in it — he didn't tell me. He only said that it was unjust, and that he would make another will which would be just to everyone. Well, he died before he could do that, but I want to carry out his wishes as far as I can. That is what I have been talking to Mr. Maudsley about.'

Mirrie had stopped crying. Her eyes were fixed on Georgina's face and her breath came quickly. Georgina went on speaking.

'Mr. Maudsley says I can't give you any of the capital, because it is left to me in trust. He and Anthony are the trustees. They will pay me the income from the money, but neither they nor I can give you any of the capital. What I can do, and what I mean to do, is to pay you over some of the income as your share of what he meant to leave you. I don't know how much it will be, because I don't know how much there will be altogether. There is always a heavy tax to pay when anyone dies, and I don't know how much that will come to. But there is no question of your going back to your uncle and aunt if you don't want to, or to the Home.'

Mirrie said 'Oh — '. Her mouth made the shape of it, and her eyes were quite round. She said, 'Oh, Georgina!' and then, 'I shall have some money of my own?'

'Oh, yes. Does that make you feel better?'

Mirrie nodded vigorously.

'I can give it to Johnny — for his garage.'

Georgina's voice had been warm and kind. It changed.

'Has he asked you to do anything like that?'

The little tousled head was shaken.

'Oh, no, he hasn't — but I'd like to. You see, he told me right away that he was quite poor and he would have to marry a girl with a lot of money. He used to joke about it. I told him about Uncle Jonathan saying he was going to treat me like his daughter, and I said if I had any money I could give some of it to him, and he said it couldn't be done, because men didn't take money from girls. I did think I would be having quite a lot of money then, because of what Unlce Jonathan said, and when Johnny told me about the garage he wanted to have — ' Her voice broke on a sob.

Georgina said in a troubled tone,

'Mirrie — when did Johnny tell you all this?'

'It was on Wednesday. It had been so dreadful all day and I'd been crying for hours, and Johnny took me out in his car. And he said the only way I could give him any money would be if we were to get married.'

Johnny certainly hadn't let the grass grow under his feet. Georgina felt a burning indignation as she wondered how soon Mirrie would find out that it was Jonathan Field's money that he had been making love to, and not penniless Mirrie Field. She was remembering Mirrie's cry of 'Oh, you won't want to marry me now, will you?' as she ran away from him and from all of them when Mr. Maudsley had finished telling them about the will. Johnny had gone after her, and she was wondering what he had said, and whether it had really come home to Mirrie that it was the money, and that he wouldn't marry her now. She said in a hesitating voice,

'Have you talked about it since?'

Mirrie nodded.

'Oh, yes, we have. I thought he wouldn't want to marry me if there wasn't any money, but he says he does. He says he would work his fingers to the bone for me, and he promised — he really did promise that I needn't go back to Uncle Albert and Aunt Grace. He said he had a little money from an aunt and he was looking for a garage he could put it into, and there would be a flat over it and we could live there. Oh, Georgina, it does sound lovely, doesn't it?'

'He knows you haven't got any money?'

Mirrie gave a final sob.

'He says he loves me a lot and it doesn't matter.'

CHAPTER TWENTY-EIGHT

JOHNNY FABIAN came back with that lightening of the spirit which comes from the feeling that a lot of very disagreeable and trying things now lie behind you, and that you can get back to ordinary ways again. He considered Sid Turner to be one of the disagreeable things. He was a good and easy mixer, but even on a desert island he didn't feel as if it would be possible to mix with Sid. He saw him follow Mr. Maudsley into a first-class carriage and wondered how long it would take a ticket-collector to find out that he had only paid a third-class fare. The thought of Mr. Maudsley's feelings when it happened cheered him all the way back to Field End.

He went up two steps at a time and along to Georgina's sitting-room. She had changed into a house-coat and was sitting with her hands in her lap and only one shaded lamp turned on. There was a pleasant small fire, the room felt warm and peaceful. He came over and dropped into a chair on the other side of the hearth.

'Well,' he said, 'they've gone. Hand in hand so to speak — the revolting Sid and the respectable Maudsley. I don't somehow feel that a lasting friendship will develop.'

Georgina's brows drew together.

'I can't think why he came down.'

'Can't you, darling? That's your nice pure mind. Mine tells me he came down to nose out how much Mirrie had come in for and to cash in on it.'

Her eyes rested upon him with rather a curious expression.

'She is afraid of him.'

'Darling, if she hasn't got any money, I shouldn't think he would have any designs. I feel we may count on Sid fading out with or without soft music.'

'I don't think she is fond of him.'

'I'm quite sure she isn't.'

'But it isn't very nice for a girl to feel that a man is only wanting her money. Even if she isn't fond of him it would leave a kind of bruise, don't you think?'

Johnny said, 'Has she been talking to you?'

'I've been talking to her.'

'What did she say?'

'What was there for her to say?'

'That I had made love to her?'

'Could she have said that? Would it have been true?'

'Oh, yes.'

'You've always been quite good at making love, haven't you, Johnny?'

He gave a rueful laugh.

'I suppose I have. And anyhow why not? Girls like it. I like it. A good time is had by all, and no harm done.'

'No one who really knew you would take you seriously, Mirrie doesn't know you very well. It's a game to you, but it mightn't be a game to her.'

There was a pause. After a moment he said,

'Suppose it wasn't a game to me — this time. It isn't, you know.'

There was another pause and a longer one. He was sitting forward with his chin in his hand looking away from her into the fire. She couldn't really see his face. In the end she said,

'Are you sure?'

He nodded.

'Surprising, isn't it? I — I'd like to talk to you if you don't mind.'

'No, I don't mind, Johnny.'

'It began when Jonathan brought her here. You know how she strikes you, how she would strike anyone — little stray thing trying to ingratiate itself, hoping it's going to be allowed to stay. It seemed only natural to make a bit of a fuss of her. Then when I saw she liked it I began to have ideas. Jonathan was falling for her like a ton of bricks, and I thought — well, I suppose you can guess what I thought.'

'Oh, yes.'

'Mind you, I'd have been good to her. I mean —'

He found it impossible to say what he meant. He had lived under the same roof as Georgina for nineteen years and there really wasn't much they didn't know about each other. She knew very well what he meant, and she said so.

'You thought Uncle Jonathan would set you up in a business of your own and say, "Bless you, my children." '

'Something like that. Mind you, I wasn't in a hurry. I was looking about for a nice little going concern, and I thought he would be getting used to the idea of my being fond of Mirrie. And then all this had to happen. One minute everything was going on all right, and the next it was all in the melting-pot and nobody knew where anybody stood. Mirrie told me that Jonathan had made a new will. She said he had told her he was treating her as if she was his daughter. I didn't mean to say anything to her then, but the converation just came round that way. She thought she was going to have a lot of money, and she wanted to give me some of it. I said it couldn't be done, and — oh, well, I expect you can see the way it went. I suppose I lost my head — I suppose I didn't try very hard not to lose it — and before we knew where we were we were talking about the flat over the garage I was going to get. I have got old Aunt Eleanor's two thousand pounds — '

Georgina said, 'Oh, Johnny!'

He looked round with a fleeting grin.

'I know, I know. Jonathan gone and Mirrie an heiress, and I don't even let twenty-four hours go by before making sure of her — that's the way it looks.'

'It does rather.'

He said,

'It just happened. You know the way things do. You get on a buttered slide and it just runs away with you.'

Georgina was looking at him. He wasn't putting on an act. She said,

'You must have had a horrid shock when you found that Jonathan had burned the will he made on Tuesday.'

'Yes — in a way. I suppose you won't believe me, but — '

'Why shouldn't I believe you?'

He gave an odd short laugh.

'I don't find it easy to believe myself! When Maudsley said that about the will being burned and your inheriting under the old one it knocked Mirrie right off her balance. She thought it meant that she would have to go back to that infernal Home, and whether you believe it or not, all I could think about was the best way to look after her and make her feel safe. When she said I wouldn't want to marry her if she hadn't got any money I knew that I wanted to marry her more than I had ever wanted anything in all my life. And I went after her and said so.'

Georgina put out her hand to him, but he didn't see it. He was staring into the fire.

'This afternoon at the funeral that horrible chap Sid Turner came up and spoke to Mirrie. I can't think what possessed him to show up. No, that isn't true. It was fairly obvious that it was because he thought Mirrie was coming into Jonathan's money. I've just been driving him into Lenton with Maudsley, and he began about it in the car. Mirrie had told him about the will, and he shot off a line about seeing she got her rights. I left Maudsley to cope with him, which he did very efficiently. But all the time he was talking — all the time, Georgina — it was coming home to me that if it hadn't been for Jonathan there mightn't have been a pennorth of difference between him and me. You know I hadn't the faintest, most shadowy claim on Jonathan. Mama was only about a seventeenth cousin, and I was just a horrid scrubby little schoolboy who was no more relation to him than Adam, but he let her bring me here, and he has always let me treat this as my home. If I'd really had to live by my wits, I don't expect there would be anything to choose between me and Sid. It came over me pretty clearly that I'd the devil of a lot to thank Jonathan for. And Mama — and you.'

Georgina said, 'Thank you, Johnny.' Then, after a little pause, 'What are you going to do now? I mean, about Mirrie. Are you engaged?'

'Well, yes, we are. Do you think we ought to give it out?'

'I don't know. She is very young, Johnny.'

He said,

'Someone has got to look after her. She can't go back to that uncle and aunt.'

'They won't want her if there's no money. You had better wait and let me talk to Mr. Maudsley.'

For the first time he turned round to face her.

'What are you going to say to him?'

Georgina laughed. She put out her hand again, and this time he took it. She said,

'Wait and see.'

The serious Johnny was gone. His eyes laughed back at her.

'You couldn't be going to give us a nice wedding present, could you, darling?'

Georgina said, 'I might.'

CHAPTER TWENTY-NINE

LATER on that evening Miss Silver had a conversation with Detective Inspector Frank Abbott. It took place, as their former interviews had done, in the study, but in what appeared to be a rather less formal atmosphere. The first sense of shock and strain had lifted a little. Miss Silver's knitting-bag lay open on a corner of Jonathan Field's writing-table, the bright paeonies and larkspur of the chintz contrasting in a most pleasing manner with a lining of primrose silk. Her hands were occupied with a pair of pale blue knitting-needles from which there depended a cloudlike pattern in a very fine white wool. A soft towel across her knees protected what was destined to be a baby shawl from contact with the stuff of her skirt. There were always babies who needed shawls, and those knitted by Miss Silver were in continual demand. She looked across the needles at Frank Abbott and said,

'I really feel that some enquiry into Mr. Turner's activities might prove rewarding.'

He laughed.

'I wasn't drawn to him myself, but he probably goes with a bang in Pigeon Hill.'

'He is certainly very well pleased with himself. What is more important is that Mirrie Field is afraid of him.'

'And what makes you think that?'

'I was watching her when he came over to speak to her in the churchyard. I was not near enough to hear what was said, but his manner was very bold and assured, and Mirrie took a step away from him and towards Mr. Fabian. Sid Turner immediately displayed a marked offence and Mirrie looked very much frightened.'

'I should have expected her to enjoy playing off one of them against the other — but, as you are no doubt about to say, perhaps not at her uncle's funeral.'

Miss Silver repeated what she had already said.

'She was very much frightened.'

'Well, he struck me as the type that wouldn't mind making quite a nasty scene. But there is more to it than that, I suppose. I take it you didn't come in here after me to discuss Mirrie Field's love-life. I have no doubt she would have flirted with Sid if he was the best she could do at Pigeon Hill, but you can't really be surprised if she prefers Johnny Fabian at Field End. Sid would naturally feel he was being given the dirty end of the stick. He is probably quite a lad in his own circles, and I expect Mirrie got the wind up as you say.'

Miss Silver shook her head.

'I do not think the situation is quite as simple as that. Mirrie has had a very dull life with the uncle and aunt who brought her up. They were not only badly off, but extremely strict. She had no pocket-money and she was allowed no amusements. She was not even allowed to go to the cinema, and would in any case have had no money to pay for a ticket. But I discovered that she had seen most of the current films. She told Georgina that Uncle Albert and Aunt Grace did not approve of Sid Turner, and that she was not allowed to go out with him, but I am quite sure that she contrived to do so. I think she is very good at contriving. She has an artless manner which is a considerable asset. Up to a certain point I believe it to be natural, but she has learned to use it with considerable skill.'

He threw up a hand.

'My dear ma'am — what a dissection!'

Miss Silver continued to knit.

'You have frequently told me that I understand girls. I should have wasted my time in the schoolroom if I had not acquired some appreciation of the different types and the probable pattern of their behaviour. Mirrie's type is not an uncommon one. Her faults have been accentuated by severity and coldness in her surroundings. She has a natural craving for comfort, pleasure, and affection. And she has learned to play a part. But as Lord Tennyson so truly says, speaking of one who veils "his want in forms for fashion's sake", nature will at seasons break through — "For who can always act?" '

'My dear ma'am, you surpass yourself!'

Her glance reproved him. She said,

'I am endeavouring to convince you that Mirrie Field was not only shocked out of playing a part by the unexpected appearance of Sid Turner, but that she had, and has, some reason to be deeply afraid of him.'

'Go on.'

She paused to draw three or four strands of wool from the ball in her knitting-bag. After which she said gravely,

'I believe Georgina told you that she had received an anonymous letter accusing her of being jealous of Mirrie and of trying to humiliate her. I think some of the material must have been furnished by Mirrie herself, though I do not suppose she knew the use to which it would be put by Sid Turner.'

'You think the letter came from him?'

'I think there is a strong probability that it did. I had a conversation with him in the dining-room after we had all returned from the funeral. The room was crowded, refreshments were being served, and as most of the people present were either relatives or old family friends, he was left in a somewhat isolated position. When I approached him he enquired in an extremely mannerless way whether I was the governess. My answer being that it was some years since I had retired from the scholastic profession, he obviously concluded that I had occupied the position of governess to Georgina Grey, and it occurred to him that he might extract information from me with regard to the disposition of Mr. Field's property. I may say that the whole tone of his conversation reflected a coarse and vulgar mind.'

'And you did not blast him?'

'My dear Frank!'

'He actually survived?'

Miss Silver did not permit herself to smile, but the line of her lips relaxed.

'I refrained from reproof.'

'The thunderbolt was withheld!'

'I wished to hear what he would say.'

'And what did he say?'

'He wanted to know whether the house was left to Mirrie. He assumed that it was, and was very much put out when I said I believed that it had been left to Miss Georgina Grey. I encouraged him to go on talking but gave him no more information. During the whole time that we were conversing it was quite plain that he regarded me as a person who need not be considered in any way, and with whom it was quite unnecessary to be on his guard. I allowed myself to appear inaccurate and easily confused in matters of detail. On more than one occasion he intervened to correct me.'

Frank Abbott was not completely serious.

'What are you leading up to?'

'The points on which he was able to set me right. You will know whether the fact that Mr. Field was shot through the heart while sitting at his writing-table appeared in the Press. It was not mentioned in either of the papers which are taken here.'

He was regarding her with attention.

'No details were released to the Press. The first mention of them was at the inquest this morning. At the time it was merely stated that he had been found shot in his study.'

'When I purposely made an inaccurate allusion to Mr. Field having been found stretched on the floor and shot through the head, Sid Turner lost no time in putting me right with the assertion that the paper had said Mr. Field was sitting at his desk. A little later he spoke casually of Mr. Field having been shot through the heart.'

Frank said frowning,

'Mirrie could have told him that.'

'She had no opportunity. I was in the car with them on the way back from the funeral. Mirrie and Georgina Grey went straight upstairs.'

'She could have written to him, or he could have picked up the information locally. These things get out, you know.'

Miss Silver coughed in a manner which he took to indicate dissent.

'When I introduced the subject of the album — '

'Oh, you introduced it?'

'I wished to ascertain whether there would be any response.'

'And was there?'

'A very marked one. I enquired whether his paper had mentioned that the album containing Mr. Field's collection of famous fingerprints was found beside him, to which he replied that he believed that it had been.'

'There was certainly no mention of the album.'

'That is what I thought. Sid Turner, having been supplied with an excuse to talk about the album, continued to do so. He wondered whether the fingerprints could have had anything to do with the murder, and seemed to be a good deal taken up with the idea that the murderer's motive might have been to get rid of some incriminating print. He then asked me whether any of the pages had been torn out.'

'Oh, he did, did he? And what did you say?'

'I enquired whether there was anything about it in the paper he had read.'

Frank Abbott spoke quickly.

'If he said there was — '

Miss Silver shook her head.

'He did not commit himself, merely saying, "Then a page *was* torn out?" I replied that I could not say, but I supposed the police would have looked into the matter. It was plain that Mr. Turner was a good deal interested. I had, throughout, the feeling that he wished to direct attention to the album, and to suggest a link with the murder. It is very difficult to convey what I may perhaps call the atmosphere of such a conversation, but I have very little doubt that he was aware of the presence of the album before I mentioned it, and equally aware that one of the pages had been removed.'

'You were left with that impression?'

'Very decidedly so. Having received it, I made some remark

upon the competence of the police, adding that you were an extremely intelligent officer, and that you would, I was sure, be most zealous in following up any clue which had come into your possession.'

'And what did he say to that?'

'He asked if you had any clue.'

'Just like that?'

'Just like that. I allowed myself to appear confused, and said I would not like it to be supposed that I had said anything of the sort. I think you must remember that he considered me to be a humble dependant, inclined to gossip but nervous and uncertain of my position. He imagined, in fact, that I had just given something away, and since he saw no necessity for being on his guard with me he betrayed the interest, and I think I may say the concern, which it occasioned him.'

'You allowed him to think we had a clue?'

Miss Silver pulled again upon the soft white ball in her knitting-bag.

'I believe that he was under that impression.'

'What happened after that?'

'People were beginning to go away. He saw a chance of approaching Mirrie Field, an opportunity for which, I think, he had been waiting. He followed her out of the room, and they afterwards went into the study together.'

There was a somewhat prolonged pause. Miss Silver continued to knit, the intricate lacy pattern apparently presenting no difficulties. Frank Abbott was leaning back in the writing-chair. He wore a beautiful dark suit and the black tie which he had put on for the funeral. His pale, smooth hair took the light from the overhead bowl and reflected it. The high forehead and bony nose emphasised an appearance of being plunged in thought. He emerged rather suddenly to say,

'A pinch of evidence would be worth a peck of horse-feathers.'

It was the first time that Miss Silver had encountered the term. She repeated it in a mildly interrogative tone.

'Horsefeathers?'

There was a sardonic gleam in his eye.

'A transatlantic expression and quite expressive. They are to be found in the neighbourhood of mares'-nests. But to continue. What, if anything, do you suggest?'

'Nothing that you will not already have thought of for yourself. Some enquiries about Sid Turner. His whereabouts on Tuesday night. The possibility that he might have heard, perhaps from Mirrie, of the story Mr. Field related a fortnight ago. You were present yourself, and so were some other people, including Mirrie. Did she seem particularly struck by it?'

'She did. A good deal of bright girlish excitement, and "Oh, dear Uncle Jonathan, you must go on!" when Georgina came along and wanted him to meet the arriving guests.'

'She could have mentioned the story to Sid Turner in a letter, or during a conversation.'

Frank had a curious irrelevant flash-back to the night of the dance. Or was it irrelevant? He began to wonder about it. Cicely had left a handkerchief in the study and had asked him to get it for her. As he put it in his pocket there had been a sound from the direction of the windows. The glass door on to the terrace had moved, as it had moved on the night of Jonathan's death. And when he pulled back the curtain, there was Mirrie on the step outside in her white fluffy dress with her eyes like saucers. She had been frightened — there was no doubt about that. Startling, of course, to have the curtain swung back on you, but all she had to say was 'I — I was hot — I just went out.' They had gone along into the supper room together, and she had paired off with Johnny. But who had she been meeting in the garden, and why hadn't he come in with her? Could it have been Sid Turner? He wondered, and kept his thoughts to himself. Aloud he said,

'Was she in the habit of telephoning to Sid?'

'I do not know, but I can make some discreet enquiries. I think perhaps you had better leave them to me.'

Frank was frowning.

'As a matter of fact I happen to know that the story did actually reach Pigeon Hill. One of the people who was in the room when Jonathan told it was a Mr. Vincent, recently settled in the neighbourhood but previously in South America. If you ever happen to want to pass right out with boredom, ask him to tell you what he did in Venezuela in '35 — or was it '37? He will take at least twenty minutes to determine the point. It appears that he has a friend at Pigeon Hill. He runs a boys' club, and last week Vincent went there, repeated Jonathan's tale to several people, and finished up by incorporating it in a speech which, I gather, he insisted on delivering. I shouldn't expect Sid Turner to frequent that kind of club, but the story having been launched in Pigeon Hill, it could have reached him. Or, of course, Mirrie may have imparted it. What, unfortunately, seems to be the fact is that there isn't a solitary shred of evidence to show that she or anybody else imparted anything at all.'

Miss Silver said in a gently immovable tone,

'He knew that a page had been torn out of the album. He was anxious to link the missing fingerprints with the crime.'

Frank Abbott said, 'Why?'

She directed upon him the glance which she would have bestowed upon a pupil who was failing to do himself justice.

'It might have been a red herring.'

Whether it was her lapse into the vernacular, or the idea which it presented, he was certainly startled.

'My dear ma'am!'

'He might have desired to distract attention from the subject of the change in Mr. Field's will.'

There was a prolonged silence. It was broken by Frank Abbott with a certain air of determination.

'Well, that is a point of view, and I won't forget it. At the moment there is something which is exercising me a good deal, and I would like to know whether you have given it your attention. It seems to me to be the point upon which the whole case turns.'

Miss Silver gazed at him in an interested manner and said, 'Yes?'

'That door on to the terrace — who opened it?'

'Since it is of the type fastened by a bolt running down to a socket in the floor and controlled by the mere turning of a handle on the inside, there is no question of a key having been stolen or fabricated. A door of that type can only be opened from within. You will, of course, have considered these points. Since Mr. Field was in occupation of his study from about half past eight onwards, the natural conclusion would be that he expected a visitor and that he himself opened the door. There might, of course, have been some occasion when he was out of the room for a few minutes and when a member of the household could have slipped into the study and withdrawn the bolt, but I cannot bring myself to believe that this took place. It would be risky, since the unfastened door would be liable to bang, as indeed it did later on in the night when it waked Georgina Grey. And it would be unnecessary, since there are three other doors, front, side and back, besides innumerable windows on the ground floor, any one of which could have been left unfastened if someone in the house had planned to admit an intruder.'

'I see you have thought it all out. I agree that Jonathan himself probably admitted the person who shot him if — I say if— it was an outside job. I haven't altogether given up Georgina, you know. After what had happened she could have had no certainty as to how many more times Jonathan might change his will, or what her position would be at the end of it. There is one thing — you will have noticed that Anthony Hallam is avoiding her. What you may not know is that he has been devoted to her for years, and that when I was down here before he didn't seem able to keep his eyes off her. But leaving that on one side, and supposing that Jonathan himself let someone in, I think we are bound to assume that this person probably came by appointment. His presence had obviously caused no alarm. There is no shred of evidence to show that the revolver which was found here was Jonathan's own. There is no evidence that he expected any attack. He was shot while he was sitting quietly at his desk. I find it impossible to believe that he was not completely taken by surprise. This suggests a friendly conversation, and a friendly conversation at that hour suggests an appointment. Then how was it made? By letter? Highly improbable. I don't think a man on such an errand would commit himself on paper or give Jonathan the opportunity of telling anyone that he expected a visitor. I think he would telephone as late as possible on the Tuesday evening. It wouldn't be difficult to think up an excuse. Suppose someone did that and spun a yarn about having some fingerprints in which he might be interested. If the tale was only an excuse for getting into the house, he could think up something pretty sensational and know that his bluff would never be called. Now it's common knowledge that Jonathan would go through fire and water to get a really good specimen for his collection. This will business is a proof of the extent to which he was prepared to act on impulse. Knowing what I do about him, I can see him making an appointment like that on the spur of the moment. It would account for the album being there on the table. In fact it would account for pretty nearly everything, including the torn-out page in the album and the removal of Jonathan's notes on the story of the man in the bombed building who, he says, confessed to two murders.'

Miss Silver had been listening attentively. She said,

'Is it possible to ascertain what calls Field End received during Tuesday evening?'

'Georgina says my cousin Cicely rang her up just before ten — something about a dress pattern she wanted to borrow. She said no other calls were received before they went up to bed. The Lenton exchange says a call was put through at about half past ten. If that was so, Jonathan must have taken it. It is said to have come from a call-box in Lenton. So you see, there is at least a possibility that this was when the appointment was made.'

'One would expect so late an appointment to be regarded with suspicion.'

Frank shook his head.

'I don't think Jonathan Field would let anything of that sort come between him and a specimen he really wanted.'

CHAPTER THIRTY

THE following day being Sunday, Miss Silver attended morning service in the church at Deeping. Georgina did not come with her, and Mirrie was much divided in her mind. She would have liked to wear her new black coat and skirt and the little hat with the veiling. Since the funeral was over, she wouldn't need to be all over dead black right up to the neck. Mrs. Fabian said she could wear a white jumper or a white blouse and the string of pearls that Jonathan had given her. And she needn't wear black gloves. That was the funny thing about Mrs. Fabian, she wore the oddest things herself, years out of fashion and quite dreadfully ugly, but she knew what was all right for a girl to wear, and what simply wasn't done. It didn't matter how old your clothes were in the country so long as they were the right sort of clothes, and she could wear her little black hat to go to church in because of it being church and Sunday, but it wouldn't do for every day. In the end she didn't go to church, because Johnny said he would take her out in his car.

Miss Silver enjoyed the quiet service, listened attentively to a kind, practical sermon, and came out into a blowing wind and the threat of rain. She was going to lunch with the Abbotts, and was relieved to find that they were able to reach the shelter of the house before a really heavy shower came down.

Lunch over and Colonel Abbott retired to the study with the Sunday papers, the two ladies ensconced themselves comfortably in the morning-room.

It was some time later, after a full and frank discussion of village affairs, that Maggie Bell's name came up. Monica Abbott was never quite sure which of them had mentioned it, but all at once it was there, and she was saying,

'I don't suppose she has had the receiver away from her ear for more than five minutes since Wednesday morning.'

Miss Silver coughed in a non-committal manner.

'Ah, yes — the party line.'

'One doesn't grudge it to her,' said Monica, 'because really I don't know what she would do without it. It prevents her feeling out of things, if you know what I mean. And it would be all right if one could remember that she was probably listening, but of course one is so terribly apt to forget. I know I have always said I didn't care who heard me ordering the fish, but of course there *are* times! When Cicely was so unhappy, for instance, and Grant used to ring her up and she wouldn't speak to him. I'm quite sure Maggie didn't miss a single word of it. Oh dear, what a miserable time that was.'

Miss Silver said in her kindest voice, 'But so happily over now, my dear.'

Monica Abbott whisked away a tear.

'Oh, yes! And Grant is so good for her. She is a proud, obstinate little thing, you know, and it would be fatal if he were to give way to her. She would only despise him, and she might get to be quite like her grandmother, which would be dreadful for us all.'

Miss Silver smiled.

'Cicely has too warm a heart for that. And she is happy. Have you ever considered that Lady Evelyn must have been a most unhappy woman?'

A spark replaced the tear.

'She was a very cruel and mischief-making one. And it's no use your trying to make me feel sorry for her, because I can't. Oh, I suppose I can, but she was so horrid to Reg, and to Frank's father and mother, and to Frank. Don't let's talk about her any more.'

Miss Silver said,

'I was going to ask you whether it would be possible for me to pay a short visit to Maggie Bell.'

Monica gazed. Her eyes were the same sherry-brown as Cicely's, but she was much better-looking. In place of Cicely's wayward charm she diffused an atmosphere of warmth and kindness. She said, quickly,

'Oh, but she'd love it! She adores having visitors, and especially on a Sunday afternoon, because if she is well enough to be left, Mrs. Bell goes over to see a sister in Lenton and Maggie is alone.'

'So I understood from Georgina. She has provided me with some magazines and picture papers as an introduction — if one is needed.'

At half part three. Miss Silver rang the bell of Mr. Bisset's private door. If she had depended on Mr. Bisset answering it her errand would have been a fruitless one, since on a Sunday afternoon by two-thirty at the latest he was plunged into a slumber too deep to be broken by any bell. It was Mrs. Bisset, whose repose was of a lighter character, who came to the door and found Miss Silver standing there. She hadn't been expecting anyone, because everyone in Deeping knew that she and Mr. Bisset liked to take it easy on a Sunday afternoon. And she wasn't best pleased when she saw who it was, because sleep as tidily as you will, there isn't anybody that looks as neat when they wake up as what they did before they dropped off. She put up a hand to pat her hair, repressed an inclination to yawn, and was about to ask what she could do for Miss Silver, when she was forestalled.

'Pray forgive me for disturbing you, Mrs. Bisset, but I heard from Mrs. Abbott that Miss Bell was likely to be alone this afternoon, and I wondered if she would care for a visitor. I have some magazines for her from Miss Georgina Grey.'

There was something so warm and friendly in the way this was said that Mrs. Bisset relaxed. Stepping back a yard, she raised a rather strident voice and called up the stairway,

'Lady to see you, Maggie! Are you awake?'

It appeared that she was, and Miss Silver being encouraged to go right up, Mrs. Bisset returned to her comfortable easy chair and to the rhythmic snores of Mr. Bisset.

Maggie Bell was on her sofa by the window. Sunday afternoon was a dreadfully dull time. Mum went over to see Aunt Ag at Lenton, and the telephone might just as well have been dead for all anyone used it. There was the wireless she could turn on, but she wasn't all that fond of music, or of talks either for the matter of that. It was people she liked — people she knew and who knew her — what they said to each other when they didn't think anyone was listening — the appointments they made, and the things they ordered from the shops. You found out quite a lot about people when you listened to what they said on the telephone, but Sunday afternoon was a wash-out. She had a magazine, which she called a book, lying open in her lap, but she had lost interest in it. There was a girl in the serial that she didn't have the patience to read about. There was ever such a good-looking young man after her, with money and a nice place and all, and all she did was to bite his nose off every time he spoke to her. Just plain silly was what Maggie called it. If it hadn't been in a story, he'd have gone off and never given her another thought, same as Annie White's young man did when she cheeked him once too often.

Miss Silver's knock was a most welcome sound. She brought two magazine's and three picture papers from Georgina and a book from Mrs. Abbott, who had had it given to her for Christmas and thought Maggie might like to look at it. It was called *Dress Through The Ages* and there were a great many pictures, so Maggie thought she would. Meanwhile she set herself to make the most of her visitor. Miss Silver had been at the funeral, she had lunched at the Abbott's', and she was actually staying at Field End, all of which combined to make her a most desirable source of information.

Miss Silver was so amiable in her response that they were soon launched upon one of those long, comfortable conversations which cover a great deal of ground and are trammelled by no special rules. At first the questions were mostly Maggie's, and the replies, nicely calculated to maintain the interest of the proceedings whilst adding very little to what had already appeared in the Press, were Miss Silver's. It thrilled Maggie Bell to be told what Miss Georgina and Miss Mirrie had worn at the funeral — everything new, the both of them.

'And time some of the ladies did the same, if you ask me. There's Mrs. Fabian — you wouldn't credit it, but that black costume of hers, well, it's one she had when Mr. Fabian died twenty years ago! That's what Mum says, and she ought to know, she's had it in I don't know how often, letting it out when Mrs. Fabian puts on and taking it in when she goes down again, to say nothing of lifting the hem when skirts go up and dropping it again when they come down. And last time she had it in, she took and told her straight, Mum did. "Mrs. Fabian," she said, "it isn't worth what I'll have to charge you for the alterations, and that's the fact," she said.'

When the murder had been discussed and the enthralling subject of clothes exhausted, the conversation, guided by Miss Silver, began to concern itself with the disadvantages of a party line.

'I am sure, with so much going on and so many police calls, you must find it very disturbing. There is that peculiar tinkle every time anyone is rung up, is there not? And of course there is always the possibility that the call is for oneself. It must be a great help to Mrs. Bell to have you here to attend to all that sort of thing.'

Falling comfortably into Miss Silver's assumption that a tinkle could be readily confused with a ring, Maggie said in a long-suffering tone that it was ever such a nuisance, but of course she had to do what she could to help poor Mum, or she'd never be able to get on with her work.

These preliminaries over, Miss Silver coughed and said,

'I suppose you would not happen to remember whether you were much disturbed on Tuesday evening? But no — it's so many days ago now, and even at the time I do not suppose you would have noticed anything.'

Maggie bridled. She was the noticing sort and nobody was going to tell her she wasn't. And as to not remembering, there wasn't one single thing that happened in Deeping or round about that didn't stay just as sharp and clear in her mind as when it happened. She said as much, and was rewarded by Miss Silver's declaring that it was a gift.

'Do you really mean to say that you could remember whether anyone rang up Field End on the Tuesday evening?'

Maggie nodded, her sharp little face intent.

'Miss Cicely did for one.'

'Do you remember what time that was?'

'It was eight minutes to ten. Miss Cicely wanted some pattern or other, and Miss Georgina said to come over and get it any time in the morning — only come the morning I don't suppose either of them thought about it because of Mr. Field being murdered on the Tuesday night.'

'And was that the only call for Field End on Tuesday evening?'

'Ten o'clock Mum started getting me to bed. The bell went twice, but we didn't take any notice. My back was bad and Mum was having a job to get me moved. She brings the phone over nights once I'm in bed. Sometimes it rings and sometimes it doesn't. When it does as likely as not it's someone ill and ringing up the doctor from the call-box at the corner, and if it's one of my bad nights I don't always bother.'

Miss Silver looked at her compassionately.

'Was Tuesday one of your bad nights?'

Maggie screwed up her face.

'Well, it was. Mum sleeps in the next room. I don't call her unless I've got to — you can't work all day and not get your rest at night. The phone's kind of company.'

'Did anyone ring up Field End after you were in bed?'

'Well, they did.'

'Do you know who it was?'

Maggie shook her head.

'Not but what I'd heard him before.'

'You mean you knew the voice?'

'I'd heard it before — not to know who it was though.'

Miss Silver sat there pleasant and composed. No one would have known that Maggie's answers were of any special interest or importance. To Maggie herself they were just a part of the nice interesting conversation she was having with Mrs. Abbott's little visiting lady. It was always nice to have someone fresh to talk to, and it wasn't everyone who listened to what you had to say as if they appreciated it. Miss Silver listened, and Miss Silver said,

'It was a man's voice? Do you know to whom he was speaking?'

'Oh, it was to Mr. Field.'

'I suppose you do not remember what they were talking about?'

'Of course I remember — as far as it went.'

'How do you mean, Miss Bell?'

It enchanted Maggie to be called Miss Bell. When you never go out and you live in a village where everyone has known you since you were a baby, it isn't a thing that very often happens to you. She became as anxious to speak as Miss Silver was to hear. Someone who really listened, someone who called her Miss Bell. A flow of words set in.

'Well, you see, it was like this. There I was in my bed, and not so bad as long as I didn't try and move, and there was the phone and I couldn't reach it without I did move. So first I thought I wouldn't, and then I thought I would, and by the time I got hold of the receiver there was Mr. Field saying, "Rather a late hour to suggest a meeting, isn't it?"'

'And what did the caller say?'

'Oh, he said he'd had trouble with his car or he'd have been down earlier — had to stop at a garage and have something done. And then he went on to say it was the best he could do — he was bound to push on to London because of having to take the first plane in the morning. "So it's now or never," he said, "And the chance of a lifetime." And then Mr. Field said, "All right, come round on to the terrace behind the house and I'll let you in. You'll see the light." '

There was a momentary pause before Miss Silver said,

'Miss Bell, did it not occur to you that the police should be informed about this call?'

Maggie sniffed.

'They've their own ways of finding out, haven't they?'

'They were aware that a call had been put through to Field End at half past ten, but the operator was unable to tell them any more than that.'

'It wasn't any business of mine — not if no one troubled to ask me!'

Miss Silver became aware that Maggie was not one of those who can be prompted to further confidences by severity. She said in her mildest voice,

'You are being most helpful. I am sure you can see that what you have just told me might be very important. When you heard next day of Mr. Field's murder it must have occurred to you that the person who made that appointment on the telephone was most probably the murderer.'

Maggie said, 'Oooh!' drawing the vowel out very long indeed.

'You are a great deal too intelligent not to have seen the connection and to have drawn your own conclusions.'

Maggie was twisting her handkerchief into a rope.

'Well, I did think —'

Miss Silver gave her an encouraging smile.

'Of course you did. Now you said that you thought you had heard this man's voice before.'

'I didn't *think* nothing about it! I knew right away I'd heard it. And that's why I thought I'd keep quiet, because I thought if it was someone that was friendly with the family there couldn't be anything to tell, and anyway least said soonest mended.'

'You knew the voice because you had heard it before? On the line to Field End?'

Maggie nodded, made a grimace as if the movement hurt her, and said,

'I'd heard it all right, and I'd know it again if I heard it again.'

'Miss Bell, when did you hear it before?'

There was no hesitation this time. Words came trippingly.

'Fortnight ago, the Saturday they gave that dance for Miss Georgina and Miss Mirrie — that's when I heard it.'

'At what time?'

'Ten minutes past seven, because she was in the middle of her dressing and she run over to Miss Georgina's sitting-room to take the call.'

'Who did, Miss Bell — who took the call? Miss Georgina?'

'Well then, she didn't. He wasn't Miss Georgina's sort — anyone could tell that.'

'Was it Miss Mirrie?'

Maggie had coloured right up. The flush made her features look very sharp and thin. She hadn't meant to give Miss Mirrie away, not if it was ever so. That bit about her having run over to take the call in Miss Georgina's sitting-room had just slipped out and no harm meant. But now that it was out she couldn't take it back. Not that she had said the name, but name or no name you couldn't miss that it was bound to be Miss Mirrie, with her room just over the way from Miss Georgina's.

Miss Silver had missed nothing.

'It was Miss Mirrie who took the call on the night of the dance?'

'Well, then, it was.'

Miss Silver smiled.

'Miss Mirrie is a very pretty girl. It would not surprise me to hear that a good many young men would be glad if she rang them up.'

Maggie nodded.

'They say she's going steady with Mr. Johnny. But this one that was ringing her up before the dance — bit of a jealous one I should say he was. He'd *got* to see her. Right up on his high horse he was about it. He would come down on his motorbike and he'd be out on the terrace just before twelve, and she was to come out and see him. She said something about showing him her dress — ever so pretty it was, all white frills. And he come in as sharp as sharp and said dresses weren't nothing to him, but he'd got to see her and tell her about new arrangements for where to write. Said the old ones weren't safe any more, and nor was the phone, and she wasn't to ring him up on any account or there'd be trouble. And he rung off without giving her time to say anything.'

'You are sure it was Miss Mirrie he was speaking to?'

'Oh, yes, there was several times she tried to get a word in and he wouldn't let her. Right away at the beginning he said he didn't want anything out of her, only to listen to what he'd got to say and do like he told her.' Maggie tossed her head. 'Well, I know what I'd have said to him, talking like that! But all she did was to say, "Oh!" and shut up like he told her.'

'You are sure about its being the same voice that was speaking to Mr. Field on Tuesday night?'

'I didn't mean to say, because of Miss Mirrie, but I'm sure all right.'

There was a vexed sound in Maggie's voice. She lay immovable on her sofa, but Miss Silver was aware of a withdrawal. She said,

'Was that the only time you heard Miss Mirrie talking to this man?'

Maggie did not stop to think. She saw what she thought was a way out and she made a dash for it. She tossed her head again and said,

'Why, she couldn't get a word in edgeways, which isn't what I'd call talking to anyone!'

Miss Silver ignored the sharpness of her tone.

'No, you made it quite clear that it was this man who was doing the talking. What I am asking you now is whether there was any other occasion when you heard the same voice speaking, either to Miss Mirrie or to anyone else.'

Maggie waited a second too long before she came back with 'It wouldn't be my business if I had!'

Miss Silver looked at her kindly.

'You do not wish to do Miss Mirrie any harm. But you may be helping her, you know. If this man has been frightening her into meeting him or giving him information she may need to be protected from him. She is a very young girl and she has no father or mother. I think there is something you have not told me, and I would like you to do so. If this man is a murderer, do you not think that Miss Mirrie may be in need of protection? I would ask you very seriously indeed to tell me what you know.'

There was a moment of indecision. Then Maggie said,

'She rang him up.'

'When?'

'Quarter past eight Tuesday evening. And it's no use your asking me what number, because I didn't get on in time to hear it. First thing I did hear was him scolding her for ringing up. "And no names," he says, "or it'll be the worse for you." Proper bullying way he'd got with him, and not what I'd have put up with if I'd been her. And she says oh *don't* — she'd only got a minute because of their all being in the drawing-room having coffee. And then a bit about her uncle having got back from London and telling her he'd made a new will and signed it and all and he was treating her just like she was his daughter. Ever so pleased she was, and no wonder.'

'What did the man say to that?'

'Oh, he said it was a bit of all right, and he'd got a friend at court that had okayed it or he might have thought it was just a bit too good to be true. Miss Mirrie asked him what he meant, and he said he'd got ways of finding out what he wanted to know and she wasn't to trouble her head, he could look after them both. And she'd better be getting back to the drawing-room, or someone would be wondering where she was.'

Miss Silver said in her most serious tone,

'Miss Bell, are you quite, quite sure that the man who spoke to Miss Mirrie before the dance was the man whom she rang up on Tuesday evening at a quarter past eight, and who rang up Mr. Field and made an appointment with him later on the same night?'

Maggie stared.

'It was the same voice. I could swear to that.'

Miss Silver said,
'You may have to.'

CHAPTER THIRTY-ONE

JOHNNY FABIAN drove Mirrie up on to the Common and off the
road along a sandy track that didn't lead anywhere. Such a long
time ago that most people had forgotten all about it a man
called Sefton had tried to build a house there. The land being
common land, he wasn't allowed to get very far with it, and
when he finally threw the whole thing up in disgust and went
away, people from all the neighbouring villages came along and
cleared the site. There really wasn't much to take away — a few
preliminary loads of bricks, a broken-down wheelbarrow, and a
pile of gravel. It didn't take long for the Common to come back
to its own with a crop of loosestrife, and later on with seedlings
of gorse, heather and birch. Today the only indication that
there had even been an invading house lay in the track which
had led up to it, the rather more luxuriant growth which had
followed the digging of the site, and the name of Sefton's
Folly.

Johnny flogged his car to the end of the track and drew up
there, remarking that Sefton would have had a fine view if he
had been allowed to finish his house. He told Mirrie the story,
and she said it would have been very lonely up here without
another house anywhere in sight.

Johnny laughed.

'Some people like being all alone on the top of the world.'

'I don't. I'd hate it.'

'Why?'

'I like people.'

He laughed again.

'Rows and rows of them — all in little houses exactly alike,
with an aspidistra in the window?'

Mirrie gazed at him.

'Aunt Grace has an aspidistra. She is very proud of it. I had to sponge the leaves.'

'And you loved it passionately?'

'I didn't! I hated it!'

'Darling, what a good thing! Because, easy as I shall be to live with, on that point my mind is made up, my foot is down, and my will is law. I won't share a flat with an aspidistra!'

She went off into a peal of laughter.

'Oh, Johnny, you *are* funny!'

They were not looking at the view selected by Mr. Sefton. The Common stood high and there was quite a wide prospect. The bells of Deeping church came up into the silence in a very pleasing manner, and the cloud which was later on to break in rain still lay crouched upon the horizon, leaving the sky agreeably dappled with blue and grey. The air was mild and the two front windows of the car stood open to it.

Mirrie and Johnny looked at each other. She wasn't wearing her new black suit but the grey tweed skirt and white wool jumper, with an old nondescript top coat of Georgina's which Johnny had fished out of the cupboard under the stairs. She was bare-headed with a black and white scarf about her neck. If country clothes were not very exciting they were certainly comfortable and warm. She also thought that she looked quite nice in them. Johnny thought so to. He kissed her several times before he said,

'Darling, this is not why I brought you here.'

'Isn't it?'

'Definitely not. The reason we are here is because I want to talk to you, and this is the sort of place where nobody is likely to butt in.'

'What do you want to talk about?'

'You — me — Sid Turner.'

She winced away from the mention of Sid's name.

'I don't want to. Johnny, I *don't*.'

'Sorry, darling, but I do. If you didn't want people to talk about Sid you oughtn't to have asked him to the funeral.'

'Johnny, I didn't — I wouldn't! He just came.'

'And you just took him off into the morning-room.'

'I didn't! It was he who took me. I didn't want to talk to him.'

'Then why did you?'

'He made me.'

'Why did you let him?'

'I — I couldn't help it.'

He took both her hands and pulled her round to face him.

'And now you're not going to help talking to *me*! That is why we are here. Nobody's going to come in and interrupt us, and if you were to scream for help until you hadn't any more breath to scream with, no one would come. So just stop looking like a scared kitten. I am going to talk, and you are going to talk, and before we start I want to make it quite clear that lies are out.'

Her eyes were like saucers.

'Lies?'

'Yes, darling. Fibs, falsehoods, tarradiddles, and what have you! They're out, and the reason they're out is that you can't put them across. Not with me. Every time you've lied to me I've known about it. You can't get away with it, so why bother? I'm an expert liar myself, and you won't ever be able to take me in. It's the same principle as set a thief to catch a thief. And that being that, darling, what about Sid Turner?'

'S — S — Sid?'

He nodded.

'Yes, darling — Sid. The boy friend! That was the way he introduced himself, wasn't it? Do you know, from what you have told me about Aunt Grace I shouldn't have expected her to approve of him.'

'She d-doesn't.'

'I'm not surprised. What does he do for a living?'

'I d-don't quite know.'

Johnny Fabian laughed.

'Don't you ask no questions and you won't be told no lies — that's about the size of it, I should say! Always got plenty of money — better not ask where he gets it! Now to start with, he doesn't always call himself Sid Turner, does he? That letter you dropped at the post office — that was to him, wasn't it?'

She raised brimming eyes to his face, and then quite suddenly she put up her hands and covered them.

'Oh, Johnny — '

'All right — that's as good as a yes. It was to Sid. Now just carry your mind back to the day you wrote that letter and pretended to read it to me.'

'I d-did read it to you.'

'Not all of it, I think. And anyhow what you told me was that you were writing to Miss Ethel Brown who had been your schoolmistress. You told quite a lot of lies about that. First Miss Ethel Brown was your schoolmistress, and then you remembered that wouldn't do because you went to the Grammar School. And then you said Miss Brown and her sister didn't exactly keep a school — they had a few pupils, and you had promised to write and tell them how you were getting on at Field End. What you wrote in the part you read out to me was that Uncle Jonathan was so kind and he was going to leave you a lot of money in his will. I don't know what was in the bits you didn't read me, but what I do know is that none of it was written to Miss Ethel Brown. Because when you dropped the letter and I picked it up, it was addressed to Mr. E. C. Brown, 10, Marracott Street, Pigeon Hill, S.E. You pretended that he was Miss Brown's brother, and that she was staying with him. And you might as well have saved your breath. You were just making it up as you went along, and you couldn't have been doing it worse. So now I'm going to have the truth. The letter was to Sid Turner, wasn't it?'

She gave a miserable little nod and two of the brimming drops ran down to the corners of her mouth.

'Did he tell you to write and let him know if Jonathan had settled any money on you?'

She nodded again.

'Oh, yes, he d-did.'

'And you always do everything he tells you? Nice obedient little girl, aren't you! Come along — just what have you been up to with Sid?'

Mirrie burst into tears.

'Johnny, I haven't — I didn't – oh, Johnny!'

He went on in the hard new voice which was making her cry.

'It's not the least use your crying. You've got to tell me just how far you've gone with him.'

'Oh, Johnny, it was only to the pictures. Aunt Grace never let me go anywhere except to tea with girls she thought it was nice for me to know. I just went to the pictures with Sid, and told her I was with Hilda Lambton or Mary Dean. That's all — it really is.'

He was watching her, his eyes as hard as his voice.

'He made love to you?'

'Only a l-little.'

'And just what do you mean by that?'

'Oh, Johnny — '

'Out with it!'

'T-treading on my foot and holding hands in the pictures, and k-kissing me good night. Oh, Johnny, I didn't like it — I didn't really!'

He continued to hold her at arm's length and to watch her. She couldn't ever tell him about the time when Sid had really frightened her. And right on the top of her thinking about it Johnny was saying,

'What did he do to scare you like this? You're frightened to death of him, and I'm going to know why!'

She couldn't tell him why. It had frightened her too much — the little dark alley between the houses and no windows looking that way, and Sid with his knife out and the point sharp against her throat. If she moved, it would go right in and she would be dead. It tickled against her skin, and he was telling her what he would do to her if she split on him. 'Near or far, I'd get at you and I'd do you in. You wouldn't know when it was coming. You'd be walking along feeling safe, and all at once the knife would be in your back and you'd be dead. Dead girls tell no tales.' That was what he had said. And then he had laughed and put the knife in his pocket and kissed her the way she didn't like to be kissed, holding her right close up against him and almost stopping her breath. She could never tell Johnny about that. And it was all because she had asked a question. There had been a policeman shot and Sid had been going on about it, saying the police were too nosey by half and a good job if one of them got what was coming to him. There was a jeweller's shop that had been broken into and she and Sid were larking — just a bit of a joke it was, him saying she was to give him a kiss, and her saying she wouldn't and pushing him away, and just for fun she put her hand in his inside pocket. It was his wallet she meant to snatch, but her hand came back with a little parcel in it instead, and when he tried to get it away from her the paper tore and something fell down between them. Too dark for either of them to see where it was, but Mirrie found it. Her hand came right down on it when she stopped, and she didn't need a light to tell her what it was. A ring with three big stones, and she slipped it on her finger and wished she could see what it looked like there. That was when she asked that question, pleased and laughing in the dark alley with the ring on her hand. And not thinking anything until the words were out, not thinking anything at all until she heard herself say, 'Ooh — that's a nice ring, and it fits me!' And then she said, 'Where did you get it, Sid, and is it for me?' That was when he reached out and caught her in that hard grip and set the knife against her throat. She couldn't ever tell Johnny about that.

She leaned away from him as far as she could, and he saw the terror in her eyes. He couldn't go on — not when she looked at him like that. He had always had a soft spot for anything that was frightened or hurt. He let go of Mirrie's hands and pulled her into his arms.

'Don't look at me like that, silly little thing! I'm not going to hurt you, I'm going to look after you. I don't care what anyone has made you do. Do you hear — I don't care. If this chap has been frightening you, I'll knock his block off. If he's blackmailing you you'd better tell me all about it. If you're in a jam we are in it together. And I'll get you out — I promise I'll get you out.'

When he held her like that Mirrie felt it was really true. All the time she was remembering about Sid and the knife she had been getting colder and colder, and stiffer and stiffer. She couldn't feel her feet and she couldn't feel her hands. But now, with Johnny holding her close, the stiffness and the coldness were going out of her. She was warm again, and she was safe. Sid and the knife were a long way off. Johnny would keep her safe. She pressed her face down into the hollow of his shoulder and told him about the dark alley, and the ring, and the knife that had pricked her throat.

CHAPTER THIRTY-TWO

WHEN Miss Silver got back to Field End she was in some doubt as to what she should do next. She was, as a rule, a person of quick decisions, but at this moment she was aware of two opposing impulses, and she felt obliged to give each of them her most serious attention before complying with either. On the one hand, she could not minimise the importance of what she had heard from Maggie Bell, and she felt that no time should be lost in passing this information on to Frank Abbott. On the other, it might be desirable for her to check over with Mirrie the two telephone conversations which Maggie had overheard. The third conversation, the one in which Jonathan Field had been a participant, must rest upon Maggie's word alone, but the talk before the dance and the call made by Mirrie herself at a quarter past eight on Tuesday evening, might, and probably would, confirm the fact that the other person on the line was Sid Turner. If Mirrie were to be unexpectedly confronted with these two calls, Miss Silver did not believe that she would be able to persist in a denial of her part in them, or of Sid Turner's identity. She had reached this point and had almost determined to seek an interview with Mirrie, when it became clear to her that she would not be justified in doing so. Frank Abbott was in charge of the case, and if Mirrie were to be questioned he had a right to be present.

She knew that he intended to drop in for tea at Deepside with his cousin Cicely and her husband, and she felt reluctant to disturb this brief family reunion. She would not even have known about it if Monica Abbott had not mentioned that she and Colonel Abbott had been invited, yet the more she thought about the matter the greater was her sense of urgency. In the end she drew the study telephone towards her and asked for Deeping 3.

It was Cicely's voice which came to her along the wire.

'Oh, Miss Silver, is it you?'

'Yes, my dear.'

'What can I do for you?'

Miss Silver slipped into the schoolroom French which it was her custom to employ when she had anything of a delicate nature to communicate.

'I think it will be better if we do not mention any names.'

Cicely continued to use her mother tongue.

'What is it?'

'Is your cousin with you?'

'Yes. You are not going to snatch him away, are you?'

Miss Silver coughed in a slightly reproving manner. If Maggie Bell were listening she would certainly be able to put two and two together. She said in French,

'Will you tell him that I should like to see him as soon as possible? That is all, my dear. Goodbye.'

Out at Deepside Frank laughed, shrugged, and said he supposed he must go. Rabbits from hats were no novelty where Miss Silver was concerned. He had his tea and departed, wondering just what she had turned up this time.

Miss Silver had also been having tea. It was rather an odd meal, with Johnny in high spirits, Mirrie happy and relaxed, Georgina very strained and pale, and Mrs. Fabian just her usual self. She said she couldn't think what had come over Anthony.

'So unlike him to go out for the whole day and not mention it to anyone. You are sure he didn't say anything about it to you, Georgina?'

'No, Cousin Anna, he didn't.'

Mrs. Fabian said,

'Very strange indeed.' She turned to Miss Silver. 'He is usually so considerate. And of course it does make a difference about meals. One more or less *is* bound to make a difference. I can't remember who it was who said, "Evil is wrought by want of thought as well as want of heart," but I remember being made to write it out twenty times when I had forgotten to shut the conservatory door and a plant my father was very fond of got a chill in the night.'

Johnny burst out laughing.

'Darling, is one of us to have a chill because Anthony hasn't said whether he will be in to Sunday supper?'

Mrs. Fabian remained perfectly amiable.

'It was just an illustration. So easy to forget things, and no use being sorry afterwards. I'm sure Anthony would never mean to upset Mrs. Stokes or any of us, but of course the Stokes go out on Sunday evening, so he won't have. And if there isn't quite enough to go round we can all take a little less.'

Johnny blew her a kiss.

'Mama, you surpass yourself! If you ever let Mrs. Stokes hear you say anything like that she'll give notice on the spot. She produces oodles of food, and you ought to know it by now.'

Mrs. Fabian looked a little bewildered.

'Well, my dear, it must be very difficult to calculate, and I don't know how she does it. I am sure I should be quite at a loss.'

When Frank Abbott arrived he found Miss Silver on the lookout for him. She took him into the study and gave him a quiet and accurate account of her visit to Maggie Bell. When she had done, he said,

'You thought she might have something to say?'

'I remembered that when I was here before Mrs. Abbott told me Maggie listened in on the party line.'

'Yes, of course — Monica makes rather a joke of it.'

Miss Silver shook her head.

'I have always thought that a mistake. A thing which is treated lightly comes to be overlooked. It occurred to me at once that Maggie might possess some important information.'

He said, 'I see — ' and then 'Did she strike you as being reliable? You didn't think she might be running a few odds and ends together and tacking them on to the murder?'

'No. She certainly was not making anything up when she told me of Mirrie's two conversations with this man. She likes

Mirrie and admires her. Mrs. Bell had made and altered clothes for her. Maggie feels a friendly interest. She is a person who makes no attempt to hide her feelings. Her likes and dislikes lie on the surface and she is perfectly frank about them. She did not volunteer the information about Mirrie. Something slipped out, and when I guessed of whom she was speaking I was able to persuade her into telling me the rest.'

He said abruptly,

'Well, I happen to have a check on one of those conversations.'

'On which one?'

'The one before the dance. It's quite a small thing, but it fits in. Cicely and I went in to supper at twelve o'clock. She had left her handkerchief in the study, and I went to get it. That glass door was ajar. I heard it knocking and pulled the curtain back. Mirrie was on the step coming in. She was in her thin white dance dress with nothing over it, and she was shaking with cold, and fright. She said she was hot and had gone out for a breath of air — which was a downright lie and a stupid one at that, but I suppose she couldn't think of anything better. What I thought was that she had gone out with a lad who had made a pass at her and given her a fright, and I thought she was just the sort of little fool to let herself in for that kind of thing, and if she wanted to have a necking party, why not have it inside where it was warm? Anyhow I didn't say any more and she didn't say any more, and that was that.'

Miss Silver looked at him in a thoughtful manner and said,

'Maggie Bell's account of the first telephone call is certainly corroborated. I think that there can be very little doubt that Mirrie had slipped out to meet Sid Turner. As to why she did not provide herself with a wrap of some kind it is idle to speculate. Girls are extremely averse from putting anything on over an evening dress. They will wear a fur coat all day, and when the temperature has fallen to well below freezing point they will put on a low-necked dress and go out upon a terrace, or into a garden.'

Frank laughed.

'Low-necked is definitely an understatement,' he said. 'Well, one of Mirrie's conversations as reported by Maggie Bell has some support. I suggest that we ask her about the other, and if that is corroborated I think we may assume that Maggie is telling the truth about Turner's third conversation, the one with Jonathan Field. Would you like to go and collect the girl? It will probably frighten her less than if we send Stokes to say we want to see her.'

CHAPTER THIRTY-THREE

Mirrie and Johnny were in the morning-room engaged in the enthralling occupation of making lists of the furniture they would need for a hypothetical flat over an as yet non-existent garage. It was to have a bedroom, a sitting-room, a kitchen, and a bathroom, and they were looking things up in a pre-war Army and Navy Stores list which gave them a beautiful if illusory feeling that a very little money would go a very long way. Johnny did murmur something about funiture being four times as expensive as it used to be, but immediately spoiled the effect by adding,

'But of course these are the prices of new things, and what we had better go for is good second-hand stuff — much better made and much better value. And anyhow it's only a game, because I haven't found a garage yet, let alone a flat to go over it.'

Mirrie gazed at him with admiration.

'But you will. Oh, Johnny, I do think you are clever!'

Johnny pushed the catalogue away.

'I tell you what, if Georgina sells this place there'll be a lot of things she won't want to be bothered with. I don't mind betting she would let us have enough to furnish our flat when we get it.'

'Oh, Johnny, do you think she would?'

Johnny nodded.

'Sure of it. Georgina's a most awfully good sort. And I'll tell you something that will surprise you — I've never made love to her in my life. There she is, an out and out lovely, living in the same house and all, and she might just as well have been my sister. I expect that is what it amounted to — she felt like a sister.'

Mirrie flicked her eyelashes up, and down again. It was an accomplishment to which she had given a good deal of time and attention, but the quiver in her voice was unrehearsed as she said,

'Have you made love to a l-lot of girls, Johnny?'

He grinned cheerfully.

'Dozens darling — starting, if Mama is to be believed, when I was six years old. I came home from a Christmas party and told the family that I was going to marry a little girl with a coral necklace and yellow curls. We swapped sweets and she gave me a chocolate kiss, but I couldn't remember her name, so it never came to anything.'

Mirrie did the eyelash trick again.

'And you've gone on kissing girls ever since?'

'That's about the size of it.'

'And forgetting all about them?'

'Darling, you don't actually *want* me to remember them, do you?'

Her brown eyes looked suddenly straight into his.

'If I went away you'd forget me too.'

'You're not going away, so I won't have the chance. You see, if I kiss you every day like this — '

They were in the middle of the third or fourth kiss, when Miss Silver opened the door. Mirrie blushed, Johnny laughed, and Miss Silver said in an indulgent voice,

'I am so sorry to interrupt a conversation, but Detective Inspector Abbot is here, and he thinks perhaps Mirrie could help him to verify a point that has arisen.'

Johnny thought. 'When the police say they think someone may be able to help them it's a damned bad sign. I'm not going to have them badgering Mirrie and trying to trip her up.' Aloud he said,

'I thought they'd asked us everything they possibly could already.'

Miss Silver repeated what she had said.

'He thought perhaps Mirrie could help him.'

Johnny thought, 'It doesn't look well to refuse. They might think she's got something to hide. I hope to goodness she hasn't.' He said,

'All right, we'll be along . . . Oh, yes, I'm coming too. I don't trust old Frank a yard — not with a girl like Mirrie. You shall be there as chaperone and I'll be counsel for the defence, and between us we'll get her off without a stain on her character.'

Frank did not look over pleased when Johnny walked in. He was immediately presented with an ultimatum.

'I don't know what you want to ask her about, and nor does she, but either I stay, or she doesn't talk. She isn't obliged to answer a single thing, and don't you Gestapo lads forget it!'

Frank looked down his bony nose.

'I am here on duty, and this isn't a joke. You can stay, but you mustn't interrupt. I want to ask a few questions about a telephone conversation which Miss Field had on Tuesday evening a few hours before Mr. Field's death.'

Mirrie said, 'Oh —' She sat down in one of the easy chairs and Johnny propped himself on the arm. Frank went on speaking.

'You rang someone up at about a quarter past eight, didn't you? Mr. Sid Turner, wasn't it? That conversation was overheard.'

Mirrie began to shake. Johnny, with a hand upon her shoulder, could feel how the tremor began at the mention of Sid's name. She said, 'Oh —' again. It wasn't really a word but a quickly taken breath. And then the words came out.

'They were all in the drawing-room, and the Stokes and Doris were through the wing-door —'

Frank said,

'I'm sure you took every precaution, but someone listened all the same. Now look here, there's nothing for you to be worried about. You weren't doing anything wrong in ringing up. It just links up with other things, and we want to get it straight. The person who listened in has made a statement, and this is what it amounts to. You rang Sid Turner up at a quarter past eight on Tuesday. You were very much pleased and excited because Mr.

Field had just come back from London and he had told you that he had made and signed a new will. You said that he was treating you as if you were his daughter, and Sid Turner said that was a bit of all right, and he had a friend at court who had okayed it, or he might have thought it was too good to be true. Now there wasn't anything wrong in your saying what you did, but, as I said, we are checking up and I would like to know whether you agree that that is a correct account of the conversation.'

Johnny's mind moved quickly. By the time that Mirrie turned imploring eyes on him it was made up. He slipped his arm about her shoulders in a reassuring manner and said,

'Well, darling, it's up to you. Is that how it went?'

She turned the gaze on Frank.

'He said not to ring him up, but I was so pleased, and I thought he would be too.'

'This statement about what you said and what he said, is it correct?'

'Oh, yes it is.'

'You rang up Sid Turner in London and told him about the alteration in Mr. Field's will?'

'He told me not to ring up, but I thought — '

'Yes — you explained how it happened. I am going to ask you if you will just sign a statement about that conversation. We want to be sure that we've got it right.'

She looked at Johnny again, and he nodded.

'Better do it.'

She said, not to Frank but to him, 'Sid will be angry.'

'That's just too bad, but you'd better do what Frank says. Nasty fellows to get up against, the police, but they'll see that Sid doesn't do anything to annoy you.'

Frank Abbott gave them time for the interlude. If Johnny was prepared to co-operate, his help was worth having. He said,

'What did you understand Sid Turner to mean when he said he had a friend at court who could okay what you told him about Mr. Field's will?'

Mirrie was feeling more confident now.

'He knew someone in Mr. Maudsley's office.'

Frank Abbott took her up on that.

'The person who was listening to your conversation says you asked him what he meant by that friend at court business. If you knew he meant this person, why did you do that?'

Her colour rose becomingly.

'He was just bringing her in to vex me, and I thought I'd let him know I didn't care who he was friends with or what they told him. And if it was that girl in the office who told him about Uncle Jonathan signing his will, then she hadn't any business to, and if Mr. Maudsley knew about it he would send her away.' Her colour faded and her voice shook. 'If she was telling him things, I didn't want to hear about it! And it was horrid of him to tell me about her!'

In a wide experience it had fallen to Frank Abbott's lot to receive the confidence of a good many damsels, mostly cousins. But for this he might have considered Mirrie's line of reasoning to be obscure. As it was, he understood perfectly that Sid Turner had mentioned the girl in Mr. Maudsley's office with intent to annoy, and that Mirrie had very properly snubbed him.

He considered that this might be the appropriate moment to make a further enquiry, one confidence being apt to lead to another. He said,

'There's just one thing. You remember on the night of the dance some of us were in here and Mr. Field was telling us about his collection. He got the albums out and told us a yarn about getting a fingerprint from a man who had confessed to a couple of murders. He said he and this man were buried under a bombed building, and that he got the fingerprint by passing him a cigarette-case. Just at the most exciting point of the story Georgina Grey came along and said that people were beginning to arrive for the dance.'

Mirrie was looking at him with sparkling eyes.

'Oh, yes — wasn't it a shame! It was a most exciting story, and I did so want to hear it properly!'

Frank nodded.

'I think we were all keyed up about it. I should have liked to have heard the rest of it myself. Now later on that evening you slipped out of this glass door to meet Sid Turner. He had rung you up at seven o'clock and told you to come out and meet him. He wanted to tell you about new arrangements for writing to him, and you wanted to show him your new dress, so you slipped out.'

Mirrie's voice reproached the absent Sid.

'It was a lovely dress, but he didn't take any notice of it. I wanted him to come into the study and see it in the light, but he wouldn't.'

'Stupid fellow! Now look here, I want to know whether you told Sid Turner this story about the man who confessed to two murders and left a print on Mr. Field's cigarette-case.'

Johnny said, 'Why should she?'

Frank lifted a hand and let it fall again.

'Why shouldn't she? It was a good story and she was obviously thrilled with it. She might have told him.'

Johnny said,

'Well, did you, darling?'

Mirrie looked from Frank to him and back again.

'Oh, well, I did.'

'What did he say when you told him?'

'He said it was a funny thing collecting fingerprints, and there might be someone who didn't like to think about his dabs being in an album, and I asked him what dabs were, and he said fingerprints.'

Frank proceeded to the business of taking down her statement and getting her to sign it. When it was done and she and Johnny had gone back to their flat-furnishing game, he turned to Miss Silver.

'It begins to look like Sid, doesn't it? He'd got his eye on Mirrie as a possible heiress and he was all set to get the earliest possible information as to the actual signing of the will. That being the case, he would have an interest in Jonathan's death. But hang it all, the will was only signed on Tuesday afternoon. The earliest he could have heard of it would be some time after five, when the girl in Maudsley's office would be free to see him or to ring him up — say somewhere between five and a quarter past eight, when Mirrie rang him up and he already knew that the will had been signed. To my mind Jonathan's murder was a very carefully planned affair. If Sid was the murderer he must have got off the mark pretty quickly. But why? From his point of view where was the hurry?'

Miss Silver said equably,

'The more quickly he acted, the less chance was there that any suspicion would attach to him. He had forbidden Mirrie to ring him up. If she had not done so, and if Maggie Bell had not overheard their conversation, it could never have been proved that he knew anything about the will which made Mirrie Field an heiress. And if he did not know about the will he had no possible motive for the crime. Since it is now certain that he did know about it, his motive was a strong one. He was, I am sure, completely confident of being able to induce Mirrie to marry him. His influence over her was obviously an established one, and he was unaware that it was being undermined by her growing attachment to Mr. Fabian. As to the need for immediate action, I feel that there were probably cogent reasons for it.'

Frank was leaning back, his eyes half closed, missing nothing. He was being taught this business, and he had no thought of resenting it. That was the astonishing thing about Maudie — she took a case to pieces before your eyes and then she put it together again, and she did it without feeling clever herself or making you feel stupid. She saw things as they were, and she took you along with her until you saw them too. And she left you with the feeling of being on the top of your own particular world.

'And what do you imagine those reasons to have been?'

She smiled.

'You will, I am sure, have thought of them for yourself. Mr. Field had shown himself to be both changeable and impulsive. We have no actual proof of how much this girl in Mr. Maudsley's office had been able to repeat, but a young woman bent on eavesdropping could doubtless have picked up a good deal. Mr. Maudsley told Georgina Grey that he had made every effort to deter Mr. Field from signing what he considered to be a most unjust will. He said that the old friendship between them had been strained almost to breaking-point. In the circumstances, there is no difficulty in imagining that the voices of both gentlemen were raised, and that Mr. Maudsley's office would have had a very good idea of what was going on. I gather that two of the clerks were called in to witness the signing of the will. This girl might have been one of them. I think Sid Turner may well have considered the possibility of another change of mind on the part of Mr. Field. Put yourself in his place. It is Tuesday evening, and he has learned that Jonathan Field has signed a will which makes Mirrie his heiress. He believes himself to be sure of her, and if Mr. Field dies tonight Mirrie is sure of the money. If Mr. Field lives he may change his mind again. But if he dies, Mirrie is an heiress and Sid Turner has only to put out his hand and take her. That is, I think, a fair deduction from the bullying tone which he adopted during their telephone conversations. Maggie Bell was extremely indignant about it, and I think it is safe to say that a man does not adopt that manner towards a girl, and without reproof, unless it has become a habit between them.'

'I expect you are right. You think he decided to strike while the iron was hot?'

'I believe that he must have done so. To a person deprived of principle and merely considering his own advantage it would appear to be a natural course of action. A truly shocking example of the consequences which attend the neglect of religion and morality.'

This was Maudie in her loftiest manner. Frank bowed to it respectfully. Whilst in one corner of his mind a modern imp cocked a snook, its more orderly inhabitants chorused, 'That is true.' Aloud he said,

'So he got on his motorbike, hared down to Lenton, rang Jonathan up from a call-box, sold him a line on fingerprints, and came over and shot him. Definitely a fast worker!'

Miss Silver said,

'Yes.' There was a short pause before she went on. 'There is no means of knowing at what period it occurred to him that the story about a murderer's fingerprint repeated to him by Mirrie could be used to his own advantage. He may have thought of it originally as a means of inducing Mr. Field to let him in. Any alarm would be fatal. He remembers that Mr. Field is a collector, and he uses the offer of specially interesting material as a bait. Once Mr. Field has taken it the rest is easy. Jonathan Field lays out the album on his table and waits for him. The talk probably begins with some reference to the story repeated by Mirrie. We know that Mr. Field was particularly fond of telling it. It is probably whilst he is engaged in doing so that Sid conceives the idea of tearing out the page concerned and removing the notes about it from the envelope which marked the place. He would argue that this would suggest a motive other than the real one. He has come determined on Mr. Field's death. He shoots him without warning, and once he has torn the leaf from the album, removed the notes, and left the house, he feels that there will be nothing to connect him with the crime.'

Frank nodded.

'He left the revolver because there was just a faint hope that the death might be put down to suicide. Jonathan's prints were on it, but an attempt to get a dead man's prints in any sort of natural position doesn't really come off. I think that is where he made a mistake. If he was going to suggest an unknown murderer intent on destroying an incriminating fingerprint, he could have left it at that and taken his gun away. He could always have dropped it in the river after he got back to town. Well, we've produced a very pretty jigsaw puzzle between us, and all the pieces seem to fit very nicely, but we've still got to make the thing stick together. Jigsaws have a nasty way of coming apart when you try and pick them up. And, to leave the metaphor out of it, we may find that Sid has got a real first-class unbreakable alibi for Tuesday night.'

Miss Silver coughed in a meditative manner.

'I feel quite sure that he will have provided himself with an alibi.'

'Any particular reason for thinking so?'

She said,

'I think Sid Turner is a very dangerous person. He plans with great attention to detail, and he acts promptly and efficiently. He takes care to establish a connection with Mr. Maudsley's office, he takes care to maintain his ascendancy over Mirrie Field, he even takes the bold step of coming down to attend Mr. Field's funeral. I feel sure that he would not have neglected to provide himself with an alibi for Tuesday night. There are a number of ways in which it could be done.'

'My dear ma'am! I tremble to think of the consequences if you had ever turned your mind to crime!'

This impropriety was rightly ignored. She said,

'There is a point which may interest you. It concerns the torn-out page and the missing notes supposed to authenticate the fingerprint upon it.'

He wondered what was coming, but was hardly prepared for it when it came.

'Georgina tells me that the story of a murderer's confession during an air raid was a great favourite of Mr. Jonathan Field's, but that he had told her it really had no foundation in fact.'

'Georgina told you that!'

'I already had grave doubts about the story. The fingerprint was supposed to have been left on a cigarette-case passed by Mr. Field to the man who, like himself, had been trapped in the ruins of a bombed building. Mr. Field in his account of the incident was said to have stated that he subsequently lost consciousness, and that when he came to he discovered himself to be in hospital with a broken limb. He would have been undressed, money and valuables removed from his pockets, and I found it impossible to believe that a fingerprint would have survived the handling to which his cigarette-case must have been subjected. In fact the murderer's confession might possibly have been made as described by Mr. Field, but reason and common sense reject the evidence of the fingerprint. When I said this to Georgina she informed me that the print on the torn-out page was that of Mr. Field's own forefinger.'

Frank said, 'The old devil!' He received a glance of reproof.

'I believe that he considered it to be a very good joke. It does undoubtedly remove the possibility that the missing page was torn out for any other reason than to divert attention from the real motive for Mr. Field's murder.'

'Bringing us back to Sid Turner. You know, he really did have desperately bad luck — bad and quite unforeseeable. No one — no one could have imagined that Jonathan would destroy his new will only a few hours after he had signed it.'

Miss Silver looked at him gravely.

'Sid Turner is a dangerous and unscrupulous man. I shall be uneasy until I have heard of his arrest.'

CHAPTER THIRTY-FOUR

FOR at least once in his life Sid Turner would have endorsed a police officer's opinion. His luck had been terrible. With every foreseeable detail thought out, every adverse contingency provided against, the one thing which could upset his careful planning had turned up against him. Jonathan Field had destroyed the will which he had signed only a few hours before, and his and Mirrie's chances had gone up in smoke. Well, no use fighting your luck, and no use crying over spilt milk. Mirrie wasn't the only pebble on the beach. There were other girls with money coming to them, and if he wanted to play safe, there was Aggie Marsh — getting on a bit, but not bad-looking and as soft as butter. Bert Marsh had left her the pub and twenty-five thousand. He knew that for a fact, because he had been to Somerset House and read the will. He had been considering her very carefully before Jonathan Field had carried Mirrie off from the Home and began to fall for her in a big way. Well, he would just have to make do with Aggie. She'd have him all right, but he'd better not let the grass grow under his feet. Thanks to careful planning he was in the clear — alibi for Tuesday night and nothing to connect him with the death at Field End as long as Mirrie held her tongue. And she'd be much too frightened to do anything else. For a moment, as he contemplated the possibility of Mirrie blabbing, his thoughts became frighteningly dark. Then they cleared again. She had known things about him before and she hadn't split. Besides it was all to her own advantage to keep a still tongue. Whatever she thought, she'd be too frightened of getting drawn in herself not to keep quiet about it.

He had reached this comforting point, when his landlady

Mrs. Jenkins called up the stair, 'Phone call for you, Sid Turner,' and he went down to take it. The telephone was in her front room, and he shut the door before lifting the receiver. It might be Aggie Marsh. There had been something said about his going round for a spot of supper tonight. Well, he didn't mind if he did.

It wasn't Aggie. It was Bertha Cummins.

'Is that you, Sid? I want to see you at once ... No — no — it's not on my account, it's on yours. Things have been happening at the office. There's been an Inspector from Scotland Yard — '

'Shut up!' He couldn't get it out fast enough. The leaky tongues women had! She was trying to say something again, but the rasp in his voice stopped her. 'I didn't get what you said just now — the line's bad. I'll be at the corner of West Street in say twenty minutes. We can do a flick.' He hung up and went to meet her.

Bertha Cummins came out of the call-box where she had been ringing up. There are hundreds just like her in any big city — neat, nondescript — the efficient secretary, clerk, manageress. She was thin without being slender, well-featured without making any effect. She had one of those smooth colourless skins which are an excellent foundation for make-up, but she had never done more for it than wash it in soap and water and dust it with powder if the day was warm. She wore neither lipstick nor nail polish. Her clothes were as drab as herself. She was forty-four years old and no man who wasn't an elderly relation had kissed her until a month ago, when she had dropped her umbrella coming out of the office and Sid Turner had picked it up.

She had let him pick her up too. Even now she couldn't think how she had come to do it. He had been most respectful in his manner. There had been a little talk about dropping things and somehow he was walking along the street beside her, and when she thanked him again and said goodbye he had given her that wonderful smile and said, 'Does it have to be goodbye?' After that it really seemed quite natural to have tea together, and then they went to the pictures, and he told her how lonely he was and she let him hold her hand. After that he met her every day, not coming right up to the office but waiting for her round the corner. No one had ever made love to her before. She couldn't believe that he cared for her, but he convinced her that he did. The barriers fell one by one. She walked in a daze of happiness and only thought how wonderful it was that he should be so interested in everything she did. She hadn't wanted to talk about the office, because she thought it would bore him, but it was wonderful how interested he was. She found herself telling him about everything that happened. He didn't know any of the people, so what did it matter? She told him about Jonathan Field changing his will. The barriers were down in good earnest.

He was waiting for her at the corner of West Street. She could see the black look on his face before she came up to him. He didn't raise his voice, but it had a cutting tone in it.

'Don't you ever say things like that on the phone again, or I'm done with you!'

'Things?'

'You heard! And we're not talking here — there are too many people about. We'll get on the next bus separately and get off at the fourth stop from here. We're not to look as if we're together.'

They finished up at the back of a very nearly empty tea-room. When the waitress had brought them tea and cakes they had as much privacy as it was possible to achieve.

She had taken only one strong comforting sip, when he said,

'Now what's all this about a police Inspector?'

She set down her cup again because her hand was shaking too much to hold it.

'He came in after we got back from lunch. He saw Mr. Maudsley, and as soon as he had gone Mr. Maudsley sent for me. He was dreadfully angry and upset. He said there had been a leakage of information from his office and he meant to find out who was responsible. I don't know what I felt like.'

Sid Turner made it clear that he took no interest in her feelings.

'Tell me what he said.'

'It's that girl — ' When it came to naming Mirrie Field she

couldn't keep her voice from trembling. 'You oughtn't to have rung her up. You ought to have kept right away from her until the will was proved — I could have told you that.'

He said in a low dangerous tone,

'When I want you to teach me my business I'll let you know. What about the girl?'

'Someone listened in when you were talking to her. They've got one of those party lines. I suppose you didn't know about that, but they have. Anyone can just lift a receiver and listen in on the others. Someone did when you were talking to Mirrie Field. She was telling you about the will having been signed, and you said you had a friend at court so you knew already. When the police asked her what you meant by a friend at court she said it was someone in Mr. Maudsley's office. Oh, how could you tell her about me! I've never done anything like it before, and I wouldn't have done it for anyone else in the world. You wanted to know, and I told you, but I never thought you would give me away.'

He said,

'Stop nattering! Does Maudsley suspect you?'

'Oh, *no*. That is what is so dreadful — he *trusts* me. And he thinks it's Jenny Gregg.'

He laughed.

'Then what's all the fuss about? You're in the clear, and Jenny gets the sack. That's all. If a girl talks out of place, there isn't anything the police can do about it.'

He looked at her and thought what a stupid woman she was. One good thing, he wouldn't have to keep up with her after this. He liked a girl to be warm and willing. He could make love to pretty well anything if it was in the way of business, but this thin, anxious woman with her scruples and the marks like bruises under dark eyes, well, it would certainly be a relief to be rid of her.

She was watching him. She hadn't been twenty-five years in a lawyer's office for nothing. She was very much afraid.

'Sid, don't you realise what this means? I'm not thinking about myself or about Jenny Gregg. The police are asking these questions because they are thinking about you.'

He looked at her with contempt.

'There's nothing for them to think about. I've known Mirrie since she was a child. She lived in my sister's house — in a way you may say I am a relation. I got to know you, we liked each other, and you happened to mention Mr. Field's name — said he was leaving a lot of money to a girl called Mirrie Field. There's nothing the police can do about that, is there?'

'It would lose me my job, and I should never get another.'

'Oh, well, there's no need to mention names. I can just say it was a girl in the office. If they press me, I'm the perfect gentleman and couldn't give a young lady away. You don't need to worry about your job. No one is going to think of you having a boy friend when there are a couple of girls around. Is Jenny the fair one?'

She said, 'Yes.'

She was cold right through and through — cold and numb. Presently she would remember what he had said and feel the bruise which the words had left. At the moment she felt nothing but the numbness and the cold.

He said,

'Well, we'd better not be seen together. You go home and take some aspirin or something and get that look off your face. Better say you've got a headache, or people will be beginning to wonder what's happening to you.'

She said,

'You don't seem to realise the police think you had a motive for Mr. Field's murder. They're trying to connect you with it. They think he was killed because he had signed that will. They think you went down there and shot him on Tuesday night because that will he had signed in the afternoon left a lot of money to Mirrie Field. I think she had told them whatever she knows.'

'She doesn't know anything, and there isn't anything to know. As for Tuesday night, the Jenkins, where I live, can tell your nosey-parker policeman I came in to fetch my raincoat about nine. Coming downstairs I caught my foot in it and took a nasty fall. They came running out and found me knocked clean out at the bottom of the stairs. Tom had to give me brandy and help me up to bed. Mrs. Jenkins gave me two of her sleeping-tablets and they put me out till the morning. Pretty bad head I had too, but no bones broken. They said to knock on the floor if I wanted anything, but I slept like the dead. Not much the police can do about that, is there?'

She had kept those strained dark eyes upon him. They searched his face. She said,

'You've got a motorbike, haven't you?'

'So what?'

'Where do you keep it?'

'In the shed at the bottom of the yard.' He met her look with a savage angry one. 'What are you getting at? You don't think I fell downstairs, had to be helped to bed, and then got up and took the bike out and went down to this place Field End to shoot a man I'd never seen, do you?'

In her own mind she said, 'I don't think you fell downstairs.' She didn't say it aloud. She went on looking at him and she went on thinking. He could have faked that fall — thrown something down, clattered down the last few steps and made quite a noise, bumping and calling out without really being hurt at all, and if he wasn't hurt he could have climbed out of his bedroom window. And the motorbike needn't have been put away. He could have left it handy and wheeled it out when something heavy was passing along the road. She didn't want to have these thoughts, but they were there in her mind. She was to wonder afterwards whether Sid knew they were there, because quite suddenly he changed. The smile that had charmed her came into his eyes. He edged his chair round a bit and slipped his hand inside her arm, running it up and down with the caressing touch which had set her heart beating, beating.

Now she was too cold to feel anything at all — too cold, and too much afraid. Presently there would be the sense of loss, the sense of shame, but for this moment there was only the fear and the bitter cold.

For the first time since she had met him she counted the moments until she could get away from his look, his touch. It was the only relief that she could hope for.

CHAPTER THIRTY-FIVE

FRANK ABBOTT dropped in at Field End on Tuesday morning. He asked for Miss Silver, and she came to him presently with her knitting-bag on her arm and the white woolly shawl now two thirds of the way towards completion wrapped up in a soft old face-towel — one of those fine white ones with a diaper pattern on it now quite out of date and superseded by cleansing tissues. The much faded date in the corner of this one was 1875, and it had been part of the wedding outfit of an aunt.

Miss Silver took out the shawl, spread the towel over her knees, and turned her attention to Frank.

'The enquiries about Sid Turner? Have they had any success?'

He gave a faint shrug.

'Beyond producing considerable alarm and despondency in Maudsley's office I should say none, if it were not for the fact that to have a perfectly good alibi for Tuesday night is in itself a suspicious circumstance.'

Miss Silver inserted a second needle into the fluffy white cloud on her lap and began to knit with her usual smoothness and rapidity.

'Sid Turner has an alibi?'

'Certainly. You will remember we agreed that he would have one. Blake went down, or shall I say up, to Pigeon Hill and saw his landlady and her husband. Retired railwayman and his wife. Nothing against them. Sid has lodged with them for about six months. Mr. Jenkins said he was all right, and Mrs. Jenkins said he was ever so nice. The alibi consists in his coming in to fetch a raincoat about nine o'clock on Tuesday evening, catching his foot in it, and falling down the best part of a flight of stairs. The Jenkinses depose to finding him unconscious in the hall. They roused him with brandy, and Jenkins helped him to bed. There were no bones broken, and he said he didn't want a doctor. Mrs. Jenkins produced a couple of sleeping-tablets and told him to knock on the floor if he wanted anything. He replied that all he wanted was to be left alone to go to sleep. So they left him. As you are about to observe, he could have got out of the window and just made Lenton on his motorbike in time to ring Jonathan up from there.'

Miss Silver gave a faint doubtful cough.

'It would have been running it very fine, and he would be taking the risk of the Jenkinses looking in to see how he was before they went to bed.'

Frank nodded.

'According to Blake there wasn't any risk of their doing that. They sleep in the basement and Jenkins keeps off the stairs as much as he can. He's got a dicky foot, which is why he left the railways, and Mrs. Jenkins weighs about seventeen stone.'

Miss Silver's needles clicked.

'Did Inspector Blake see Sid Turner?'

'He wasn't at home. Asked where he was likely to be, Mrs. Jenkins bridled and said she wouldn't wonder if he was at the Three Pigeons. Very friendly with the lady there he was — a Mrs. Marsh. Her husband had been dead about a twelve month, and there were those who thought she might be going to make it up with Sid. And he'd be doing well for himself if she did. Nice bit of money the husband had left her, to say nothing of the pub.'

'So Inspector Blake went round to the Three Pigeons? Was Sid Turner there?'

'He was, and so were a lot of other people. And do you know what they were doing? Celebrating Sid's engagement to Mrs. Marsh — drinks on the house and a good time being had by all. Sid is a quick worker!'

Miss Silver looked thoughtful.

'If one of the girls in Mr. Maudsley's office was friendly with him to the point of giving away confidential information, do you not suppose that she would have let him know about Inspector Blake's visit to the office?'

'She probably did. Why?'

'I was thinking that it would be a clever move to announce his engagement to this Mrs. Marsh. It would cast doubts on the likelihood of his having had designs upon Mirrie and upon anything she might have inherited from Jonathan Field.'

'It may have been that, or it may simply have been that Mirrie being out of the will, and therefore out of the running, Sid was declining upon the not unattractive Mrs. Marsh, her bit of money in the bank, and her flourishing pub. Blake reports him as being very well pleased with himself — in fact cock-a-hoop to the point of impertinence. Pressed as to his movements on Tuesday night, he gave the same account of his fall as the landlady and her husband. He said it knocked him clean out and left him muzzy in the head. Put his hand to the place and said the bump had gone down but it still felt tender. He had crawled into bed, and certainly had no desire or temptation to leave it. Well, there you are, and we haven't got a case. We can prove his knowledge of the fact that Jonathan had signed a will in Mirrie's favour, and that's all we can prove. Maggie Bell says that the voice which made the appointment with Jonathan Field during a call from Lenton at ten-thirty on the night of the murder was the same voice which had replied to Mirrie's call at a quarter past eight. Mirrie admits that the person she called was Sid. The number he had given her for an emergency is the number of Mrs. Marsh's pub, the Three Pigeons. But what Maggie says is just her opinion, and even if it was admitted as evidence, which I should say was doubtful, I don't think a jury would look at it unless it was backed up by something a good deal more conclusive. You see, we can't prove that Sid ever set foot in this house, and to have a case against him that is what we have got to do. We could prove motive, but we should have to prove opportunity. We have got, in fact, to prove that he was here in this room on Tuesday night.'

Miss Silver had been listening with an air of bright attention. She now laid down her hands on the mass of white wool in her lap.

'The album!' she said.

'The album?'

'If it was Sid Turner who tore out the pages, he could not have done so without handling the album and leaving his prints upon it.'

'The album was, of course, examined for prints. You've got to remember that it had Jonathan's own prints all over it.'

'And no one else's?'

'I don't think so.'

'But, Frank, that is in itself a very suspicious circumstance. Someone tore out that page and took Mr. Field's notes out of the envelope which marked the place.'

He shrugged.

'Well, someone shot Jonathan and was careful to leave no prints. He could have worn gloves, or he could have protected his hand with a handkerchief.'

She said with unusual earnestness,

'Think again, Frank. To have worn gloves must have appeared highly suspicious. So suspicious that it might have led Mr. Field immediately to ring the bell and alarm the house. To carry out the murderer's plan, Mr. Field must be lulled into a state of security, induced if he has not already done so to get out the album, and to sit down at the table. I think the murderer would certainly have been obliged to remove his gloves. He may, as you suggest, have protected his hands in some way after the murder had taken place, but I think there must have been a time when his hands were bare, and however careful he was he may during that time have touched some object, let us say a table or a chair. Amongst the prints which were taken from this room on Wednesday morning, are there none which have not been identified?'

'You mean — '

'I have remembered something which should have occurred to me before. When I was speaking to Sid Turner after the funeral we were standing to one side of the dining-room against the sideboard. During the first part of our conversation Sid Turner's hands were a good deal occupied with his drink. He sipped from it, changed it constantly from one hand to the other, and appeared nervous and jerky in his movements. In answer to his questions I had intimated that, as I understood it, Georgina Grey was the principal legatee under Mr. Field's will. Looking back, I can see he must have been on the rack of anxiety as to whether Mirrie had misled him, or if she had not, as to what after so short an interval could have happened to the will under which she inherited.'

'In fact quite a nasty moment.'

'When Sid Turner had set down his drink his restless mannerisms increased. He put his hands in his pockets and took them out again, and then, whilst suggesting that Mr. Field could have been murdered and the page in his album torn out by someone who might be compromised by the fingerprint preseved upon it, he began a kind of nervous tapping upon the edge of the sideboard. He appeared, in fact, to be tapping out a tune. But the tapping was done in an unusual way, and it is to this that I wish to draw your attention. During all the time that I was observing him his hand was held sideways and the tapping was on the under surface of an overlapping edge. It came to me to wonder whether he might not have left his prints in this room, under the arm of the chair in which he sat or under the edge of the table. I do not, of course, know whether this way of tapping was a constant mannerism with him, but he employed it at a moment of tension when he was talking to me, and when I recalled this just now I considered that I had better mention it.'

He said quickly,

'Oh, yes — yes — I'll go into it with Smith. As to there being any unidentified prints, there were some he was enquiring about.'

Miss Silver inclined her head.

'If it can be proved that Sid Turner was in this room, it will have been proved that he had the opportunity of murdering Mr. Field.'

Frank Abbott drew the telephone fixture towards him and rang up Lenton police station. There was a little coming and going before Inspector Smith was on the line. Miss Silver had resumed her knitting. Frank said,

'That you, Smith? Abbott speaking. Those prints in the Field End case — there were one or two which hadn't been identified. There was something about a man coming up to take measurements for curtains, wasn't there? You thought they might be his, but there was a difficulty in tracing him — gone off to another job. Have you caught up with him? ... Oh, you have? Good! Well, what about it? Are those unidentified dabs his? ... Oh, they're not? Well, well — All right, I'll come in and have a look at them. Be seeing you.'

CHAPTER THIRTY-SIX

MISS CUMMINS had always made a point of arriving early at the office. This Tuesday morning just a week after Jonathan Field had come in about the final instructions as to his new will was no exception. She could indeed have been a couple of hours earlier, since she had not slept all night. She had her own key. When she had let herself in, taken off hat, coat, and gloves, and ordered her already tidy hair, she sat down to wait for Jenny Gregg and Florrie Hackett, who would be on time but not before it. Mr. Maudsley would not appear until the half hour had struck, if then, and in his absence Miss Cummins was in charge. She sat down to wait.

The thoughts which had prevented her from sleeping were still agonizingly present. During the night a few hard-won tears had forced themselves beneath her straining eyelids, but now in this desert of ruined hopes they were as dry as if its dust were physical. She had seen the last of Sid Turner. A cold shudder went through her at the thought that she did not even want to see him again. She had ruined herself for him and she didn't want to see him again. As she sat talking to him in the back of the empty tea-room a number of things had come home to her with dreadful finality. He did not care for her. He had never cared for her. He cared for money, and he cared for Sid Turner. He had used her, and now he would drop her. She thought that he had murdered Jonathan Field.

Florrie and Jenny came in. Jenny had been crying. She was a pretty, fair girl with fluffy hair and a fine skin. She had powdered over the tear marks but they showed. Everything showed when you had a skin as fine as that. She sat down at her desk and began to be busy.

When Mr. Maudsley arrived he went straight to his room. Jenny said in a high, thin voice,

'He'll ring in a minute, and when I go in he'll give me the sack.'

Florrie said comfortably,

'Well, suppose he does — there are lots of good jobs to be had.'

Jenny dashed away a tear.

'Not without a reference there aren't. They'll want to know what I've been doing, won't they? I've been here three years, and they'll want to know why I've left, and when he tells them it was for talking out of turn, who's going to take me on?' She dragged a handkerchief out of her pocket and dabbed her eyes. 'I wouldn't mind, only I can't afford to be out of job with Mum the way she is. And I swear I never said a word — not to anyone!'

The sound of Mr. Maudsley's bell came in upon them. Bertha Cummins had been standing by the window with her back to the room. She turned round, saw Florrie Hackett with an arm round Jenny's shoulders, and spoke.

'I'll see what Mr. Maudsley wants. I have to see him anyhow.' She went through the connecting door and shut it behind her.

Mr. Maudlsey was at his table. He lifted a frowning face and said,

'Oh, it's you, Miss Cummins. Good morning. Send Miss Gregg in to me, will you. I suppose she's here. I'd better see her now and get it over. It's a most unpleasant business.'

She stood in front of the table, her fingertips touching the edge.

'What makes you so sure that it was Miss Gregg who talked, Mr. Maudsley?'

He looked up at her. He was still frowning.

'Why, the whole thing. She's just the sort of girl this Sid Turner would try and pick up with — pretty, not too many brains, a bit of the come hither in her eyes. She's been here how long — three years, and there's been nothing to complain of in the office. Naturally, you would see to that. But I've passed her in the street before now, giggling with some young man or other. Then there was the way she took it when I spoke to her about the leakage — burst into tears right away almost before I'd got the word out.'

Bertha Cummins said in a forced flat voice,

'She would be afraid of losing her job. She has an invalid mother to support.'

'Really, Miss Cummins, I think that is beside the point! This office is not a charitable institution. You can't expect me to overlook a thing of this kind, now can you?'

She said,

'No. But it wasn't Miss Gregg who talked, Mr. Maudsley. It was I.'

Mr. Maudsley gazed at her in a quite stupefied silence. He had heard what she had said, but his mind was refusing to accept it or to deal with it in any way. He looked at her, and became aware of her pallor and of the fixity of her regard. As an alternative to taking in what she had said, he snatched at the idea that she was ill. She never had any colour, and he was used to that, but she now looked — the word that came into his mind was ghastly. He heard himself say,

'Miss Cummins, you are ill.'

She just stood there, her eyes fixed upon his face.

'Oh, no. It wasn't Miss Gregg who talked. It was I.'

The unbelievable truth began to penetrate his thought.

'Do you know what you are saying?'

'Oh, yes. I told him about the will.'

'I can't believe it!'

'I told him.'

'What made you do such a thing as that? It wasn't — money?'

She shook her head.

'Oh, no. I thought he — cared for me. He made me think he did. I thought he wanted to know about what went on in the office because he liked to know what I was doing — because he cared. It was the first time anybody had ever cared what I did. I thought he cared. I know now that he only wanted to find out about — the — will — ' Her voice got slower and slower and the words just faded away. It was like hearing a gramophone record run down.

Mr. Maudsley did not know when he had been so much shocked. If there was anyone in this world for whose integrity he would have vouched, it was Miss Cummins. He did not know what to say to her. He only knew that he must bring this painful interview to a close. He must have time to adjust himself, to think what must be done next. The thought of Jenny Gregg presented itself, and he snatched at it.

'I had better see Miss Gregg,' he said. 'This has been a shock. I must think what I had better say to her. Do you happen to know, is she under the impression that any distinct accusation has been brought?'

'She knows that she was suspected. She has been a good deal distressed.'

Even now he couldn't break himself of the old habit of consulting her. He said,

'How would it be if I had her and Miss Hackett in together and just told them I was quite satisfied that they are not responsible for the leakage? Then after I have seen them I will ring again for you. Oh, and by the way, Mr. Atkins will be here at eleven about the winding up of that family trust. You were going to let me have a memorandum so that I can give him the whole thing in a nutshell.'

She said, 'I'll see about it,' just as if this was an ordinary day. But as she went out of the room it was in her mind that this might be the last time she would leave it as an employee of the firm. Now that Mr. Maudsley knew she was not to be trusted he would probably want her to leave at once.

Jenny and Florrie went in and he said his piece to them, cutting it as short as he could. They came back with beaming faces, and obviously with no idea that the blame had been transferred.

'I'm sure you must have spoken up for us. You did, didn't you, Miss Cummins?'

'I did what I could, Jenny.'

Florrie said,

'He was quite different this morning. He said not to think about it any more. Thank you ever so, Miss Cummins!'

She sat at her table, putting the notes about the Atkins family trust in order and waiting for Mr. Maudsley's bell to ring, doing her accustomed work just as if nothing had happened, and thinking that it was for the last time. After today there would be no more work, and no more money coming in. She hadn't saved a great deal. There had been what she thought of in her own mind as calls. A helpless younger sister left a widow with four children — she couldn't say no to Louie. At least she couldn't go on saying no, and there was no end to the asking.

Mr. Maudsley sat back in this chair and endeavoured to order his thoughts. The sense of shock dominated everything. His mind went back over the twenty-five years during which the plain, shy girl of nineteen had been developing into an invaluable head clerk. During all those years he had never known her to fail in the most conscientious application to her duties. And as to honesty and trustworthiness, he had taken them so completely for granted that he would as soon have thought of questioning his own.

She would, of course, have to go.

His reaction to this was immediate and vehement. She would be quite irreplaceable. Experience recalled the discomforts of her annual holiday, and provided even more vividly and pertinently a recollection of the time she had been laid up for six weeks with a broken leg. He had not been able to put his hand on anything, he had not known where anything was. He had completely forgotten a memorandum which might have made all the difference in the Smithers case. Fortunately, Miss Cummins had come back just in time to enable them to use it. He had never had to remember these things. Miss Cummins remembered them for him. She forgot nothing, overlooked nothing. She was devoted, reliable, indispensable. He had a sudden picture of her standing on the other side of his table, telling him that once in those twenty-five years she had given something away, and waiting for his judgment. He remembered her ghastly look as she waited. And she was waiting still.

Indispensable.

The word pushed through all these thoughts and stood there boldly with its feet planted upon the hard dry ground of common sense.

He stretched out his hand and rang the bell.

CHAPTER THIRTY-SEVEN

MISS SILVER came down on the same Tuesday morning to find that a note had been dropped in the letter-box for her. It ran — 'Off to town to compare fingerprints. Interesting possibilities. Smith has produced three or four prints which may be S.T.'s. They don't belong to the fellow who came to measure the curtians. There is rather a smudged set just under the edge of the writing-table in the study. Blake has S.T.'s prints, and we'll see how they compare.' There followed a scrawled F.A., and that was all.

Miss Silver went on into the dining-room. Finding nobody there, she read the note again and dropped it into the fire. The post arriving just afterwards, she became occupied with a letter from her niece Gladys Robinson, who was Ethel Burkett's sister but so very unlike her in character. Since Gladys only wrote when she had got herself into difficulties and was looking for someone to help her out of them, she opened the envelope with no very pleasant anticipations.

Mrs. Robinson wrote:

'DEAR AUNTIE,

I believe you have more influence with Andrew than anyone else has. He is being most unreasonable. All my friends say they don't know how I put up with it. He does *not* give me enough for the housekeeping, and it isn't any good his saying he does. Betty Morgan says . . .'

Miss Silver had really no need to read on. The letter followed a pattern which had varied very little for many years. There were always the same complaints about her husband, about money. There was always the unwise friend who encouraged her. A particularly mischief-making one who had recently been eliminated appeared to have been replaced. Betty Morgan was a new name. Reflecting that it was a pity Gladys had not half-a-dozen children to occupy her, and then checking herself with the thought that Providence in its inscrutable wisdom had doubtless hesitated to entrust them to her care, she replaced the letter in its envelope, committed it to her knitting-bag, and turned to bid Captain Hallam good morning.

The word good, though customary, is sometimes lacking in appeal. It did not appear at all probable that Anthony was regarding the morning in that or in any other favourable light. He had returned to Field End at a late hour on the previous evening, and he now presented a gloomy and preoccupied appearance. Georgina, coming into the room a little later, said,

'Oh, you've got back?' After which neither of them seemed to have any further observation to make.

Fortunately Johnny and Mirrie had plenty to say, and Mrs. Fabian, who was last, could always be relied upon for a trickle of conversation.

Johnny had had a letter from a friend with particulars of a very nice little garage business out beyond Pigeon Hill, and Mirrie was being alternately thrilled by a description of the flat that went with it and put off by the reflection that if there was a place she never wanted to see again it was that particular suburb. They wrangled about it in a lively manner all through breakfast.

'Darling, you'll adore being able to drop in on Aunt Grace and Uncle Albert.'

'I shan't! I shall hate it!'

Johnny shook his head in a reproving manner.

'Never neglect your relations. You don't know when you may want to borrow a fiver.'

'Aunt Grace wouldn't give anyone a fivepenny bus fare!'

'She hasn't come under my softening influence.'

Mirrie made melting eyes at him.

'I don't want to go back there — I don't!'

'Darling, it's miles away really. And listen – the flat has three rooms and a kitchenette. I'd better catch the first train from Lenton and go up, or someone may snatch it.'

Mrs. Fabian, making the tea and forgetting to fill up the pot, remarked brightly that she hoped Johnny would be careful and not do anything at all without consulting a solicitor.

'Because you know, my dear, there are some very dishonest people, and all sorts of things to look out for like being charged a premium because here's a bit of torn linoleum on the bathroom floor. I knew a Mrs. Marchbanks who took what she thought was a most delightful flat, but there was a chair which had been left behind, she thought because it was broken, in the bedroom, and some cocoanut matting in the passage — such a terrible dust-trap and of course not at all what she wanted. And I think there was something else but I don't remember what it was, only they wanted her to pay quite a large sum down, and her solicitor said it was an imposition and not to have anything to do with the people.'

Johnny blew her a kiss.

'All right, Mama, I have been warned. No cocoanut matting, no broken chairs. We will go to auctions and pick things up cheap.'

He and Mirrie ate their way gaily through a large breakfast. Georgina drank half of a very nasty cup of tea and crumbled a piece of toast. Anthony ate a sausage with a gloom which it really didn't deserve, and drank the tea squeezed out by Mrs. Fabian from an unwatered pot as who should say, 'If this be poison, let me make an end!' Miss Silver, conversing amiably, reflected that young people really had an uncommon talent for making themselves miserable.

Frank Abbott rang up at two o'clock. He asked for Miss Silver and spoke in the manner of one who is remembering Maggie Bell.

'That you, ma'am? ... I thought I'd just let you know that the whatnots are the same. Our friend was certainly there, and Blake and I are hoping to collect him this afternoon. Keep your fingers crossed.'

Aware that this expression was unlikely to meet with approval, he rang off before Miss Silver could express her views upon the subject of what she would certainly regard as a vain superstition.

Johnny Fabian, standing in a queue at Pigeon Hill waiting for a bus which he had been informed would take him within a hundred yards of Rooke's Garage at the four crossways just beyond the Blue Lion, received a slight set-back at seeing what he took to be Sid Turner emerging from a small eating-house on the other side of the road. Having no desire to renew what could scarcely be described as an acquaintance, he looked away. It occurred to him that however desirable Rooke's Garage and the flat over it might be, he wouldn't really want Mirrie to be in the way of knocking up against Sid if she happened to shop in Pigeon Hill. The effect of this wore off presently when he had met Jimmy Rooke and discovered a liking both for him and for the terms on which he was willing to dispose of the garage. It wore off, but it had been there and it was to recur.

What he didn't know was that Sid Turner had seen and recognised him. At the time Sid was not interested. He recognised Johnny, felt an angry pricking grudge against him, and thought no more about the matter until later, when it suddenly became important. He was not at this time seriously worried about the police and their enquiries. They would nose about for a bit, and when they didn't get anywhere they would come off it. They might suspect him, but there wasn't anything they could prove. Absolutely nothing. He had a dangerous smouldering anger against Mirrie Field for blabbing about those two telephone calls. *Women!* Couldn't keep their mouths shut, not even when they'd be getting themselves into trouble by talking. All the same they were. He wasn't all that easy about Bertha Cummins. A pound to a tanner she'd be slopping over to old Maudsley and spilling the beans.

The thought jabbed him, but only for the moment, because if it came to that the beans were spilled already and no great harm done. All she could tell Maudsley that he didn't know was that it was she and not Jenny Gregg who had given away the terms of Jonathan Field's will. And all she would get out of that would be the sack, and if she got another job she'd be lucky. But anyhow, and suppose she was bent on her own ruin, he didn't see how she could do him any particular harm. The police already knew that Mirrie had told him about the will. And so what? He was her aunt's brother and an old friend — why shouldn't she tell him, and why shouldn't he know? The fact that Bertha had told him the same thing was neither here nor there. It was Mirrie who had made a damned fool of herself by blabbing about those two telephone calls. He thought she should have known better than to split on him. He remembered holding her close up to him in a dark alleyway and setting the point of his knife against her throat. He thought she would have remembered it too. Perhaps the time had come to give her another lesson.

CHAPTER THIRTY-EIGHT

IT was just after opening time on Tuesday evening that Aggie Marsh came out of her comfortable sitting-room at the Three Pigeons, crossed a narrow passage, and opened a door which led to the space behind the bar. She had a pleased, flushed look, and she would rather have stayed in her comfortable parlour and let Sid Turner make love to her, but business before pleasure was her motto, and it wasn't any good letting Sid get too free. She was a respectable woman, and it wouldn't do him any harm to remember it. So she tidied her hair at the gilt-edged mirror above the mantelpiece and put her dress to rights before going through to give Molly Docherty a hand. But she had hardly got the door half open, when she heard Sid's name. Something made her step back. She stood there and listened. Molly was laughing — a big red-haired girl and a very good barmaid.

'Sure he'll be here, and why not — they're courting. But whether he's here this identical minute I couldn't be telling you, for I've not set eyes on him myself.'

Aggie closed the door softly and stepped back across the passage. Sid Turner was on his feet straightening his tie.

'What's up?'

She shut that door too.

'Two men asking for you in the bar. One of them was here last night. A plain-clothes tec, you know, but the other one's new.'

'What do they want?'

'I didn't wait to hear. Molly said she hadn't seen you, and I didn't know whether you'd want — '

'Well, I don't! Why can't they leave a chap alone? I don't know anything, and I'm not going to have them say I do! Talk to them for a bit and jolly them along. I'll slip out the back way.'

She began to say something, but he pushed past her and was gone. Didn't so much as give her a kiss or say he'd be seeing her. She stood for a minute and remembered that poor Bert hadn't ever really liked Sid Turner. Too slick by half and a bit too much on the make, that was what Bert used to say. And he used to tell her she'd got too soft a heart, and to be careful of herself or she'd be getting into trouble when he was gone. Bert had been good at sizing people up and she had been very fond of him. She went into the bar and gave the two Inspectors a sober 'Good evening.'

'Detective Inspector Abbott and Detective Inspector Blake, Mrs. Marsh. I'm afraid we are here on business. We are anxious to see Sidney Turner.'

She was a comely, pleasant-looking woman — nice fair hair, nice colour, nice curves. The colour demonstrated its natural origin by a sudden fade-out as she said,

'What do you want him for?'

'We think he may be able to help us in connection with the death of Mr. Jonathan Field.'

There were only two other people in the bar, young fellows having a joke with Molly Docherty. Aggie Marsh said quickly,

'What's it got to do with Sid? Anyhow he isn't here.'

Frank Abbott said,

'Mrs. Marsh, I am sure you won't want to put any obstacle in the way of the police. You are the licensee, are you not? I must tell you that we have a warrant for Turner's arrest.'

The door into the passage stood ajar. She wondered whether Sid had heard. She wondered whether Sid was gone. She said, 'What for?'

And the tall fair policeman said, 'For the murder of Jonathan Field.'

She felt as if he had hit her. The Three Pigeons had always

been a respectable house. Bert had always kept it respectable. Murder had a dreadful sound. She ought to have listened to Bert and remembered what he said. She oughtn't to have let Sid make love to her. Bert had warned her, and she had gone against him. She oughtn't to have done it. She said in a slow, dull voice,

'I'm afraid I can't help you.'

There was a yard behind the Three Pigeons, and a door in the wall which gave upon a narrow alleyway. Following this as far as it would take him, Sid Turner came out upon a street of semi-detached houses, very neat and comfortable, with lace curtains in the front rooms and a fair sprinkling of aspidistras.

When he had put a good distance between himself and the Three Pigeons he considered what he should do next. He had lingered to hear what the busies wanted with him, but at the word 'warrant' he did not wait to hear any more. From being fatuously secure he tumbled into a panic — what to do, where to go, how to escape. He didn't dare go back to his lodging for fear of its being watched. Tom Jenkins had looked at him once or twice in a queer sort of way. No, he had better not go back to the Jenkinses. And that meant he couldn't pick up his motor-bike, or his money, or anything that could be turned into money. He had a few pounds, but they wouldn't go far. And he must get out of London, and get out quick. He went into the next pub he came to, bought himself a drink, and got down to making a plan of escape.

There are plans which are built up a bit at a time, shaping themselves as you go along. And there are plans which come into mind, as it were, ready made. Into Sid Turner's mind there came such a plan. What was the last place on earth where anyone would look for him? Field End. And with this as a start the whole plan was there, waiting to be carried out. Field End, the money he was going to need, the satisfaction of teaching Mirrie a lesson, the clever twist which would bring her under his hand — everything was there to the last detail. He finished his drink and went out to find himself a car.

CHAPTER THIRTY-NINE

FIELD END dined at half past seven, a concession to modern conditions to which Jonathan Field had been brought by his own fair-mindedness and the representations of the invaluable Stokes.

'Eight o'clock or half past eight was all very well with a full staff, sir, but dailies just won't stay so late for the washing up, and it's more than me and Mrs. Stokes can undertake with so many in the house. Now if it was to be half past seven —'

Jonathan had dined at somewhere between eight and half past ever since he came out of the schoolroom, but he gave way with a good grace.

When the half hour struck and Mirrie had not put in an appearance, Georgina went upstairs to see what she was doing. She came running down again to say that Mirrie hadn't changed, and that she wasn't in her room. Her outdoor coat was gone and a pair of outdoor shoes. The house was searched, and it was plain that Mirrie was not in it.

Miss Silver had a word with Stokes.

'Miss Mirrie seems to have gone out. Do you know of any telephone calls she might have had?'

'There was someone called up for Mr. Johnny. Getting on for half past six that would be.'

'There was not any call for Miss Mirrie?'

'Not just then, miss. A little later on there was.'

'Did she take it?'

'I told her there was a gentleman on the line, and she went into the study to take it there.'

'After you spoke to Miss Mirrie, did you go back to your pantry?'

'Not at once, miss. Mrs. Fabian came out of the drawing-room, and she was talking about whether Mrs. Stokes had made any arrangements about eggs for the preserving, and whether we should get them the same as we had always done or go in for

230

a change. It took a little time, because if you'll excuse my saying so, there's nothing upsets Mrs. Stokes like changes and I was trying to get Mrs. Fabian to see it her way, so by the time I got back to my pantry Miss Mirrie had got off the line, and they had put that nasty howler on to show there was my receiver left off. A very annoying practice, if I may say so.'

It seemed that no one had seen Mirrie since just after seven o'clock, when Georgina met her on the stairs and she was going up to dress.

Miss Silver went into the study and rang up Maggie Bell.

'Miss Bell, this is Miss Silver speaking. You will remember that I came to see you on Sunday. You were so very helpful then that I am tempted to believe that you may be able to help me now. We are troubled about Miss Mirrie. She received a telephone call a little while ago, following which she seems to have gone out without telling anyone where she was going. Now I wonder if you happen to know who called her up.'

Maggie hastened to be helpful.

Oh, yes, Miss Silver — it was Mr. Johnny.'

'Mr. Johnny Fabian?'

'Oh, yes, Miss Silver. So I'm sure there isn't anything for you to worry about. He rang up and he said, "Johnny Fabian speaking." And Miss Mirrie said, "Oh, I can only just hear you. The line's dreadful — you sound about a million miles away. And tell me," she said, "what about the garage?" she said. "Is it what you want? And is there really a flat over it like you said? And will you be able to buy it? And, oh darling, I'm so excited!' And Mr. Johnny said, "Now listen," he said. "This is very particular, and you're to do just what I tell you, or there won't be any garage or any flat, or any you and me for that matter. I've got to put down a deposit, and I must have the money tonight or he'll close with somebody else. How much money can you raise?"She said something about money in the bank and tomorrow, and he said that wouldn't do, he'd got to have it tonight. So she said she'd got ten pounds in the house, but Miss Georgina might have some she could let her have. And Mr. Johnny said she wasn't to say a word to Miss Georgina or to anyone, most particularly she wasn't. It was a top secret between him and her, because if anyone else got to know about it, there would be a lot of talking and arguing, and there wasn't time for that. It was all he could do just to pick up the money and get back, or he'd have missed his chance. He said she was to take the ten pounds and be out at the gate with it just before half past seven and he'd tell her all about it then. And she had better bring the pearl necklace she had on the night of the dance, because the man might take it as a pledge until they could raise the money — "and mind, not a word to a soul!" he said.' Maggie rattled it all off with obvious enjoyment.

'Seems funny to me,' she concluded, and as she heard her own voice saying the words there was a clouding of that pleased sense of being clever and helpful. There seemed to be a coldness in the room. Miss Silver said something very odd indeed.

'Miss Bell,' she said, 'are you sure it was Mr. Johnny?'

Maggie felt as if someone had hit her. She really did. She said, 'Oh!' And then, 'That's what he said, "Johnny Fabian speaking," and Miss Mirrie she couldn't hardly hear him, the line was so bad.'

'Miss Bell, did you think it was Mr. Johnny's voice?'

Now that she came to think about it, it might have been anyone's voice. She had had to listen as hard as she could to do no more than pick up the words. No more than a whisper it was really. When she had told Miss Silver this there was a grave 'Thank you, Miss Bell,' and the connection was broken. That was the part Maggie hated so much, when the line went dead and other people went away and did things but she had to stay on her sofa and remember the pain in her back.

Miss Silver came out of the study and saw Georgina and Anthony in the hall. They were not speaking to each other, they were waiting for her. But before she had time to say anything the front door opened and Johnny Fabian walked in. He looked from one to the other of them and said,

'What's up?'

Johnny was quick — he had always been quick from a child. There was something he didn't like, something about the way Miss Silver was looking. She said,

'Mr. Fabian, where is Mirrie Field?'

CHAPTER FORTY

It was just before half past seven when Mirrie slipped down the back stairs and let herself out by the side door. She was feeling clever and excited, and very, very pleased with herself and with Johnny. They were going to have their own darling flat, and she would be helping him to get it. And she had thought of everything. About not coming down the front stairs or through the hall in case of meeting anyone. She hadn't lived all those years with Aunt Grace and Uncle Albert without knowing all about slipping out of the house without being seen or heard. She was wearing her pearl necklace and she had ten pounds in her pocket, and it was all most romantic and interesting. She went just outside the left-hand gate and stood there hugging herself in her warm tweed coat and waiting for Johnny to come. It was a dark evening without moon or stars, cloud overhead and a light wind blowing. It ruffled her curls and she put up a hand to them. She ought to have brought a scarf to tie over her head, but it was too late to go back for one now. The wind blew her hair about, and she hoped Johnny wouldn't be long.

The car came up smooth and silent. It stopped beside her, the beam of a torch slid over her from her head to her feet Then it went out with a click and the door swung open. She said, 'Johnny!' and he said, 'Quick!' Just the one word in a whisper and she was up on the running-board and an arm pulling her in and shutting the door. The engine hadn't stopped. The car shot forward and they were away. The hand that had pulled her in came across her and shut the window. And in one horrid flash of time Mirrie knew that it wasn't Johnny's hand.

She didn't say anything, because she couldn't. She couldn't make the smallest sound, but if she could have screamed it wouldn't have made any difference. She leaned back in a dizzy silence and felt how fast the car was going. If she were to open the door and try to get out she might be killed, or she might be a cripple for life like Maggie Bell. She didn't want to be killed, and she didn't want to be a cripple. It was easier to sit quite still and wait for what was going to happen next. The car ran on for a time, then slackened speed and drew in to the side of the road and stopped. Sid Turner said,

'Did you bring the money?'

Of course she had known it would be Sid. It it wasn't Johnny, there wasn't anybody else it could possibly be. It was Sid who had told her to bring the ten pounds and the pearls. It wasn't Johnny at all. If he had spoken louder, she would have known that it wasn't Johnny, but he had just whispered, and you can't tell who anyone is in a whisper. He had said he was Johnny, and it hadn't come into her mind to think it might be anyone else. You don't think about things like that — not until they have happened.

He took hold of her arm and shook her.

'You've got a tongue in your head, haven't you? Did you bring the money?'

Two big frightened tears began to roll down her cheeks.

'Oh, yes, I did.'

'Hand it over!'

It was all in nice clean notes fresh from the bank. She took them out of her pocket and gave them to him.

'And the pearls!'

Frightened as she was, Mirrie was prepared to put up a fight for the pearls. Her breath caught on the words, but she got them out.

'I d-didn't bring them.'

His voice went quiet and deadly.

'Do you think you can lie to me? I've known you too long for that, and you ought to know *me*!'

His hands came feeling about her neck. The pearls slid into one of them. The other came up and squeezed her throat. The pressure only lasted for a moment, but it put the fear of death into her.

'Try any games with me, and that's what you'll get — or worse! Remember me tickling you with my knife? You didn't like it, did you? Now you and me have got to talk! If you do what you're told you won't come to any harm, but try just one trick and you'll wish you'd never been born!'

He let go of her and she shrank there like a little wild creature that is caught and can't get away. She didn't dare to move, she hardly dared to breathe, obeying the age-old instinct that sends its message along the frightened nerves — 'Keep still — make yourself small — melt into the earth — pretend that you are dead.'

Mirrie froze where she sat. Sid Turner was putting the pearls away in his wallet. When he had done he turned on her again.

'Where are we — suppose you've been out driving with your fancy boy! What's this place?'

She had to speak, because he would be angry if she didn't. It didn't do to make Sid angry. Her lips were stiff and her breath whispered as she said,

'It's Hexley Common.'

'There was a track going off to the left — we just passed it. Where does it go?'

'Nowhere. There's an old gravel pit.'

The word came into his mind and made itself at home there. Tangled up overgrown places those old pits — handy if there was anything you wanted to hide. His sullen resentment and anger against Mirrie Field had been piling up since yesterday. She had misled him about the will, she had tried to fob him off at the funeral, and she had given him away to the police. The darkness and the anger in him were piling up. If they were to break — if he were to let them break — well, there was the gravel pit as you might say to his hand. He said,

'That'll do us fine. We'll get off the road, then we'll talk.'

He backed the car to where the track led off and for a little way along it. Careful, that was what he was. That was why nobody had ever tripped him yet. Nor they weren't going to.

When he thought he had gone far enough he shut off the engine and the lights. Then he got out, came round to Mirrie's side, and opened the door.

'You and me have got to talk. And just in case anyone comes along and gets nosey about the car, we're going a bit farther from the road. How far did you say it was to that pit?'

She held back trembling.

'I — don't know. Can't we talk here?'

She didn't want to go any nearer to the pit. Johnny had pointed it out in the wintry dusk, a dug-out place grown over with blackberry and gorse. She hadn't liked it then — it terrified her now.

Sid Turner took her by the arm and yanked her out of the car. He set her down so hard that the jar of it ran right through her up to the top of her head. She didn't dare cry out, but she stumbled as he pulled her along, and he swore and held her up. He had a torch in his pocket, but he didn't put it on. He had good night sight and the sandy track showed up against the dark heather on either side. The sky is never without some light, and it is astonishing how much you can see once your eyes have adjusted themselves.

The track got rougher as they came near the pit. They were now about fifty yards from the car, and he judged it to be far enough from the road. He said, 'This'll do,' and stopped. He kept his hand on her arm and pulled her round to face him.

'I asked you just now in the car whether you remembered me tickling you with my knife. D'you remember why I did it? It was to remind you what would happen if you ever thought of splitting on me, wasn't it? Remember that? And on the top of it you go blabbing to the police about talking to me on the phone and what you said to me and what I said to you!'

'I didn't, Sid, I didn't! It was Maggie Bell. She listens in. She hasn't got anything else to do and she listens in all the time. She had an accident and she can't walk, and she just lies on her sofa and listens in.'

Fear pricked her, as Sid's knife had pricked her. The words came tumbling out.

'You told the police about ringing me up and telling me how your uncle had made a new will and left you a lot of money!'

'Maggie told them. It wasn't me — it was Maggie. They knew all about it.'

'And what they didn't know you told them, just in case this Maggie had left anything out! You can lie all right when it suits you, but you tumbled over yourself to give the busies what they wanted! You could have said this Maggie Bell was making it up, couldn't you?'

'It wouldn't have been any good. Everyone knows she listens.'

He flung her away from him with an angry shove, then caught at her wrist.

'Everyone knows — and you go blabbing! Now listen, you little piece of dirt— anything you said to the police, you've got to take it back, that's what! You can lie cleverly enough when you like — practised for years on Grace, didn't you? Well, now you can turn it to some account! Whatever you told the police, you'll go over it and mess it up! Whatever day you told them you rang me, you'll get down to telling them you're not sure what day it was! What you've got to get across is you never told me anything about the old man having signed his will! D'you hear — you never told me! That's what you've got to stick to! And if this Maggie Bell says different, she's the one that's lying, and not you! You never rang me up on Tuesday night — it was next day, after he was dead, and you just told me that, and when the funeral was going to be! If Maggie says anything more she is making it up!'

As he heard his own words he knew that it wasn't any good. He could scare her, and she would promise whatever he asked, but she wouldn't stick to it. As soon as she got back it would all come tumbling out — how he'd frightened her, and what he'd told her to say. He would have to finish her off. There was no way out of it, and with the rage that was in him now he'd be glad to do it. He said in the soft dangerous voice which terrified her more than any loud one,

'No, it's not any good — I couldn't trust you.' His hand went into his pocket for the knife. 'You little blabbing slut! Suppose I show you a cure for a leaky tongue — suppose I cut it out!'

She gave a faint high scream, twisted her wrist away from him, and ran wildly, blindly, desperately, without aim, without thought, without sense of direction.

CHAPTER FORTY-ONE

JOHNNY FABIAN stood with the open door behind him and looked across the hall. He saw Anthony and Georgina. And Miss Silver, who had just asked him where Mirrie was. That meant Mirrie wasn't here, but he had to hear it said.

'Isn't she here?' The words sounded stupid and empty, because he knew already that something had happened to her.

Miss Silver came towards him.

'Mr. Fabian, you are supposed to have rung her up.'

'No.'

'Someone rang up who gave your name. The line is said to have been very bad. Maggie Bell was listening in. I got on to her as soon as Mirrie was missed. She says Mirrie began by asking you what about the garage. Was it what you wanted? Was there really a flat over it, and would you be able to buy it? The man on the line said, "Now listen —' And then he went on to say that there would not be a flat or any garage unless a deposit was paid tonight, because there was someone else after it, and Mirrie was to slip out of the house with all the money she had and her pearls, and she was not to say a word to anyone.'

Johnny said short and hard,

'When?'

'Just before half past seven.'

He looked at his wrist-watch.

'Twenty minutes start.'

He turned and went out as he had come in, with Anthony Hallam after him. They exchanged a word or two in the dark. Anthony said,

'Three ways they could have gone — to Lenton, or by this road, up or down. We had better separate.'

Johnny said,

'All right, you take the Lenton road. It's Sid Turner. He must have seen me across the street at Pigeon Hill — knew I wasn't here — tried it on. If he's on the run he'll be heading away from town. If he's got a car it'll be stolen, and he'd steal a fast one.'

He went round the car to get in, and as he did so Miss Silver slipped into the passenger's seat. She had picked up the first muffler that came to hand in the cloakroom off the lobby, and a coat used by Mrs. Fabian for walking in the garden or stepping across the road to post a letter. The fact that she had come out without a hat and in her evening slippers with their beaded toes bore witness to the urgency of the occasion. She could have guessed Johnny Fabian's expression from the tone in which he aid, 'I must ask you to get out. I can't possibly take you.'

She replied in words which he had been about to use himself.

'There is no time to be lost. I may be of some assistance. I have excellent sight, and I am provided with an electric torch.'

Johnny ceased to regard her presence. The words filled his mind — 'No time to be lost.' But the time might already be lost. Mirrie might be lost. He set his mind away from that. He set it to drive the car, to get the last ounce out of her. They shot past the straggle of houses at Field End and ran on towards Hexley Common.

From the first moment it was the Common that had been in his mind. He didn't know why. He ought to be able to think, to find a reason, but he couldn't. He could feel. Or he could shut off the feeling and just drive the car. But he couldn't think. From the darkness beside him Miss Silver said,

'I have reason to believe that there is a warrant out for Sid Turner's arrest. Inspector Abbott and Inspector Blake were going down to Pigeon Hill this afternoon. It looks as if he had received some warning and had got away. As I heard you say to Captain Hallam, he has probably stolen a car. I cannot see that he has anything to gain by harming Mirrie, but he will not risk driving through a town with her in case she should attract attention. Having taken the money and her pearls, the most obvious thing for him to do would be to put her down in an unfrequented place from which it would take her some time to find her way home. He would naturally wish to secure as long a start as possible.'

Her words and the quiet, composed tone which had carried them passed over the hard surface of Johnny's mind and found no entrance. He heard what she said, but implicit between them was the dark thing which she did not say. There was one means of securing that Mirrie Field would not return to Field End with any tale for the police. There was the dreadful means of murder — as old as Cain, running like a scarlet thread through all the history of every nation upon earth — the one final answer to every murderer's need. Johnny shut his mind against it.

They ran up the long slope to Hexley Common. It lay dark under the sky. A chill breeze passed over it. Miss Silver was aware of it as she leaned from the open window to scan the side of the road. She saw the track going off to the left.

'Mr. Fabian, there is a path — '

But he was already slowing down. He got out, and she followed him. She said,

'Where does it go?' And he, 'There's a gravel pit.'

And with that, faint and high, there came the sound of Mirrie's scream.

CHAPTER FORTY-TWO

WHEN she had run from Sid Turner she was in no case to think or plan. A blind panic drove her. The track led straight to the gravel pit and she followed it. It was only when her foot went over the edge and she lost her balance that she knew anything at all. What came to her then was thought in its simplest, most elementary form — 'I'm falling.' And with that she fell, out of thought and out of consciousness.

The first thing she knew after that was something pricking her. She didn't come to all at once. She had been very badly shocked and frightened, and she had had quite a fall. The pricking became more insistent. Her face and hands were scratched, her shoulder hurt. She heard Sid calling her, softly, cautiously. She lay as still as a rabbit and saw a small round disc of light go dancing by. Sid had a torch and he was looking for her. The thing that was pricking her was gorse. She had rolled, and slipped, and slithered down the side of the pit, and she was lying between two gorse bushes. They covered her against the dancing light, and it passed over her and was gone. The fear that had been holding her rigid relaxed and let her go. She lay in a soft trembling heap and prayed that the light would not return. If she was very good always, if she never told another lie in all her life, if she always remembered to say her prayers, perhaps God wouldn't let Sid find her.

She drew herself up very, very carefully. She was stiff and sore, but there wasn't anything broken. When she peered from between the bushes she could see the light going away to the left, sliding to and fro over the gorse, and the blackberry trails, and the yellow side of the pit. Sid was walking away from the place where she had fallen. As he went he shone the light over the edge and looked down and called her name.

'Mirrie, you little fool, where are you? I was only joking, you know. You wouldn't be afraid of me — not of Sid. Just call back, and I'll get you up. You don't want to make me angry, do you? Mirrie!'

She began to crawl out from between the bushes. If he went on round the pit — if she could get out whilst he was on the other side — if she could get back on to the road . . . She hadn't fallen very far, but if he heard her he would come back and kill her with the knife. She knew what his hand had gone into his pocket for — it was to get the knife. It opened with a spring. She had seen him open it before, the time he had set the point against her throat. If he caught her now he wouldn't stop at frightening her, he would kill her dead.

She couldn't climb in her coat. She slipped it off and let it go. The slope where she had fallen was not a steep one. She crawled on it an inch or two at a time, sometimes a little to the left, sometimes a little to the right, according to the lie of the ground. And then just as she got to the top, the flickering light and Sid's voice calling her. They turned and began to come back again. She got her knee over the edge, her other knee, her foot. If she stood up he would see her. If she didn't stand up she couldn't run away. The dancing light would pick her up — Sid would catch her and she would feel the knife.

She stumbled to her feet and ran screaming down the track. It was rough and rutted under foot. She didn't think, 'I mustn't fall,' she knew it with a kind of shuddering intensity. If she tripped, if she slipped, if she fell, the knife would be in her back. She kept her hands stretched out before her as if they could save her from falling. They did just save her from running into the back of the car. She called out as it brought her up with a jerk, her hands sliding on the paintwork, but she didn't fall, and through the sound of her choked breathing she could hear the running steps behind her. She made her last, most desperate effort, pushed back from the car, and stumbled round it, feeling her way, banging into a mudguard, getting clear, and staggering on again towards the road.

She ran right into Johnny Fabian's arms. He said,

'Mirrie! Oh, *Mirrie*!' and she said his name over and over again as if she couldn't stop saying it, as if it was something that would keep her safe as long as she held on to it and didn't let go. They stood on the edge of the track and held each other.

Miss Silver, coming up at a more sober pace, was aware of them. She had put on her elecric torch, but she turned the beam away. And then quite suddenly it was cutting the dark again and she was calling out,

'Mr. Fabian — the car — it's moving! Take care!'

There was the roar of the engine behind her words. It startled him to action. He jumped Mirrie off the track among the heather roots and saw the black shape of the car lurch past them and out on to the road. With the lights coming on and a dangerous reeling swerve to avoid Johnny's car Sid Turner was out on the tarmac and away.

Miss Silver, who had also stepped into the heather, now emerged from it. She addressed Mirrie Field.

'My dear child! You are not hurt? It was indeed providential that Mr. Fabian should have been led to come this way. You are quite safe now, and you must try to compose yourself. There must be no delay in getting in touch with the police.' She directed herself to Johnny. 'I endeavoured to take the number of the car as it passed me, but the plate had been, no doubt designedly, obscured by what looked like splashes of mud.'

Johnny shrugged.

'He'll get rid of the car as soon as he can. He'll have pinched it, so the number wouldn't have been much help in tracing him. And he'd have had the legs of us even if we could have got off in time to follow him. He'd pick a fast one while he was about it.'

They got into Johnny's old car and ran back to Field End. Just about the time that the lobby door swung to behind them and they came into the lighted hall Sid Turner went blinding round the corner of Jessop's Lane into the main road and crashed into the Hexton bus. It was fortunately not very full. The driver had a miraculous escape, and of the few passengers no one was seriously injured, though old Mrs. Brazely lost her front teeth and could never be persuaded that her son-in-law had not trodden on them on purpose. But the stolen car was what the conductor described as a mess, and Sid Turner was dead.

CHAPTER FORTY-THREE

ANTHONY rang up from Lenton. The first sound of Johnny's voice was enough to tell him that Mirrie had been found and was safe.

'And you'd better come back quick or there won't be anything left to eat. 'We're not waiting for anyone, and personally I could cope with an ox.'

Anthony hung up and came out of the call-box. He hadn't reckoned on Georgina being so close to him. She had insisted on coming, but they had hardly spoken until now when he almost ran into her and she caught him by the arm and said,

'What is it?'

'She's all right. They've got her back.'

Just for a moment they stood close together like that, her hands on his coat-sleeve, her face tilted up to him and the greenish light of a street-lamp turning her hair to silver. She was bare-headed, with a coat thrown round her, and there was no colour about her anywhere, not in her face nor in her lips, nor in the pale glimmer of her hair. Only her eyes were dark and fixed upon his own. She said,

'Thank God!' Then her hands fell and she stepped back from him, and they got into the car and drove away.

But as soon as they were clear of the town she spoke again.

'Anthony, I want to talk to you. Will you draw in to the side of the road?'

'Not here — not now. They'll be expecting us back.'

There was a moment's silence before she said,

'Does that matter to you so much?'

'I think we should get back.'

She had the feeling that if she let him put her away from him now, there would be no time in which they would come together again. She said,

'Anthony, will you stop now if I tell you that it is very important to me?'

They had been so near, and for so long, that she could feel him resisting her. And then quite suddenly the resistance lessened and the car slowed down and stopped. He said without turning towards her,

'I shall be going away tomorrow. I only came back to get my things.'

'Yes, I thought that was what you were going to do. You didn't feel there was anything you had to say to me?'

'I was going to write.'

'You were afraid to come to me and say that you had let yourself be carried away — that you don't really care for me the way I thought you did.'

'You know that's a lie.'

'I know you said you loved me. But you didn't, did you? You only said so because Uncle Jonathan had hurt me so much and you thought it would comfort me. And now, of course, I don't need comforting any more.'

'Georgina!'

'That doesn't get us very far, does it? You are Anthony, and I am Georgina, and I thought you loved me. You did too. I want to know when you stopped. Have you fallen in love with someone else?'

'You know I haven't.'

A little warmth came into her voice and shook it.

'Of course I know! I shouldn't be talking to you like this if I didn't. You've loved me for a long time. I knew when you began, and I should know if you were to stop. You haven't stopped. You're just offering us both up as a burnt sacrifice to your pride, and it's a horrible, cruel thing to do and completely senseless.'

'You don't understand.'

'I understand perfectly. Everyone understands but you. Uncle Jonathan did. That last evening when I talked to him he told me he did. He said he had always wanted us to get married some day. He said he thought we should be very happy, and he had left you something in his will as a mark of his trust and confidence.'

He turned round then for the first time.

'Did he say that? Are you sure he meant it that way? I thought — '

'What did you think?'

'I thought — No, it doesn't matter. It sounds — '

'You thought you were being put on your honour to keep away from me?'

'No, no — of course not — '

'I knew it was that. You see, I do always know what you are thinking — at least I always have until now. And when you began to lock your doors and bolt yourself away, and I couldn't get near you — ' Her voice broke off short.

He could see that she turned away from him, catching at the edge of the open window and hiding her face against her hands. If he touched her he wouldn't be able to hold out any more. He had only to take her in his arms and all that obstinate ingrowing pride would melt. He sat where he was and heard the sound of her weeping.

It was not for long.

She sat up, straightening herself and leaning back. Then she said,

'I don't think you love me very much. I just want to say that there wouldn't be a terrible lot for your pride to swallow after all. Mr. Maudsley says I can't give Mirrie any of the capital, but I can make her an allowance of five hundred a year if I like, so that is what I shall do. I don't quite know how much there will be left by the time all the duties are paid, and Cousin Anna's legacy. Mr. Maudsley doesn't know yet, but he says I shall have to pay the income tax on Mirrie's allowance. Goodbye, Anthony.'

She had spoken in a soft, tired voice and without any expression. On the last word she turned the handle of the door and stepped out into the road. Since he had been trying not to look at her, he was not really aware of what she was doing until it had been done and he saw her walking away from him into the darkness.

Anger. An absolute fury of anger putting paid to the struggle in his mind. She would walk out on him, would she? Walk three lonely miles on the Lenton road in thin evening shoes rather than sit by him another moment and let him drive her home! Didn't she know how impossible it was for either of them to leave the other? He had wrenched mind and body to do it, only to find how damned impossible it was. He was out of the car, banging the door behind him and catching her up before she had gone a dozen yards.

Georgina heard him come. She went on walking, neither quickening her step nor slowing down. If she had been quite alone she would have walked like that, without hurry and without delay. He took her by the arm and she did not turn her head.

'Come back and get into the car!'

Her heart leapt at the fury of his tone. If this was to be a battlefield, she could fight and lose, or fight and win. It was being alone in a cold wilderness with no voice nor any that answered which had brought her to the breaking-point. She wasn't afraid of Anthony when he was angry. She wasn't afraid of anything as long as he was there — not half a universe away in some cold hell of his own making.

'Did you hear what I said? Come back at once!'

'Thank you, I would rather walk.'

Her tone made him the merest stranger.

'Georgina, are you mad?'

'I don't know. Would it be anything to do with you if I was?'

He experienced a horrifying resurgence of the emotions of primitive man. There was nothing but a little matter of perhaps half a million centuries between him and the male creature who knocked his woman over the head with a lump of stone and dragged her senseless to their cave. A gratifying experience if there ever was one! But the centuries had done their work. He merely stopped her where she stood and made her face him with a bruising grip upon either arm.

'Don't be such a damned fool!'

She said in a whispering voice,

'You may go away from me, but I mustn't go away from you?'

'You mustn't ever go away from me! I can't bear it! Georgina, I *can't*!'

She began suddenly to laugh very softly.

'Darling, you don't have to. You don't really, you know. Not unless you want to.'

He put his head down on her shoulder, and they stood like that for a long time, until the headlights of an oncoming car picked them up and dazzled them out of their dream.

CHAPTER FORTY-FOUR

JOURNEYS end in lovers' meetings. Anthony and Georgina came in with so radiant an air that no one could have mistaken them for anything else. Mrs. Fabian was delighted.

'And so would dear Jonathan be, I am sure. And of course perhaps he is — we don't know, do we? But he was so fond of

Anthony, and I am sure he would have been quite delighted. Because so many girls get engaged to someone they have only known for a few weeks, if that, and then perhaps it doesn't turn out at all well, and you can't really be surprised. Whereas, when you have known each other practically since one of you was in her cradle, you do feel that you know what to expect. I remember old Mrs. Warren telling me her grandmother had a rhyme about it —

> "Marry a stranger,
> Marry for danger,
> Marry at home,
> No ill will come." '

Johnny blew her a kiss.

'Pause, darling, or you'll be putting your foot in it. Now you'll have to think up a nice quotation for Mirrie and me.'

Mrs. Fabian smiled in her most amiable manner and replied that for the moment all she could call to mind was a Scottish song which began — at least she thought that was how it began —

> "Bonnie wee thing, cannie wee thing,
> Lovely wee thing, wert thou mine,
> I would wear thee in my bosom
> Lest my jewel I should tine."

'And I believe the last word means *lose*. So it is really very good advice for you, my dear boy, because a young girl does need quite a lot of looking after, especially if she happens to be a very pretty one.' She beamed upon Mirrie and continued, 'It must be at least forty years since I heard anyone sing that song. My mother had cousins in Scotland, and one of them had a very good tenor voice. I remember his coming to stay with us and singing a number of these Scottish songs until my father was quite put out and wanted to know whether we couldn't have an English air for a change. It was most embarrassing, because he used the expression "Barbarian music only fitted for the bagpipes," and Cousin Alec wasn't at all pleased and wouldn't sing again. It really was very uncomfortable.'

Frank Abbott came in to see Miss Silver next morning. He found her pledged to come and stay at Abbottsleigh for a double wedding in June.

'I am returning to town this afternoon, but Georgina is most insistent that I should come down again for the wedding.'

He looked at her with a gleam of malice in his eye.

'Extraordinary the attraction these morbid occasions have for what is called the gentler sex. In the days of public executions I believe that quite three quarters of the assembled crowds were women.'

Miss Silver was putting the finishing touches to the white baby shawl. They included a finely crocheted border. She looked across it at Frank and smiled.

'Then you will not be attending the wedding?'

'Well, as a matter of fact Anthony seems to want me to be his best man, and since the case will be closed there isn't really any reason why I should refuse.'

'None at all. It will be pleasant to meet you on a purely social occasion.'

He leaned back in his chair.

'I think we may all be thankful to be so well out of the affair. There were some nasty moments, and if Sid Turner hadn't managed to get himself killed in that smash with the Hexton bus, we should still have the trial hanging over us. Mirrie might have been given a nasty time in the box by the sort of chap Sid's solicitor would have put up for the defence, but as it is, the whole thing can just go down the drain and be forgotten. What I should like to ask you is, how did you tumble to that fingerprint business being a red herring, and when?'

Miss Silver continued to crochet the frail shells which bordered the shawl.

'It is always difficult to say at what moment the faint suggestion of a possibility becomes something more definite. Whereas you had been actually present when Jonathan Field related the supposed history of a murderer's fingerprint, it only reached me at second hand and without the dramatic emphasis with which he no doubt contrived to invest it.'

Frank laughed.

'Oh, he made it convincing enough, the old blighter! You should have seen us! We were fairly lapping it up! He was a good showman, and he put on a first-class act, I'll give him that.'

'To my mind the whole thing appeared to be a little too dramatic. It was, of course, necessary to give it the most scrupulous attention, and one or two points presented themselves. According to this story of Mr. Field's, after getting the murderer's fingerprint on his cigarette-case a second bomb came down in the neighbourhood and he lost consciousness. When he came to he found himself in hospital with a broken leg. As I said before, I found it difficult to believe that any fingerprint would have survived the handling which the contents of his pockets must have received. I also doubted very much whether the existence of a single print with no more to authenticate it than the hearsay evidence of a man who had been taken unconscious out of a heap of ruins in which no trace of any other person had been found could possibly be supposed to carry sufficient weight to supply the motive for a murder.'

This formidable sentence having been achieved, Miss Silver paused to loosen some strands from the ball in her knitting-bag, but before Frank could say anything she resumed.

'As Lord Tennyson so truly says:

> "The end and the beginning vex
> His reason; many things perplex
> With motions, checks, and counter checks."

From the moment Maggie Bell informed me that Mirrie had an appointment with Sid Turner on the night of the dance it was plain that she would have had an opportunity of repeating this story about the fingerprint. It undoubtedly made a deep impression on her. This was clear from what you had told me and from what Georgina was able to add to it. When it came to a choice between believing that Jonathan Field had been murdered either in order to destroy the fingerprint or to prevent him from revoking the will which made Mirrie his heiress, I could not really consider the fingerprint motive as sufficient or even credible. But if Mirrie within an hour or two of hearing it repeated the story to Sid Turner — and we know now that she did repeat it — it could, and no doubt did, provide him with the idea of using Mr. Field's collection as a pretext for obtaining an interview. By the Tuesday night of the murder the will in Mirrie's favour had been signed, but since it might at any time be revoked, Mr. Field's death was determined upon. Owing to the fact that Maggie Bell overheard the conversation in which Sid Turner introduced himself, we know that he obtained admittance at an unusually late hour by exploiting Mr. Field's interest in his fingerprint collection. He was admitted by the terrace door and accomplished his wicked purpose. There may have been some talk before the shot was fired — there probably was. Mr. Field was, I think, quite unsuspicious. He had got out his album, and had no doubt opened it and displayed some of the more interesting prints. He may himself have referred to the supposed bombing incident, or the subject may have been introduced by Sid Turner. Be that as it may, we must, I think, assume that the album was opened at that particular page, and that the murderer was prompt to avail himself of the opportunity of diverting suspicion from the real financial motive. By tearing out that particular page and destroying the notes used by Mr. Field to substantiate his story of a murderer's confession Sid Turner undoubtedly hoped to ensure that the police enquiries would be turned in quite another direction. His own danger lay in any possible connection with Mr. Field's will and Mirrie's financial interest in it.'

Frank nodded.

'There's no doubt his girl friend in Maudsley's office had given Sid to understand that Mirrie's chance of inheriting under the will which Jonathan had just signed was a pretty shaky one. Maudsley made no secret of his opinion as to the injustice of cutting Georgina out, and Jonathan, having acted on impulse, was likely enough to go back on it as soon as he had time to think. If Sid wanted to make sure of an heiress he had to strike while the will was valid, and he had a shrewd idea that it wouldn't be valid for long. So he thought he would go whilst the going was good and came sprinting down here on Tuesday night. As it happened, he was a couple of hours too late and the will had already been destroyed. So he had his crime for nothing, and the Hexton bus has saved the hangman a job.'

He got to his feet.

'Well, I must be off. I suppose you wouldn't like to invite me to tea on Sunday?'

Miss Silver gave him an indulgent smile.

'We still have a pot of Lisle Jerningham's honey, and Hannah has the recipe for a new kind of scone.'

THE END

PATRICIA WENTWORTH

POISON IN THE PEN

Tilling Green was a charming little village nestling in the Ledshire countryside. Not at all the sort of place you would expect to find an anonymous letter writer. And when one of the recipients, a young woman, was found drowned in the lake belonging to the Manor House, Miss Silver was persuaded to go and investigate.

It was difficult to believe such evil lay beneath the surface as the village prepared for the marriage between Valentine Grey, the pretty young heiress from the Manor House—and one Gilbert Earle. Then, on the night of Valentine's pre-wedding party, things came unexpectedly to a head. Jason Leigh, Valentine's former love, returned after months without a word. Valentine discovered Gilbert in a compromising situation with her guardian's wife. And several people received extremely nasty letters. Ronnie Brooks knew who had written these letters. But on the same night, she was murdered...

Post·A·Book

A Royal Mail service in association with the Book Marketing Council & The Booksellers Association.

Post-A-Book is a Post Office trademark.

PATRICIA WENTWORTH

THE CLOCK STRIKES TWELVE

New Year's Eve was a strange evening for the Paradine family. Departing from the normal routine, James Paradine made a speech that changed the trend of many lives. Valuable blueprints had disappeared. Some member of the family had taken them, and he gave the culprit till midnight to confess and return the prints to him in his study. That was James Paradine's announcement!

A few minutes after twelve James Paradine was dead.

Faces mirrored the deep shock and dismay. Open mouths gaped incredulously. Murder. And then the mouths closed tight on composed faces and the alibis, like castle walls seemed impenetrable. It was left to Miss Silver to unravel the mystery and to disentangle the threads that bound the Paradine family in a strange web of dislikes, hatred and fear.

CORONET BOOKS

PATRICIA WENTWORTH

THE LISTENING EYE

No one could have guessed that Paulina Paine was stone-deaf. Her ability to lip-read was astonishing. So the two men who met that day during the showing of a new art exhibition did not realise until too late that the middle-aged tweedy figure sitting quietly out of earshot had understood every word they said. And it had been no ordinary conversation. In fact Paulina was so shaken by its implications that she went to see Miss Silver. It was the last thing she did ...

Subsequent events soon involved Miss Silver in murder and robbery. And a very tense house-party where all the members were linked in some way to Paulina – and one was a killer ...

CORONET BOOKS

OTHER TITLES BY PATRICIA WENTWORTH

☐ 21792 8	Poison In The Pen	£1.10
☐ 21794 4	The Listening Eye	£1.75
☐ 02932 3	The Traveller Returns	£1.25
☐ 17832 9	The Clock Strikes Twelve	£1.75
☐ 24515 8	Latter End	£1.25
☐ 25057 7	Ladies Bane	£1.25
☐ 25357 6	Pilgrim's Rest	£1.25
☐ 18776 X	The Girl In The Cellar	£1.75
☐ 17833 7	Spotlight	£1.75
☐ 26372 5	The Case Of William Smith	£1.25
☐ 26373 3	The Benevent Treasure	£1.25
☐ 12361 3	The Brading Collection	£1.75
☐ 16949 4	The Gazebo	£1.75
☐ 28101 4	Through The Wall	£1.25
☐ 16953 2	Miss Silver Intervenes	£1.25
☐ 15951 0	Miss Silver Comes To Stay	£1.50